BREATHLESS IN LOVE

The Maverick Billionaires, Book 1

Bella Andre & Jennifer Skully

BREATHLESS IN LOVE

~ The Maverick Billionaires, Book 1 ~

Meet the Maverick Billionaires—sexy, self-made men from the wrong side of town who survived hell together and now have everything they ever wanted. But when each Maverick falls head-over-heels for an incredible woman he never saw coming, he will soon find that true love is the only thing he ever really needed...

Will Franconi has a dark past that he's kept a closely guarded secret—very few people have ever heard his real story and he plans to keep it that way. After surviving a hellish childhood, he's now living the dream life where everything he touches turns to gold. But something's missing. He doesn't quite know what, until a simple letter from a teenage boy brings Harper Newman into his life—a woman who just might fill up the empty places inside him...if only he could ever be worthy of her love.

When a man has more money than he could spend in five lifetimes, Harper has to ask herself what Will Franconi could possibly want from a woman like her. She's learned the hard way that rich men always get what they want no matter the cost. If it were only herself she had to worry about, Harper would manage, but she's guardian to her younger brother, who depends on her for everything. After he nearly lost his life in a car crash, she's vowed never to let anyone hurt him ever again.

Still, sometimes Harper can't help but long to change her story from that of the always cautious woman to an adventurous tale of a heroine who's wild and free...especially when Will's kisses and caresses make her utterly breathless. And as he begins to reveal his story to her, she discovers that he's so much more than just another wealthy, privileged man. He's kind and giving, and he fills up all the spaces inside her heart that have been empty for so long. Together, can they rewrite their stories into a happily ever after that neither of them would have believed possible?

A note from Bella & Jennifer

We are beyond thrilled to introduce the Maverick Billionaires!

For those of you who have read Bella's series about The Sullivans, you might remember hearing about The Maverick Group in *Come A Little Bit Closer* (Smith Sullivan's book) and then again in *One Perfect Night* (Colbie and Noah's book). Bella has wanted to write about the Mavericks for years and couldn't be happier about getting to finally write each story in this new series with one of her very good friends, Jennifer Skully, who also happens to be one of her favorite writers!

We hope you fall as hard for our super-sexy heroes as we have.

Happy reading,
Bella Andre & Jennifer Skully

CHAPTER ONE

Will Franconi gunned the engine of his classic 1970 Dodge Challenger and the rush of speed exploded through his veins.

He had built a billion-dollar luxury goods business by respecting his customers, his suppliers, his business partners, and his employees. After he'd learned the hard way as a kid how lies and cruelty could ruin a life, he'd worked like hell to turn his own around. Today, though his meeting was with a kid instead of a power player, he was just as intent on getting there on time.

And if that meant pushing the powerful car even faster, all the better.

Jeremy Newman's letter to Will had been scrawled on spiral notebook paper that looked like it had been ripped out of an elementary school binder. Having watched Will's clip on the TV show *Hot Cars*, Jeremy had written that he loved cars, had seen every movie and TV show ever made about cars, and begged to see Will's collection.

The boy's longing had touched something in Will that he couldn't define. And only a total jerk would say no.

Powering into the turn off the freeway, his tires spat gravel while the back end held firm as he blew through the open gates of the municipal airport on the San Francisco Peninsula. The speed sent another rush through him—a rush that he'd always needed, lately more than ever.

Down the row of hangars, the two specks ahead coalesced into a woman and a young man, taller than she was and younger, too—a teen. The boy was bouncing on his feet with nervous energy.

Will had been expecting an eight-year-old. Could this teenager be Jeremy? Will took his foot off the gas and tapped the brakes, slowing as individual features came into focus. The two had similar bone structure, but where the teenager had brown hair, the woman was blond, and not out of a bottle, either.

Rolling to a stop beside them, Will focused on her, the bump in his pulse having nothing to do with his earlier burst of speed. It was all about her—the lush lips, the blond hair cascading in waves over her shoulders, and the business suit that failed to disguise her sweet curves. She wasn't dressed Saturday casual the way Will was, but all straitlaced and buttoned up. The hair gave her away, though, flowing free and sexy in the breeze blowing off the bay.

"Mr. Franconi, Mr. Franconi!" The teen began waving his arms, practically jumping out of his sneakers. In one hand, he gripped an orange spiral notebook, shaking it wildly. It could very well have contained the torn-out page Will had in his jeans pocket.

So this *was* Jeremy Newman. He had to be seventeen or eighteen, even though the printing in the letter had been, at best, at a third grade level, and the tone was the same, one of an exuberant child on a mission.

Will climbed out of the restored white Challenger. The car was the reason he'd almost been late. He'd been up in San Francisco that morning checking over a shipment of caviar. An exclusive from Russia, he'd paid a fortune for it and had done the inspection himself. Driving the Challenger to this meeting had been a last-minute decision, and the Bay Area traffic had been bumper-to-bumper on the detour back to his home in Portola Valley to pick up the car. Spring was here, and everyone seemed to be out for a drive on the first clear, sunny Saturday in weeks.

Fortunately, the excitement on the boy's face as he raced around the car was worth the extra trouble.

"Wowowowow." Jeremy spoke so fast it was almost one word.

"Jeremy, calm down," the woman said, but she was smiling at the boy as she did so. Her voice was as smooth as the award-winning Japanese single malt whiskey Will imported.

If Jeremy had been younger, she could have been his mother—the same nose, the same blue eyes. But at somewhere in her late twenties, she was far too young to be the mother of an eighteen-year-old.

"I'm Will," he said as he left Jeremy to his raptures over the car for a few moments and turned to focus his attention on her. "Will Franconi."

"It's nice to meet you, Mr. Franconi."

She shook his hand and he was struck not only by the strength of her handshake, but also by how soft her skin was. So soft that he didn't want to let go, especially when he caught the flicker of awareness—and heat—that sparked in her eyes when they touched.

"I'm Harper Newman." She carefully drew her hand away from his. "My brother Jeremy is obviously too excited for a proper introduction." She smiled fondly again at her brother, who was kneeling to study the rim on the right rear tire, lovingly running one finger over it. "I really appreciate your taking the time to show us your car collection. With your busy schedule, we don't want to keep you too long."

"First of all, call me Will. And second, it's my pleasure." He hadn't expected to meet a gorgeous woman—and single, judging by her bare left hand—here today. She had no idea just how great a pleasure this meeting had turned out to be.

Jeremy raced back over to them. "It's just like the Challenger Barry Newman crashed in *Vanishing Point*." His speech pattern was slightly off. Not slurred so much as overpronounced, as though his mouth had to work harder at making the sounds come out right, and his inflections were out of sync with his words. "Barry Newman," he repeated, then poked his own chest. "Jeremy Newman, get it?"

Will was thinking that Jeremy was way too young to know about the classic movie from the early seventies, when Harper told him, "He's watched all the great car chases, from *Vanishing Point* to *Bullitt* and every one of the *Fast and Furious* movies." Her hand lay on the boy's back, rubbing between his shoulder blades, a calming gesture. Sweet and simple affection for her brother.

But Will knew firsthand that there was nothing simple about affection...and that it wasn't necessarily a given between family members. Jeremy was very lucky indeed to have Harper as a sister.

"I've also seen the new *Transformers: Age of Distinction*." Jeremy said the last word carefully and Will didn't have the heart to correct it to *Extinction*. "That chase with the evil bad cars was cool," Jeremy enthused, his eyes wide.

Harper didn't correct the movie title, either. Or maybe she didn't know the difference, given that Will didn't see her as a Transformers fan. Besides, maybe *distinction* was a better word in this case, considering that Harper Newman was already a woman of distinction in Will's estimation—both because of how well she treated her brother and the way her natural beauty shone through despite the rather severe outfit.

"Was having the same last name as the star of *Vanishing Point* what got you started as a car enthusiast, Jeremy?"

"Cars are cool. I can't drive, but if I could, I'd go fastfastfast." Jeremy didn't quite answer the question, and again, there was that odd cadence in his speech.

"I like to go fast, too," Will agreed wholeheartedly.

There was nothing like speed to make you feel alive. Will knew he'd never completely outrun his past, and that he'd always be his father's son no matter how much he wished he wasn't. Nonetheless, he'd worked long, hard years to put as much of his past behind him as he could, with all his focus, drive, and energy bent on taking control of his future.

For a good decade or more, success had been enough for him. Yet in the last few months, something had changed—a feeling of emptiness that working harder hadn't been able to fix. When even millions in profits from a new product couldn't get him excited, a fast ride was the only sure-fire way to get his blood pumping again.

Until now, at least, when Harper Newman was having the exact same impact on him.

"He's always liked cars," Harper answered for Jeremy. "I can't say I feel the same way." She offered an apologetic smile and politely said, "But the collection we saw on TV is impressive."

Would she be equally polite in the bedroom? *Mr. Franconi, could you please touch me here?*

Jesus, that thought was hot. So hot that he forced himself to push it away, since they were standing in front of her brother.

"When you're able to drive," Will said, turning back to Jeremy, "I'm sure you'll want to obey all the traffic rules." But his tone was tongue-in-cheek. At Jeremy's age, he'd broken all the rules. Now he made his own.

Will found himself wondering what kind of rules Harper had...and which ones she might be willing to break with him.

"I can't drive." Jeremy's brow knit seriously. "Harper drives me. But she doesn't like to go fast. Not like we do." He nudged Will's arm with his elbow as if they were a conspiracy of two.

Harper smiled indulgently, and Will could easily guess that Jeremy had told her to go faster one too many times. She didn't offer an explanation as to why Jeremy couldn't drive, but Will had realized by now that while the boy might be in his late teens physically, his mental capacity hadn't caught up for some reason.

She glanced at her watch. "In the interest of time, maybe we should look at the cars."

Will smiled at her as he said, "I have all afternoon."

He didn't actually have much time at all to spare, but like hell if he was rushing this meeting. Not only because he wanted some time to get to know Harper better before he asked her out, but also because Jeremy was bouncing on his toes again, bursting with excitement. Will understood that kind of passion, and appreciated it.

"I store six cars here," Will told them both. He had eight more classics in Portola Valley, plus his personal vehicles.

Jeremy opened his notebook, flipping through, then held up a picture pasted to a page. "James Bond. Aston Martin DB5. I love James Bond."

"Sorry, buddy, I don't have that one here." Will kept that car at home because the Aston Martin was great on the rural roads of Portola Valley, like driving through the French countryside of a Bond movie.

The boy's features drooped. But not for long. "That's okay, Will. I love the Challenger, too."

Smiling at Jeremy's eagerness, Will opened a metal box on the hangar wall and punched in the security code. When the red light flashed to green, he tapped another button for the roll-up door. Inside, two rows of overhead lights popped on one after another, stretching to the back of the hangar, spotlighting each classic car in turn.

"Wow." Jeremy's voice went soft with awe.

Harper merely smiled her appreciation, though not with Jeremy's delight. She was clearly the indulgent older sister, here to make her brother happy, and Will liked that about her. Liked it as much as he liked looking at her.

Jeremy tiptoed between the two rows of cars arranged at an angle, each ready to be driven out of the hangar at a moment's notice. Rolling tool chests lined the metal walls, along with a couple of floor jacks for lifting the cars. Will had a full-time mechanic, Leland, who kept the engines tuned and clean, and the bodies spotless. Leland worked both here at the airport and out at Will's Portola Valley property.

"1965 AC Cobra," Jeremy recited as if he'd memorized a list. "Wow." His gaze was bright in the lights shining down on him as he held his notebook close to his chest, his mouth open slightly.

First on the left, the Cobra was cream in color. Will had thought about topping the paint job with a blue racing stripe, but Leland had rolled his eyes heavenward as if commiserating with the paint gods, then asked if Will wanted to be like everyone else. Of course, Will had never been like anyone else, and Leland had an excellent eye. The cream finish was like glass.

"It's a very nice car," Harper said in that polite voice that totally revved Will's engine. "And it looks brand new."

"It's a kit car," Will explained. "I had all the parts shipped here, and assembled it from the frame up. It's a replica of a '65 Cobra." The project had taken a year. He could have done it faster, but he'd enjoyed the work and hadn't wanted to rush. There was pleasure not merely in the end result, but in watching something grow.

"You built this yourself?" She looked surprised to hear it. She ran a finger along the finish, as if finally perceiving the beauty that Will saw.

"Cars are my thing."

Very few people knew Will's story—that he'd been barely eight years old when his father had taught him how to hotwire his first stolen car, with illegal drag racing coming a handful of years later. It wasn't until Will had turned eighteen that he'd vowed to turn his life around. Now, though he still spent his free time playing with cars, he always did it on the right side of the law.

"What's that one?" She pointed to the model opposite.

"1965 Mercedes 300 SL Roadster," Jeremy said before Will could supply the answer.

"He's been studying you. Your classic car collection, I mean."

Maybe she was afraid he'd think her brother was coming across like a stalker, but it was the farthest thing from Will's mind. On the contrary, he was flattered. Jeremy seemed so open, so hopeful, so happy. All the things Will had never been in his youth. He couldn't actually say he felt those emotions now either, despite how far he'd come from the derelict Chicago neighborhood of his childhood.

He also liked watching the bond between the two of them, the way Harper looked at Jeremy, the light but warm touches, her affection easy to read on her face. The bonds of blood could be meaningless—or worse, they could utterly destroy you if you let them—but Harper clearly loved her brother with everything she had.

Will had the same kind of connection with the Mavericks. That's what the five of them—Daniel, Sebastian, Evan, Matt, and Will—called themselves. *The Maverick Group.* Back in Chicago, they'd been five kids brought together by misfortune and neglect. Their bond had been forged in need, not by blood. Most people believed blood relations automatically deserved devotion, but he knew better. Devotion had to be earned, and family and blood didn't go hand in hand, not in his experience. Susan and Bob Spencer—Daniel's parents, who had taken them all in—were exceptions, just as Harper Newman and her brother were.

"Is that a kit car, too?" she asked, gesturing toward the Mercedes.

"No. It's the real thing."

Jeremy moved down the line, Harper following, her arms crossed. Her high-heeled shoes tapped on the concrete with every step, her hair shifting across her shoulders, the light from above catching the changing hues of blond.

"Oh man, a 1956 Jaguar XKSS." Jeremy turned to smile brilliantly at Will. "BRG."

"Right." Will cocked a thumb at Harper. "Maybe you'd better tell your sister what that means." He winked conspiratorially, while hoping Jeremy knew the answer. It wasn't his intention to embarrass the boy.

Sure enough, he knew. "British racing green." Jeremy's voice echoed, overly loud in the hangar, from his excitement. With that, he sprinted down the center aisle, pointing as he went. "1968 Lamborghini Miura." The gold tones of the car gleamed under the lights. "1954 Austin Healey 100S." And finally to the last one. "1965 Stingray Coupe."

Harper beamed. "He got them all right." She was clearly proud, and Will experienced an ache under his ribcage that he hadn't felt since his mother died when he was six.

They made him want in. In on their bond. In on the pride and adoration in Harper's gaze.

Watching Harper and her brother together made him need things he hadn't craved in thirty years. His father had bullied those cravings out of him.

Harper's gaze was still on her brother, the light of some special emotion shining in her eyes, when he asked them both, "You want a ride?"

CHAPTER TWO

Harper froze. She'd known it was coming, but she'd expected the question about getting into one of Mr. Franconi's cars from Jeremy. *Not* from the billionaire!

She had her excuses lined up. Mr. Franconi couldn't possibly have time. He didn't even know them and couldn't be expected to let just *anyone* ride in one of his cars. She'd imagined the powerful businessman would readily agree with everything she said, likely because he'd be angling to get out of there and back to making more billions as soon as possible.

But now that he'd made the unexpected offer, though Jeremy was already jumping up and down shouting his glee, she couldn't possibly take him up on it.

"Thank you for the lovely offer, Mr. Franconi, but Jeremy and I have already taken enough of your time."

"Like I said, I've got all afternoon." He smiled at her again. "And it's Will."

Sweet Lord, that man had a smile on him. It was cocky, sexy, and somehow sincere, all at the same time. He had to be aware of the effect it had on the female gender. She guessed he used it knowingly, undermining resistance, so that he could get whatever he wanted.

But why would he be using it on her?

"I don't think—"

"Come on, Harper." Jeremy gave her his best hangdog expression. "We want to go out in the fast car!"

"Yeah, come on, Harper." Amusement laced the billionaire's voice as he echoed her brother. Will's gaze was deep, startlingly blue, like the Mediterranean ocean of his heritage. "We really *do* want to go out in the fast car."

His hair was as dark as the devil, his features more handsome than a man with his wealth deserved. She'd half expected to be met today by a flock of Franconi Imports publicity reps. After all, she'd figured the slick, filthy-rich business owner giving his time to a young man like Jeremy would be a publicist's goldmine.

Yet Will had come alone and was dressed casually in jeans and a dark T-shirt—one that emphasized his muscled biceps, but was as far from a five-thousand-dollar suit as anything could be.

Just as Jeremy had researched Will's cars, Harper had researched the man himself. There was a great deal of information online about how he'd built his business, but very few details about his personal life or past.

None of her research had helped her understand why someone as wealthy and powerful as Will Franconi would even bother to answer Jeremy's letter. The invitation to meet at his hangar had floored her. After all, he was a luxury importer—and she wasn't even sure what that meant, exactly. How could a man make billions off *luxury*? And all his cars she'd seen profiled on the *Hot Cars* show Jeremy had made her watch smelled of money. Will was a collector of things, so she'd assumed he probably collected people, too...until he got tired of them.

But then she remembered the way he'd looked at her and Jeremy, with a longing that she didn't quite understand, but felt all the same, right in the center of her chest where her heart was beating just a little too fast from nothing more than the look in his eyes.

Plus, she hadn't expected him to be so *nice*. He didn't laugh at Jeremy. In fact, Will hadn't looked at her brother as if there was anything wrong with him at all.

And now he wanted to take Jeremy for a ride in one of his super fast cars.

Knowing they were both staring at her, waiting for her answer, she finally said, "Where would you take him if I said it was okay?"

"Just down the runway. I'll check with the control tower to make sure there won't be any planes coming in. You can watch us the whole time."

"Please, Harper," Jeremy pleaded, not at all afraid of going fast even though speed had taken so much away from him.

Will didn't know their story, even though Harper sometimes felt like everyone else did, as though it was the only thing that defined her and Jeremy. Eleven years ago, her brother had been hit by a car driven by a rich teenager who was driving *way* too fast. The teenager's father had not only bought him out of a prison sentence, he'd also forced her parents to accept a payoff in lieu of the litigation that they'd been told would have dragged on for years otherwise.

Harper had never blamed her parents for their decision to take the money. Jeremy had suffered irreparable brain damage and now he was an eighteen-year-old who had never progressed mentally past the age of seven. She understood why economics won out over justice sometimes. Her brother's road to recovery hadn't been cheap, but thankfully, as long as she was careful with her investments and earned enough with her salary as a recruiter, there was still money left to support his current needs, like the special school he attended.

When her parents had died six years ago, Harper had made it her mission to carry on their legacy and protect Jeremy. But in many ways, on the day of the car crash she hadn't only lost her little brother, she'd also lost her parents to financial worry and emotional turmoil, years before they'd passed away in a private plane crash.

Speed had taken so much from her and her brother, but Jeremy was a good kid. He always had been, and she couldn't help giving in to him when he wanted something badly. Surely one ride here today had to be a safe way for Jeremy to experience that speed he so longed for...and if she had any longing left inside of *her* for just that same thing, she shoved it down.

It was up to her to be the responsible one, after all.

"All right, Will." She wanted to keep on thinking of Will as Mr. Franconi, but somehow he made that impossible with those smiles of his and his charming insistence that she call him by his first name. "But not too fast."

Will's expression was solemn as he crossed his heart. "I promise. No faster than my mechanic would allow."

"How fast is that?"

He smiled again. "Nothing that would hurt the pristine engine."

She had no idea what that meant, but she was helpless against the combined power of his smiles and promises. "All right, fine. But I'll be watching."

"I'm thinking the Cobra for our first ride." He turned to Jeremy. "Sound okay to you?"

"Yay!" Jeremy crowed.

Harper suspected Will had chosen the Cobra because it was the one he'd personally labored over, the one that held the most meaning for him.

"Let me call the tower so they're ready for us."

Once again, Will keyed a code into a pad next to an office door. The lights inside turned on automatically, illuminating a desk and bookshelves crammed with manuals, the names of the cars written along their spines. There were trophies and framed photos, mostly of the cars, with only a few including Will. He punched a couple of numbers on the phone, spoke quietly into it, then turned back to them with that killer smile while he waited for the person on the other end to respond to his request to clear the runways. Harper's heart beat faster despite herself.

"All clear." He put the phone down, then grabbed a key off a board on the wall, tossed it up, and caught it in his fist. "Let's go."

Jeremy followed him like a smitten puppy and worry swept through her stomach again. Will Franconi had a hangar full of ridiculously expensive cars, a personal mechanic, and one call to the control tower allowed him to take over the runways.

So why was he wasting so much time with them?

Harper knew she was sometimes a little too careful with her brother. It was just that if anything happened to him, she'd never, ever forgive herself. But here in the hangar with all the amazing cars, Jeremy was so happy and excited that she couldn't bear squashing him down.

Will opened the Cobra's door. "Hold onto the roll bar back here to get in." He demonstrated with a pat on the curved bar behind the passenger seat. "Don't use the windshield."

The car had no top, just the roll bars behind each of the two seats. The interior was brushed metal, with no carpeting, and the seats were a simple leather bucket. After Jeremy was in, Will leaned over the passenger door to secure the buckle, which was much thicker than a normal seatbelt.

Clapping Jeremy on the shoulder, Will said, "There you go, buddy," then rounded the hood. He climbed into the driver's seat after a jaunty salute to Harper.

The engine roared to life, and Will pulled onto the tarmac with Jeremy vibrating with eagerness and sheer joy in the seat beside him. It was a small airport for light planes, not big commercial airliners. Two runways ran down the center with a long row of hangars on either side. Some had business signage over them—carrier services, flight insurance, maintenance, and one for a local flying club. It hadn't occurred to her that a person could actually rent a hangar to store anything other than a plane, not until Jeremy had received Will's return letter.

She watched the classy race car cruise down the closest runway. True to his word, Will kept his speed down. He turned at the end and headed back on the opposite runway, picking up the pace as they came around to pass her. Jeremy waggled a thumbs-up over the windshield. His lips moved a mile a minute, talking Will's ear off.

Harper smiled, feeling much better about everything...at least, until she realized the car was going faster. And faster. When they made the next turn, she heard tires squeal.

Her stomach jumped and she rolled her bottom lip between her teeth, biting down hard, as if the pain would distract her.

Ever since her parents had passed away at the end of her senior year of college, Jeremy had been her responsibility. He was the only family she had left. He had difficulty learning new skills, and while he loved the computer, he needed a lot of help. In the morning, he went to a special school, and he bagged at the local grocery store on weekday afternoons. She hadn't gotten Jeremy the job because they needed the money, but because her brother needed to feel useful. It was good for his self-esteem. She did everything she could for him.

Yet she'd just let him get in a car with a madman.

Some guardian she turned out to be, she thought as Will and Jeremy roared along the runways as if they were on a racetrack. Her heart hammered as the *whoosh* of their passing blew her hair across her face.

She hated speed after what had happened to both Jeremy and her parents. Or at least, she *should* have hated speed. Yet her heart, a traitor to everything she knew to be right, secretly ached to be in the car with them, to taste the rush of air as it raced right through her...and to feel the same rapture that was now shining on Jeremy's face.

The Cobra made two more laps before Will slowed and eased to a stop beside her.

"Careful getting out," he said to Jeremy. "The pipe down on the side is hot and I don't want you to burn yourself."

Before she could rush around the car to make sure Jeremy didn't touch the big black exhaust pipe, he was already pushing himself out, using the roll bar, not the windshield, just as Will had told him.

She crossed her arms over her chest and gave Will a narrow-eyed gaze as he also climbed out of the car. "How fast were you going?"

He answered her with the solemn, sincere look he'd used on her earlier when he'd promised not to go too fast. "Fifty on the straightaway."

"No way."

"I swear." He crossed his heart, just like before.

"Well, then, fifty is too fast out there." It probably wasn't, but she had to argue, because Jeremy was her responsibility. Or maybe it was because Will was so darned gorgeous and persuasive that she felt as though she had to fight the urge to automatically give in to him.

Jeremy bounded around the car. "Wasn't that cool, Harper?"

He'd had to learn to talk again after the accident, and even now, all these years later, his speech was careful, almost strained sometimes, as if he was searching for the right words. But he'd clearly been feeling great today—almost like the eighteen-year-old he should have been. And she could see that he'd just had *so* much fun. His elation was bursting out of him like an excited puppy who'd just been let out of his crate.

"Was it good?" she asked in a gentle voice. The wind had gusted his hair into spikes and tangles, and she smoothed down the soft brown locks.

"The best." Jeremy's eyes gleamed, his gaze bouncing between her and Will, then finally settling on her. "Your turn now, Harper."

She shook her head. Hard. "I'm not getting in that car."

Will smiled winningly. Or cunningly. She honestly wasn't sure at this point, her heart beating fast at even the *thought* of getting into the sports car with Will.

"I promise I won't take you any faster than I did Jeremy," he told her. "And you just saw for yourself that he didn't come to any harm."

Another easy promise. There was a challenge there, too. And for a moment of pure insanity, she wanted to take the dare, feel the exhilaration, inhale it. She wanted to go fast, feel the wind beating her face, feel her blood rushing wildly through her veins.

But she was *not* insane.

Safe. She needed to keep everyone safe. Not only Jeremy, but herself, too. Just because she might want something didn't mean she could have it. Not if it was something that was bad for her or for Jeremy.

Unfortunately, the best refusal she could come up with in the face of both of them looking at her so expectantly was, "I'm wearing a skirt. There's no way I can get down into that seat." But even as she said it, a part of her—a *really* big part—wanted to take what he offered.

Just once, she wanted to close her eyes and race with the wind.

"I'll help you." Will held out his hand.

"It's fun, Harper." Jeremy had to add his two cents.

"Once around," Will said, his voice low, his gaze deep, his hand still held out to her as if he had no doubt she'd eventually agree. "That's all it will be. A fast ride that you're going to love. I promise. Once around," he said again, before smiling and adding, "Unless you want more."

As if he'd known how close to the edge she already was, his coaxing words had her falling right into his blue gaze, like a cliff diver hurtling down to water as smooth as glass.

For the first time in forever, Harper wanted to forget about what was bad for her and just do what felt good. Which was why she finally said, "I'll go with you for one turn around the runway." She made sure to add as a reminder for them both, "But I won't be wanting more than that."

Only, she wasn't sure he believed it any more than she did.

CHAPTER THREE

Oh yes, Will Franconi was dangerous. *Extremely* dangerous as he drew her to the passenger side of the car and her stomach fluttered with the hand-to-hand contact.

Harper hadn't dated in over a year, ever since she'd realized that she was an easy target. Not only for men who wanted to get at her brother's trust fund, but also because after so many years of working to take care of herself and Jeremy, she hadn't had much time left over to nurture her other relationships. First she'd become involved with a man who wanted Jeremy's money but not Jeremy. *Why can't you just send him to a home for people like him?* he'd said. And then she'd rebounded into a relationship with a guy who had sworn he would always be there for her and Jeremy—at least until he'd found a far lower-maintenance woman. Jeremy's heart had been broken when her boyfriend no longer came around to see him.

After that, Harper had decided love and marriage simply weren't in the cards for her.

And that was okay. Because, honestly, she wanted to know for sure that Jeremy wasn't going to be hurt by anyone else, rather than risk dating again.

Not that getting in the car with Will was akin to dating him, of course. She couldn't imagine what a rich playboy like him would want with a completely ordinary woman like her. It was just that she hadn't been this close to a good-looking man in a very long time. That had to explain why her heart was pounding hard and her skin felt flushed.

Will put her hand on the roll bar. "Hold on tight right here."

Everything he said seemed to have a double meaning, turning something ordinary into something sexual. But she knew it had to be her sex-starved brain adding the extra meaning.

She lifted her skirt slightly to step inside, then slid down into the leather seat. Picking up the ends of the seat belt, she looked at them, unsure how the contraption worked.

"It's a five-point racing harness," Will explained as he got into the driver's seat beside her. "Normally it would come up between your legs and down over your shoulders, but I think we can skip the leg harness for you today, given that you didn't come dressed to drive in a race car."

When she started fumbling with the hooks and levers on the harness, he said, "Let me help you."

The next thing she knew, he was settling a strap over her shoulder, his fingers brushing her collarbone as he brought it down across her chest. Thrill bumps raced across her skin with the near contact. She inhaled his scent—shampoo and soap and *very* sexy male—and her body tingled. Pulling the harness down to her lap, he flicked the latch closed with a snap, and she felt the pressure of his touch just below her belly. Low enough—and intimately enough—that her pulse rate shot up.

As he started on the other strap, his fingers skimmed the air just above her breasts, not quite touching, but barely short of a breath away. Harper didn't look up, didn't dare meet his gaze, just in case he realized the effect he was having on her. He snapped the second latch, buckled the belt across her lap with a simple flip of the two pieces she'd already connected, then cinched the strap.

Had he spent this much time getting Jeremy into the harness or putting the shoulder straps on? At this point, her head was spinning so much from his nearness and all the almost-touches that she honestly couldn't remember.

"Comfortable?" With the sun behind him, his eyes were shadowed, but she could have sworn heat sparkled in their depths.

"I'm fine." Her answer was low, breathy, too close to a moan. She cleared her throat. "I'm great. Thank you."

He pulled back slowly, his gaze still dark and intense, making her pulse beat even harder. After he secured his belt, he started the engine with a roar, and put a hand on the gear shift. "Ready?"

With a man like him, she didn't think she'd ever be ready. But she managed a nod.

He took off with a burst of speed, and she hung on to the door with one hand, clutching the seat tightly with the other, down by the gear box where he wouldn't see.

"Don't worry," he yelled over the rush of wind, "I won't go too fast."

Didn't he get that everything he was doing was already too fast?

Her hair whipped around her face, and she had to let go of the seat to pull it back. She needed two hands to bunch the thick locks at the back of her head, out of her eyes and her lipstick. She was flying free beside him, held in only by the harness, as the wind screamed past her ears.

And he was smiling, watching her.

"Look at the road," she shouted at him.

She felt him brake as he went into the turn at the end of the runway. It felt like they were going too fast, but the back end didn't slide as he went into the second turn, heading down the opposite runway. Her body swayed and jostled in the leather seat. She could taste the salt air on her lips. In the distance, she could see Jeremy jumping up and down, punching his fist high.

Will went faster and faster, making her blood pound in her ears and the wind beat against her chest. She should have told him to slow down, to stop and let her out. She should be calling him a maniac, even screaming at him.

Yet right then, Harper had the insane urge to raise her arms in the air like a teenager on a roller coaster. A crazy voice inside her whispered, *Do it.*

Unable to resist the pull of excitement and the thrill of the speed racing through her, she let herself go, throwing her hands up and her head back.

It was as exhilarating as it was terrifying. Maybe it was the combination of fear and danger and the pure joy of soaring through the air that made her feel so alive, with every nerve firing.

Or...maybe it was the man beside her.

* * *

Harper was utterly gorgeous, the sun sparkling in her wind-tossed hair, ecstasy glowing on her face. She didn't shout or cheer— but she did hold up her arms. And she smiled.

The most beautiful smile Will had ever seen.

He wasn't even near freeway speed, yet the shriek of the motor, the rumble of the pipes, and the open sky above them made it seem as if the car were flying at over a hundred miles an hour.

Just as he'd promised, he took her around only once. He didn't want to push her limits.

Not yet, anyway.

While harnessing her in, it would have been so easy to touch her, to let his fingertips graze her gorgeous skin. His heart had hammered with the desire to put his hands on her. Even now, his fingers sizzled with her heat, and her sweet scent filled his head. But he could tell that she wasn't like the women he usually spent his time with—women who knew the score and were in it for what they could grab before he moved on.

Harper Newman was different. And he liked that, liked knowing that wooing her would be unlike anything else he'd ever done in his life. Even if a voice in his head reminded him that he shouldn't be looking for anything more than a quick roll between the sheets with her.

Not because she didn't deserve more, but because she *did*. So much more than a fundamentally broken man like Will could ever give her.

He slowed after the last turn, heading back to her brother. Back to sanity for both of them.

For now.

She let her arms drop, and her sleeve brushed his arm as she said, "That was fast."

She was trying for a noncommittal tone, but he could hear the breathlessness she was trying to hide. She might normally be good at hiding her feelings, but Will was too interested in her to miss one single thing. Especially the thrill of the speed still coursing through her veins.

"Too fast? Or just right?"

Her eyes met his and sparks jumped between them again. Sparks that had been there from the very first moment they'd looked at each other.

Finally, she admitted, "It was good," her words a little huskier than he imagined she wanted them to be.

Ahead of them, Jeremy was hopping, skipping toward the car. He looked so happy. Which, Will was glad to see, made Harper very happy, too.

They rolled to a stop and he said, "Let me give you a hand."

But she didn't wait for his chivalry, simply unbuckled before he could help her and said, "I'm fine, thanks," then turned to grab the roll bar and hoist herself up.

Jeremy ran over to them. "Wasn't it cool, Harper?"

"I enjoyed it."

Her answer was far too tight-laced, but Will knew that for a few moments out there, she'd been one with the car and the rush of speed. Just as he had.

"But once was enough," she added, smoothing her jacket, then her skirt, and finally her hair.

"Once is never enough," he said softly.

Despite how hard she was working to rein herself in, he heard her breath catch on the slightly sensual undertone to his words. Will knew that if her brother hadn't been standing right there, he would have done something crazy, like grab her and kiss her.

No, he wasn't good enough for her. But that knowledge didn't keep him from wanting her. If anything, he was even more powerfully drawn to the good in her, to the sweetness and warmth she shared with her brother.

"I don't have to be anywhere special for another couple of hours. I can show you the Aston Martin at my place."

In truth, Will had a dozen important things to take care of today, but Jeremy was like a bright, mystical sphere that beckoned him closer, a breath of something clean that made him feel young instead of jaded.

And then there was Harper.

Beautiful, unique Harper with all that tightly leashed passion inside of her just waiting to be set free...

"We really can't," she protested at the exact moment Jeremy said, "That would be way cool."

The traces of the woman with her arms over her head in his car were disappearing fast. Much too fast, as she said, "We've imposed long enough. This was far more than we expected."

"Spending time with both of you hasn't been any imposition at all." He grinned at Jeremy. "No one has ever enjoyed my cars as much as you have. And the truth is that I like showing them off."

"Can we, Harper? Please." Her brother rocked on his toes, hands behind his back, his notebook clutched tightly in his fingers.

"You can follow me over in your car and leave when you're ready," Will added.

"Where do you live?" Her tone was wary, but at least she wasn't still completely shutting down his idea.

"Portola Valley."

Jeremy's notebook was now tucked under his arm, his palms pressed flat together. He stood right in front of Harper mouthing, *Please, please, please.*

Will knew it was dirty pool to let Jeremy do all the convincing, but the boy wanted it as much as Will did. He recognized the moment Harper relented. She shot out one sharp breath, and shook her head in a quick move as though she was telling herself she was an idiot—or a softie.

"All right. But we can't stay long, Jeremy. Mr. Franconi is a busy man."

"I thought you were going to call me Will."

"Sorry, I forgot."

But he knew she hadn't. She didn't forget a thing, he could easily see that. She was simply trying to put distance between herself and that fast ride in the car. And *him*, most of all.

"We'll follow you," she said, "but please don't drive too fast or I might lose you."

Oh, he wasn't about to let her lose him. Just like he wasn't planning on losing her. "No fast driving on the way over," he promised.

One thing she'd learn about him was that he always kept his promises. Will had been anything but honest in his youth—far from it, as he'd done countless things that had given Susan and Bob gray hairs—but they'd also been the ones to teach him the power of his word. Will hadn't broken a promise since he was eighteen. His tattoo burned on his arm as a perpetual reminder of the things he'd done and the people he'd hurt.

"Can I go with Will?" her brother asked.

"Jeremy," she admonished softly. "You shouldn't invite yourself along like that."

"But I already invited myself to see Will's cars," Jeremy said logically, "and he said yes to that."

Jeremy certainly had a way about him, Will thought with a smile. The kid's great attitude was contagious. "No problem, buddy, you can drive with me."

As for Harper, he'd make sure she drove with him again, too. Only next time, he'd take her so far and so fast, and make it so good, that she wouldn't dream of asking him to slow down.

CHAPTER FOUR

It wasn't just a house. It was a whole compound. The private road leading to Will's home was a twisting half-mile up into the hills, past rolling fields of grass, scrub, trees, and other natural vegetation. Harper followed his car into the circular drive surrounding a rock fountain.

The house was like something out of a Frank Lloyd Wright photo book, with a wide, sweeping pathway of slowly rising brick steps surrounded by meticulously shaped flowering shrubs and artful rock formations. What she could see of the massive house was on two levels, one set farther back than the other, almost as if they were completely separate. A continuous line of windows flowed across the front, turning fluidly at the corners. Perched on a hill, there was an expansive valley view out the back. From the angle of the house to the drive, she could see an infinity pool, water pouring over its edge like a waterfall. Below that was a putting green.

Sticking behind Will, she steered her car into another drive, around a rock garden adorned with cacti and succulents, and headed up an incline. The garage he'd spoken of was actually two buildings, one opposite the other. She counted eight doors in each as she tailgated Will into the interior concrete pad between the two structures. One door slid up silently, and he pulled the Challenger inside.

She climbed out of the modest sedan she'd purchased several years ago based solely on its excellent safety record, and her heels clicked on the concrete as she headed to the open garage door. Lights came on inside, revealing several expensive cars whose value she could only guess. Probably a million dollars in gleaming metal, at the very least.

Will swept out a hand. "Welcome to my playground."

Jeremy was already racing down the row of cars. "It's down there." Will pointed. Then her brother was gone, shooting toward the silver Aston Martin he'd been drooling over for ages.

"I see he likes speed," Will mused, "in more ways than one."

"After the accident," she said softly, "he had to learn to talk and walk again. So now he feels he has to keep moving so his joints don't rust up like the Tin Man." Those were Jeremy's words, ones that always made her smile.

Will turned his gaze from Jeremy to her. "What happened?"

Harper swallowed, feeling herself choke up. It had all been a long time ago, yet the kindness in Will's eyes touched her. "A car accident when he was seven. A speeding teenager in his daddy's sports car." A teenager from a family that had nowhere near as much money as Will. "Jeremy was on his bike."

"I'm sorry, Harper." He looked upset on their behalf. And more than a little angry, too. "I can't imagine how difficult that was."

"He was in a coma for several weeks and suffered brain damage. In many ways, it's like he never grew older than seven." Jeremy would perpetually be a child. But he was alive. And she was more than grateful for that. "He's a happy guy, though. And he's doing well. I love him just the way he is."

"He's a good kid. Your parents obviously did a great job helping him through."

"They did," she agreed, still watching Jeremy skip around the Aston Martin, examining every detail. She'd already told Will this much of their story, so she might as well finish it for him, even though sometimes it felt like there was nothing else to her but this tale of one crash after another. "Our parents died a few years ago in a plane crash. So he's all mine now."

Will had come closer to her while she spoke. She was average height, but he was so tall, so strong, that he made her feel petite. "That must have been really hard on you."

He was right, it had been *horrible.* But she'd concentrated on Jeremy, on doing everything she could for him and, eventually, the ache had become a little less each day. "I miss my parents a lot. My mother was always so good at giving advice, and my father was always so calm about things." She would have given anything for them to be here.

Will reached for her hand and squeezed it as he said, "They would both be very proud of how you've done, Harper."

His touch seared her. She was suddenly aware of every breath she took, the slight bump in her heart rate, and the heat of his body. He was so completely *there* as he used their connection to steer her toward Jeremy, keeping their pace a leisurely stroll down the line of cars.

"Your garage is amazing." It seemed the polite thing to say and had the dual purpose of taking her mind off the loss of her parents and the focus off Will's hand over hers. Almost.

The facility was spotless, with not a single oil stain in sight. Vinyl pathways had been laid down between the cars and along the rear wall. The tool chests were shiny red, with every tool put away or hanging on pegboard above the workbenches. Electrical cords in roller bins hung down from the ceiling. There was order rather than the chaos of a normal garage. Particularly *her* garage.

She moved ahead of him so that his hand fell away from hers. Without his touch, she felt close to normal again, just a slight tingle of awareness remaining. But at the same time, she couldn't deny that a part of her missed it.

"You have so much space here," she noted. "Couldn't you also house the cars you have down at the airport?"

"Leland owns the hangar, and he'd been trying to rent out those spaces for a while. I'm glad to be able to use them."

She recalled that Leland was his mechanic. "So you have a mechanic *and* you fix the cars yourself?" She waved a hand along the row of tool chests. "Not to mention building them."

"Leland does the routine maintenance, while I get to do most of the fun stuff. But he helps out on a project if something requires more than two hands. Besides," Will added, the dark intensity back in his eyes as he looked at her, "I'm a hands-on kind of guy."

Harper remembered the way he'd fit the harness over her, nearly caressing her as he'd done so, and she flushed again. She didn't like this awareness of a man she could never be with in a million, billion years. Her cravings for a rush, for thrills, were shoved way down into a secret place—whereas his were out in the open. She'd seen dozens of photos of him on the Internet, a different woman on his arm each time. They all had hourglass figures and wore sexy designer dresses that had probably cost as much as her car. Clearly, he was a player.

Yet, he was kind to Jeremy and obviously took great pride in building things with his own hands rather than simply hiring minions to do it for him.

Harper couldn't put the pieces of the puzzle that was Will Franconi together in a way that made sense. Maybe if she knew more of his story the way he already knew hers, things might become clearer. But since she doubted she or Jeremy would ever see him again, Will Franconi would have to remain a mystery.

Needing another distraction from the heat still rising inside her, she pointed to grease-stained overalls hanging on the wall. "Looks like you've been doing a whole lot of work on your cars recently."

"Like I said, cars are my thing. They always have been, since I was a kid. Even now, I can always count on them when I'm looking for a rush."

"Can I sit in the car, Will?" Jeremy called from across the garage.

"Sure, go ahead." Will leaned against a workbench, his arms crossed, drawing her attention to his broad chest. "So Jeremy lives with you?"

She forced herself to concentrate on his words, not his impressive muscles. "Yes. We live in our parents' home in Palo Alto. He's better with familiar things around him."

"And what do you do for a living?"

"I'm a corporate recruiter." She felt she ought to explain why she was wearing a suit today. "I had an interview this morning."

"On a Saturday?" He looked impressed. "Dedicated."

"I enjoy my job." And she truly did love matching people up with the job perfect for them.

"No brothers, no sisters?"

"Just me and Jeremy. No cousins, either."

"So you take care of him all on your own?"

"Yes. And we're fine that way."

Thank God Jeremy chose that moment to run back to them. She felt like she'd been under Will's magnifying glass. He was even better at asking questions than she was, and that was pretty impressive, given that she asked questions for a living.

Why, she had to wonder again, was Will at all interested in her and Jeremy when they were never going to see each other again? Perhaps she shouldn't be so wary when he'd been nothing but nice so far, but after her experiences with the last two men she'd let get close—and after she'd watched the way the wealthy father of the teen who'd hit Jeremy had used his money to buy them out of any trouble—Harper simply couldn't trust blindly anymore.

"Can we see the other garage, Will?" Jeremy was a bundle of energy, even more so than usual. As though he felt he had to take big bites of Will's world before it was gone.

"Sure," Will said as he fished in his pocket for a remote. "But there's no Birdcage Maserati over there."

"I know," Jeremy said sadly. "Maybe if I close my eyes and wish hard enough, there could be one day." He did, squeezing his eyes shut.

Will laughed. "Sorry, I'm no genie in a bottle. Not today, at least." He pointed his remote at the closest door and it rolled up to reveal a sporty red vehicle.

"*The Ferrari*," Jeremy said in whispered awe before running toward the sports car. To Harper, his feet always seemed one step away from stumbling, but thankfully, Jeremy didn't fall.

"You don't have to do all this," she said apologetically.

"I'm enjoying it," he said again. "I like your brother. I don't often meet people who are as excited about cars as I am." He grinned at her. "He told me I should build a Birdcage Maserati."

"He's crazy for that car. He's got pictures of it all over his bedroom wall."

"I hated having to tell him no one makes a Maserati kit car." Will put his hand on the small of her back as they followed her brother at a more reasonable pace. "He showed me his notebook on the drive over."

The warmth of his touch was too much, too powerful. Wanting it so much more than she knew she should, she turned slightly, pulling away, trying to focus on what he was saying instead of his heat, his scent, and the things his hand on her back was doing to her insides.

"Even after you told him you couldn't get a kit for it, he wouldn't stop talking about that car, right?"

"Right."

Why Jeremy had fixated on the Maserati, Harper didn't know. She couldn't see anything special about it—at least, no more than any other sports car. "I'm sorry about that."

"You don't need to keep apologizing for him. Like I said, I like your brother." Another one of those gorgeous smiles curved his lips. "And I want to take you out, because I like you, too."

Rushing ahead of them, Jeremy hadn't stumbled, but Harper almost did just then. "Excuse me?"

"Dinner. Tonight. You and me."

The shock of his invitation—and just how badly she wanted to say *Yes!*—sent her pulse into the danger zone. "I don't think that's a good idea."

"Don't think, Harper. Just say yes." He gave her another smile, this one a little devious. "I already asked Jeremy, and he said it was fine if I took you out."

"You're joking."

"I'm perfectly serious. Hey, Jeremy," he called, "didn't I ask on the drive over if I could take Harper to dinner?"

"Yup. I said okeydokey."

Knowing that she was *seriously* out of her depth with this man, Harper said, "I can't date you."

"Why not?" he asked reasonably. "You're not afraid, are you?"

"Of course I'm not afraid," she said quickly. Too quickly, perhaps.

Because the truth was that she *was* afraid. Afraid of just how much she wanted to go on a date with Will. Afraid of just how badly she wanted to feel his mouth on hers. Afraid of just how much she loved seeing him smile at her. Afraid of being so starved for male affection that she'd be tempted to let herself become a plaything for a billionaire who couldn't possibly want her for anything more than that.

In the end, given the jumble of emotions inside of her, the best reason she could come up with was, "I don't like to leave Jeremy alone at night. And it's too late to get anyone to stay with him."

"Then how about tomorrow night, so that you can find someone to watch your brother?"

"Tomorrow night is okay, Will," Jeremy called from inside the garage, and she wondered how on earth he'd heard the conversation.

But she wasn't ready to concede. "This is ridiculous. I don't even know you. We just met, and only because my brother wanted to see your cars."

"That's why people go to dinner, isn't it?" He smiled again, clearly a deliberate tactic, given that he had to know his smiles made her heart jump around inside her chest. "To get to know each other better."

"Come on, Harper, say yes," her brother added. "And then I can come back to see more cars."

She shot Jeremy a shocked glance. She might have to ground him when they got home. Permanently.

"If you say yes," Will said in a low voice, "I promise I won't drive faster than you want me to."

But that was exactly what she was afraid of. That she *would* want him to go faster. That she might even *beg* him to go faster. All because those thrilling moments sitting beside Will in his fast car this afternoon had been the best ones she'd experienced in a very long time.

Only, even though there were at least a dozen reasons she should say no, when she opened her mouth the word that came out was, "Yes."

* * *

Will knew he shouldn't lead Harper on. She was a good girl. She was someone who deserved the fairytale, a guy who was as good as she was. Not an ex-thief who still battled his demons, who knew that he could never change the blood he came from, no matter how much he wished he could.

Speed had taken away far too much from Harper already—her brother's independence and her parents' lives. And yet, he could feel that she craved it all the same. Craved the rush, the thrill, just as much as he did.

Just as much as he craved *her.*

Will wanted Harper with an intensity he'd never felt before. And maybe if he hadn't felt that same intensity from her, even as she'd tried to hide it, he could have let her go. But as he stood in the late afternoon sun watching them drive away, with Jeremy waving madly out the window as they took the downhill curve and disappeared, Will knew he couldn't let her go. Couldn't let either of them go, truth be told.

Will had never known anyone with such high spirits or as much freshness as Jeremy. He had almost died all those years ago, and he'd probably been in rehab for a good part of his life since. Yet he had a boundless nature.

A Birdcage Maserati. On the drive over from the hangar, Jeremy had enumerated all the reasons why Will should build the car, most of which came down to the fact that it was awesome. And Jeremy was right—it was a truly incredible car. Having finished the Cobra a few months before taping *Hot Cars*, Will could use another project now. The problem? As he'd told

Harper, there was no such thing as a Maserati kit car.

Then again...his friend Daniel Spencer had recently told him about a guy in Europe who could scrounge up just about anything.

Will started to get an idea, one that fired him up. He'd told Jeremy he wasn't a genie, but maybe he could grant the boy's wish after all.

He pulled out his phone to call Daniel, and his friend answered on the second ring. "You're interrupting."

"What? You watching paint dry?"

"More like a dozen cameramen all groaning since we're going to have to do this take over," Daniel told him. "Whatever you've got to say, make it snappy so that I can get back to it."

Despite their razzing, Will knew his friend was happy to hear from him. They didn't get together nearly enough lately, not since success had pulled the five of them in so many different directions. It was why Daniel had picked up Will's call in the middle of a take for his home improvement show. Will would drop anything for any of the Mavericks, even if he was in the most important business meeting of his career. They, along with Bob and Susan, always came first.

Daniel owned the largest home improvement chain in the United States. He operated four plants across the country, manufacturing his own line of machines and tools. But the last time he'd held a paintbrush or a hammer—and used it for more than a shot on his TV show—had been in the previous decade. Will had started to wonder if that was a good thing for Daniel, who'd always been the guy that had not only *liked* working with his hands, but had also seemed to *need* it.

Just the way Will needed speed.

"You have the contact info for that guy in Italy?"

"Rupert?"

"Yeah. Sheet metal. Fiberglass fabrication. You said he's damn near an artist."

"Sure, I'll text it to you now. That all you want?"

"Yeah, thanks. See you on Memorial Day. Bring beer."

The conversation ended. They didn't have deep discussions every day. But the Mavericks were always there for him no matter what. And vice versa.

The Maserati wasn't a life-and-death issue that he needed to discuss. It wasn't a business problem he wanted to mull over with one of the guys. Meeting a new woman didn't usually rank up there, either. Yet there was something about Harper...

Something special.

CHAPTER FIVE

The following evening, the tattoo high on Will's right arm disappeared from sight as he pulled a long-sleeved shirt over it.

The tattoo was of a muscle car with the words *Road Warriors* curved over it in stylized lettering, small drops of red dripping off the *W* and the second and third *R*. He never let anyone see it, not even the women he slept with, making sure that it was either dark in the room or that he didn't take off his shirt. Even when dressed at his most casual, he chose T-shirts with sleeves of the necessary length.

When he was eighteen, Susan had suggested that he could get the tattoo removed. But he needed to leave it as a reminder of where he'd come from.

And of who he really was.

No matter how much Will changed on the outside, how many people he helped, or how much money he made—he knew he would always be his father's son. A father who was a liar, a thief, and a bully. *You're a chip right off the old block,* was what Gino Franconi had told him many, many times. And even though Will hadn't seen his father in more than twenty years, he never wanted to forget that his blood ran dirty—didn't want to think he could ever turn cocky and let his guard drop just because he hadn't screwed up for two decades. He'd easily need a lifetime to make up for the liar and thief he'd been.

And yet, sometimes his need for that rush was just so damned strong...

Will had never put anyone in the hospital the way the teen who'd crashed into Jeremy had, but he'd still hurt a hell of a lot of people when he was younger, people who hadn't deserved to have their cars stolen or their kids' lives turned upside down by being dragged into a gang by a punk like Will. He'd hotwired stolen cars, drag-raced, fought hard, drunk hard. And that had been *after* his father had gone to prison and Will had moved in with Daniel's parents. At the time, Susan had been a couple of years younger than Will was now, but she'd started going gray because of him. And Bob, the same age as Susan, had lost what little hair he'd had. Without Susan and Bob and the Mavericks, Will would have remained his father's son for the rest of his life, still living in that dirty, neglected Chicago neighborhood.

Will wasn't proud of the kid he'd been. And he definitely wasn't proud that it had taken him so long to change. Way too long. And way too late.

He tucked the shirt into his dark jeans and buckled his belt, thinking about the pact he'd made with the other Mavericks. The day they'd made that pact was the day he finally understood he'd found his true family in the Mavericks, never the Road Warriors. He, Daniel, and Sebastian were eighteen, almost out of high school. Evan and Matt had another year to go, but they were all ready to turn their backs on Chicago and everything in it, except Susan and Bob. They'd sworn to get out, to make it big. They'd come from hell, aimed for a heaven gilded in gold, iced with diamonds, and they'd done it, all of them. If it weren't for the fact that Susan and Bob refused to leave their hometown, Will would never go back there. Thank God Daniel had at least convinced his parents to move to a decent suburb and accept a house the five of them could well afford to buy for the couple.

Yesterday, Harper had seen the entrepreneur, the businessman, the cars, the house, the money. She hadn't seen the *Road Warrior*, and he planned to keep it that way. He was glad that she'd told him her story and he hoped to learn even more about her tonight. But he knew with utter certainty that *his* story wasn't one he should ever tell her.

Not if he wanted her to stick around with him for even a little while.

And though he'd only spent a couple of hours with her, he already knew he wanted her to stick around a hell of a lot longer than that.

* * *

What was she supposed to wear to dinner with a billionaire?

Dressed only in panties and bra, Harper stared into her meager closet. A pile of discarded clothing lay on the bed—jeans, shirts, a couple of dresses. Nothing seemed right, certainly not any of her staid work clothes. She had one serviceable cocktail dress, but Will had been just as mysterious about where he was taking her as he was about everything else. For all she knew, he had something outrageous planned, like a hot air balloon ride in Napa, or a flight to Tahoe in his private jet for an intimate dinner in an exclusive casino restaurant. Didn't rich men on TV always do things like that to show off on first dates?

Jeremy banged on her door. He did everything exuberantly, which she usually loved. Tonight, however, the loud pounding was reverberating a little too loudly through her brain. "Harper, he'll be here soon. Aren't you ready yet?"

She was showered, her hair washed, and her makeup done. She just had to decide on her outfit—hopefully before the next century rolled around. "I'll be out in a minute."

Jeremy had talked nonstop about Will since yesterday. His cars, his garage, his tools, how nice he was. And secretly, she had to admit she'd been just as thrilled about how attentive Will had been to her. She didn't scold herself for that, though. After all, what normal woman wouldn't be affected by his attention?

Speeding beside him in the car, with the wind whipping her hair all around, had made her feel wild. And *free*. More free than she'd been in a very long time. For so long she'd been so careful, but Will had aimed right at the heart of all her secret desires, and in the end she'd been helpless to turn down dinner with him.

Just one night to pretend that she was a normal woman, with a normal life.

Surely, taking her eye off the ball for one short dinner couldn't hurt anything, could it?

Jeremy banged on the door again. "Are you ready?"

She closed her eyes and stuck her hand in the closet, grabbing a hanger. Whatever it was, that's what she'd wear. It turned out to be a flowing, brightly printed skirt that hit her at midcalf. Maybe just a little too sweet, so she paired it with a form-fitting cream-colored sweater and a pair of heels.

At long last, she picked up her purse from the dresser and opened her bedroom door. "Yes, I'm ready now."

"Wow, you look really pretty!" Jeremy said, which told her he must have chosen well, since he rarely commented on her outfits. Then again, she rarely ever dressed up, since it was always just the two of them.

"Thank you," she said, but he was already running off to get a snack from the kitchen.

They lived in a three-bedroom, two-bath house, plenty for her and Jeremy. Rather than waste the formal dining space, she'd converted it to her home office. They never used her mother's untouched living room, though, preferring the den. Their family room was open to the kitchen, with a bar and stools in between that they could use for meals. More often than not, they ate in front of the TV, mostly because she had trouble keeping the bar clean of the junk mail and completed homework assignments that accumulated there.

The TV was tuned to one of Jeremy's favorite car channels. A coloring book lay on the coffee table, surrounded by a huge box of crayons, from which he'd removed almost every one. He'd been working on an orange rooster. Coloring was an exercise assigned by his teacher, Miss Richards, to help his dexterity, though he often had trouble staying within the lines.

Harper eyed the two baskets of laundry plopped at one end of the sofa. She'd have to get to those sooner or later. Glancing at her watch, she decided there wasn't time now to do the hated task.

The doorbell chimed, and she actually jumped. Okay, maybe she was a little nervous. After all, it had been over a year since she'd gone out with a man. And Will Franconi wasn't just any man, was he?

"It's Will!" Jeremy raced to the front door.

Harper grabbed her jacket off a chair, then scooped a few things off the hall table and into the drawer as she passed. When Jeremy opened the door, Will immediately took her breath away. His white button-down shirt was open at the collar, revealing a dusting of hair climbing up from his chest, and he should have been a jeans model, they looked so great on him.

Jeremy was dancing around him on the front stoop. "She took forever to get ready, Will. I had to keep pounding on the door."

Harper closed her eyes briefly in mortification.

"That's a woman's prerogative," Will said with a smile she saw once she braved opening her eyes again.

"Well, I'm ready now," she said brightly.

"Not just ready, Harper," Will said in that low voice that sent tingles coursing through her, head to toe. "*Gorgeous.*"

He held out his hand and she let his warm fingers close around hers, palms resting together. It felt good. Too good. But she simply couldn't make herself pull away. Not when it felt like there hadn't been nearly enough good things in her life...and certainly nothing *this* good.

"I'll have her back home safe and sound, Jeremy, don't you worry."

"I wasn't worried," Jeremy said with all seriousness. "She gets to stay out as long as she wants because she's an adult."

"Trish will be here in half an hour," Harper reminded Jeremy.

She didn't mind his being alone for half an hour, but certainly not a whole evening. Number one, Jeremy didn't like the dark. And two, though she'd trained him to use 911, she wasn't confident about his reaction time. Harper always had Trish, their neighbor's college-age daughter, come in for a few hours if she was going to be late.

"I know, Harper." Her brother gave an exaggerated wave as Will led her down the front path.

She'd expected a muscle car like the Challenger. Even an expensive Ferrari or a Porsche. But he held open the door of a BMW for her. Nothing flashy or showy, though it was elegant and luxurious. He helped her with a hand to her elbow, and she felt his heat through her jacket. She couldn't remember ever being this aware of a man—the true-blue color of his eyes and the thickness of his black hair, wondering how soft it would be against her fingers.

As he closed her door and walked around to the driver's side, she firmly reminded herself that she needed to maintain dignity and control tonight.

Because something told her that Will Franconi not only had plenty of practice in sweeping a girl off her feet and making her feel completely breathless, but for some reason she couldn't understand, he was planning on putting those skills to use tonight.

With her.

CHAPTER SIX

Beside her, Will filled the car with his overwhelmingly male presence. When he was near, it felt to Harper as though everything and everyone else was eclipsed. Case in point: Despite her intention to be happy with her life the way it was—just her and Jeremy—she was heading out on a date with a man she barely knew and still wasn't at all sure she could trust.

As Will headed up Sand Hill Road, out to the freeway, he said, "I hope you like Italian. I know a great place in Woodside, not far from here."

"It sounds lovely." Though her job was talking and bringing people together, she felt horribly tongue-tied. What was so different about Will that simply sitting next to him made her heat up all over and her brain go blank?

"Why recruiting?" he asked into the silence after he'd merged into the freeway traffic.

Glad that at least one of them was able to think straight enough to start a conversation, she said, "I've always liked connecting people and helping them find a career that's just the right fit. Plus, it's a fairly flexible job, so I can work from home or arrange meetings around Jeremy as I need to."

They exited at Woodside and headed west. The roads were winding and two-lane here. The town was small and quaint, surrounded by horse farms and large estates. They passed a small vineyard with bright green leaves and grape clusters just starting to appear.

"I know you're not looking for anyone to give you credit, but you've obviously done an amazing job taking care of your brother." He glanced at her, and she was surprised to see admiration in his expression. "Especially when you're so young. And with all his special needs, not many people could handle that."

But she didn't feel particularly young. She'd grown up fast after Jeremy's accident. "He's got school and a job at the local grocery store. So he keeps pretty busy without me, actually." And she felt guilty letting Will think she'd taken miraculous care of Jeremy on her own. "The truth is that I couldn't have managed without the trust."

"Trust?"

She'd already told him too much in his garage. But he was obviously quite good at realizing when there was more—and at getting her to share it. "The father of the teenager who hit Jeremy set up a fund."

Will was silent a long moment before saying, "I wanted to ask you before, did the kid go to prison?"

"No one saw anything. And my parents had to take the money because they couldn't pay for everything that Jeremy needed." Though she knew it might sound defensive, she couldn't stop herself from adding, "My parents did what they had to do."

Will took his hand off the stick shift and placed it over hers for a moment. One that was too brief before he had to change gears again, but long enough for her to be seared by his heat—and touched by his obvious compassion.

"Of course your parents did what anyone would have done in their position."

It meant a lot to her that he didn't seem to be judging either her or her parents for using the trust to take care of Jeremy. Still, she felt as though she'd told him pretty much everything about herself at this point. Now she wanted to know *his* story. Because even if this was just one night away from real life, she couldn't help but want to know where he'd come from and how he'd gotten here.

"Tell me about you, Will."

A muscle jumped in his jaw right before he gave her a crooked smile. "My life is already out there on the Internet."

But all the Internet said was that he was a self-made man from Chicago who'd dated several gorgeous models and actresses. She also knew that he was part of a consortium called The Maverick Group, whose members were all self-made men like him.

Everything else about Will Franconi—the man, not the billionaire—was a mystery. One that she couldn't help but want to solve.

And yet, at the same time, she knew she shouldn't let herself get invested in him. They weren't going to fall madly in love, get married, and live happily ever after—it was just a drive and dinner, after all. Not the first night of the rest of their lives together.

As if by design, before she could ask anything more, he pulled into a parking lot and said, "We're here."

She was pleased to see that the restaurant looked homey, a place she'd be comfortable in, rather than a flashy see-and-be-seen kind of place. The small yard of the yellow Victorian house with a wraparound porch and dormer windows was filled with flowering bushes and a carved wood sign that read *Ristorante Cannelli*.

Will got out, but Harper didn't wait for him to come around and open her door. Not that she minded men holding doors for her, but it seemed odd to sit there waiting for it. Seeing that she'd taken care of herself, he retrieved something from the backseat, then offered her his arm like a gentleman as they crossed the gravel lot.

Had he learned his manners from his mother? Or maybe he'd modeled them after his father? Yet again, she found herself wanting to know the answers despite herself.

"Mama Cannelli makes a duck ravioli to die for." He kissed his fingers in a very Italian gesture.

A young hostess greeted them as they entered. She was obviously of Italian descent, with long dark hair, dark eyes, and a full hourglass figure. "Mr. Franconi, Mama will be so happy to see you. We've held your special table."

"Thank you, Katerina." Harper shouldn't have cared that he didn't react to the other woman's beauty. But she couldn't help but be pleased that he only seemed to have eyes for her tonight. "Please tell Mama Cannelli I have a surprise for her." Will held up the tin he'd taken from the backseat.

The house hadn't been gutted to make a large dining room. Instead, tables with red-checked cloths had been set up in each of the rooms, the formal dining room to the left and the front parlor to the right. A big picture mirror over the fireplace reflected the patrons. Candles in glass jars and small pots of flowers gave the room a homey touch. Harper wasn't overdressed nor was Will underdressed.

It wasn't what she'd expected at all. No show, no flash. No private jets or hot air balloons.

And she loved it.

She also loved the tang of tomato sauce, garlic, and spices that trailed behind them as

Katerina led the way upstairs and along the landing. Will's special table was by the window overlooking a back garden awash in azaleas and hydrangeas.

Katerina laid down the menus as Will pulled out Harper's chair. "Your usual drink, Mr. Franconi?"

"Please."

"And for the lady?"

"A Riesling would be lovely if you have it."

The girl left, and Will set the tin on the table as he sat. Harper could see only the back label, the print too small to read.

"This place looks fabulous." Harper expected that they'd be fawned over, the center of attention. But Will was treated just like any other diner in the room.

"Great food. Good price." Will unrolled his utensils from the napkin. "I'm a big believer in value."

"Is that what you do? In your business, I mean. Give people value?"

"I give them what they *want*. I pay attention to current fads, but I've always had an eye for the good stuff. Something exclusive and expensive. The value is in how badly people want something unique. And that's all in the perception."

Glad that he didn't seem to mind talking about his business, at the very least, she asked, "Like what?"

"Some people will pay anything to be able to say something is one of a kind, so that they've got bragging rights. They don't want to walk into a store and buy it or get it on the Internet. It's designer couture. Like an award-winning Japanese single malt whiskey of which only fifty bottles were produced. Or a Turkish rug that took two years to weave. My customer is happy to pay for that one-of-a-kind perceived value, and then I pass it on to the artisan and make my profit at the same time." He spread his hands. "Everyone's happy."

It couldn't be standard business practice to share the wealth with the people who did the actual labor, but she already knew from her time in his garage with Jeremy that Will wasn't typical. Not when most rich men would have tossed Jeremy's letter in the trash—or treated him like there was something wrong with him.

Still, she didn't entirely understand. "What kind of people would pay so much?"

"The kind of people who have more money than they can possibly spend."

He'd compared luxury goods to designer couture, the fifty-thousand-dollar designer dresses celebrities wore to the Oscars. But the exorbitant amounts were beyond her.

Just like *he* was beyond her.

Harper had a perfectly good sense of self-worth, and yet she wasn't going to lie to herself and say that everything about Will's world didn't make her head spin. She couldn't imagine living a life like his.

"Do you regularly travel to Japan and Turkey?" She'd never been outside the U.S. She'd had dreams, of course, but after her parents died, it wasn't a luxury she could afford. Not yet, anyway, though she was saving up. One day she and Jeremy would see all the places she'd read about curled up on the couch at night.

"It's one of the perks of what I do." Smile crinkles appeared at the corners of his eyes.

"And do you have any brothers or sisters?"

"No." The crinkles disappeared. His face shut down. The muscle in his jaw jumped again. "Not by blood, anyway."

Clearly, he was far more comfortable talking about his business than he was about anything personal. And she hated that she'd said something that had clearly prodded old wounds, especially when she knew how difficult it was to have to tell people the hard stuff over and over again.

Fortunately, just then a woman burst through the doorway, chattering in Italian to the wait staff. She swished through the tables, a tray balanced on her hand with Harper's wine and a frosty mug of beer for Will.

"Mr. Franconi." She set down both drinks with a flourish.

"Mama Cannelli." Will rose to hug her.

She was the stereotypical Italian mother from the movies, with a round face, round body, and dark hair sprinkled with strands of silver. Her dress was something out of the 1950s, protected with a black apron.

"This is my friend Harper."

Mama Cannelli beamed. "Very nice, very pretty," she said in melodious, Italian-laced English. "I hope you don't eat like a bird."

"I very much enjoy eating good food," Harper said with a smile. "Will recommended the ravioli."

The woman's entire face smiled—her forehead, her laugh lines, her mouth, even her dimpled chin. "Oh, he loves that duck."

"I certainly do. And I brought you a present, Mama." Will held out the tin.

"You don't need to bring me presents whenever you dine with us. All you have to do is enjoy our food." But she took the round tin in her hand, dipping into her apron pocket for a pair of reading glasses. *"Mio Dio.* I cannot accept. This is far too much."

He touched her hand. "It's a gift. I have an entire shipment. One small tin is nothing."

"It's a *pound*." Her voice rose. "A *fortune*."

"Why don't you make us a special hors d'oeuvre with it? Make some for yourself, too, and then save the rest for your very special customers."

What was in the tin? Harper still couldn't read the label.

"Please?" Will said.

"You're a terrible one." Mama Cannelli turned to Harper, her eyes sparkling. "You watch out for this one. He's a charmer. He gets his way with everyone." She turned back to Will and gave him a kiss on the cheek, one that clearly pleased him to no end. "*Grazie*, Mr. Franconi. It demands a simple preparation so as not to overwhelm the flavor. I will return shortly with the delicious treat."

"I'm dying to know," Harper asked after Mama had left them. "What was that?"

"It's a surprise for you, too."

She shot him a mock glare at keeping the mystery spinning out—something he was very good at—as the waiter arrived, introducing himself as Antonio. The Cannellis were friendly with Will, and he was very polite and considerate. No cocky finger-snapping. Maybe she'd seen too much TV, where rich people treated the help like second-class citizens who were not even worth a thank-you.

But Will wasn't like that. At least, as far as she could tell. Because as they talked over their wine and beer—a little more about his cars, about the amazing weather they'd been having, about some of her best and worst clients over the years—he managed not to say much about himself at all.

Soon, Mama Cannelli arrived with her simple yet elegant creation. "I have taste-tested. Magnificent." She kissed her fingers just as Will had earlier. "Any garnish would be a travesty."

She placed a small pot in the center of the table. Beside that she laid a plate of toasted bread slices and set a spoon by the pot. "Mother-of-pearl. We must not influence the flavors." She threw out her hands expressively. "Now eat." Then she leaned down to Will. "The ravioli tonight is on me. And a bottle of our best champagne."

"That's not necessary," Will protested, but Antonio was already popping the cork.

"One cannot have caviar without champagne," she declared. "And now I leave you alone with your beautiful lady."

"You brought her caviar?" Harper examined the pot filled with tiny golden eggs.

"I found this about six weeks ago. It's Ossetra caviar. The golden color is quite prized. And, as a bonus, the fishery is known for its conservation policies, given that the sturgeon is a threatened species." He picked up the mother-of-pearl spoon, scooped up the caviar, dabbed it on the toasted bread, and brought the slice close to her lips.

"Taste," he urged.

The action was intimate. *Sexy.*

Her heart began to beat loudly in her ears. Just as he wanted her to, Harper ate from his fingers, her lips touching his skin. But the flavor that exploded on her tongue was far more decadent than caviar.

The most delicious flavor by far was *him.*

CHAPTER SEVEN

Will felt an ache grow in his gut as he watched Harper taste caviar for what he guessed was her very first time. Her cheeks flushed as she chewed, savored, and swallowed, her tongue slipping out to lick away the excess.

The delicacy had a rich, buttery, slightly salty flavor. Mama Cannelli was right on with the preparation—no adornment, no garnish.

Harper didn't need fancy clothes or glittering jewelry, either. She shone all on her own. Shone so brightly that he wanted more and more from her by the second. Not just a dinner out. Not just one hot night.

Will wanted her to stay and fill the empty spots inside of him. And so that he might also be able to do the same for her.

He knew that he shouldn't let himself want those things from her. Nor could he argue with the voice of reason that told him he should let her find some perfect guy who had never seen or done the things from Will's hellish past. Maybe he could have lived with the things his father had made him do. But Will couldn't forget the things he'd done all on his own after the old man went to prison. He should have left the Road Warriors behind and committed to the Mavericks right then, to Bob and Susan, to his new family. But he'd gone on making mistakes for years. Until things had happened —terrible things—for which he could never forgive himself.

But none of those truths were doing a damned thing to make his desire disappear.

After he fed her another slice and relished the caress of her lips on his fingers, she said, "You're not having any."

"It's better feeding it to you."

"I can't eat it all myself." She selected a slice of toast, ladled on a spoonful of caviar, spread it, and handed over the morsel.

She deliberately kept her hand too far away to feed him. But he couldn't resist wrapping his fingers around her delicately boned wrist and pulling until she was close enough for him to catch the crisped bread between his teeth. Biting down, he took half, stroking her wrist with his thumb as he demolished the caviar.

Sweet Lord, it was *far* better now than when he'd tasted it on Saturday morning. All because of what Harper brought to it. "You're right," he said. "It's excellent."

Her hand still imprisoned, he bent to take the other half, his lips lingering on her fingers, tasting her. The salty caviar was like a chaser to her sweetness. She was breathing harder now, and he very much liked the way her skin had flushed pink with the light caress of his lips. But as they finished the caviar between them, she made sure not to prepare another slice for him. And when he spooned one for her, she inserted her hand before he could put it to her lips.

He was getting too close in more ways than one. And Harper was backing off. The problem was that one taste of her had him dying for more. Just as he'd known it would.

Mama's food demanded a diner's attention, and neither of them disappointed as they polished off everything on the plates put before them.

"Are you sure you don't want dessert?" he asked after Harper waved Antonio away. "The crème brûlée will melt on your tongue." The sight would have driven him crazy but it would have been well worth it just to see the look on her beautiful face when she tasted heaven.

"It was all so good, but I'm stuffed."

Mama refused to bring a bill, as Will had known she would. But he'd wanted the sweet lady to enjoy the caviar.

"You're too good to us, Mr. Franconi."

Will folded an arm around her shoulders, hugging her close. She reminded him of Susan, with her big heart and her love of family. She even patted Harper's cheek, and said, "Please come again."

"I will."

Yes, she definitely would, if Will had anything to say about it.

As they'd eaten, he'd dominated the questions while managing to brush aside Harper's for him. And he'd learned that everything she did was for or about her brother. Her job choice, where she lived, how often she got out on her own—all of it was about what best suited Jeremy's needs. Again and again, she'd waved away Will's admiration, saying it was all because of the trust fund some rich guy had used to appease his conscience. But he could see how much of herself she'd devoted to her brother. He'd hinted about whether there were any other men in her life, but it wasn't hard to guess that there, too, Jeremy took precedence.

Except that in their case, Jeremy had given Will his stamp of approval to take her to dinner—as well as saying that Harper could stay out as long as she wanted, because she was an adult. Remembering the solemn statement made Will smile.

Hell, yes, Harper was an adult, a gorgeous woman who gave him the kind of rush he'd only ever had from fast cars before. And it was a very good thing that she could stay out late tonight... because Will was *far* from done with their evening.

"Let's go for a drive." It was pitch black outside as they got into the car. "I'll put the top down and crank up the heater."

"I should get home."

Harper, he'd noticed, used an awful lot of *should*s and *shouldn't*s. And the more she piled on, the more he wanted to blast through all of them, wanted to see her eyes light up and her skin flush, to watch her let go just as she had on their short ride around the runways.

"I promise not to drive too fast."

"It's not that," she said, even though he knew it had to be, after what she'd been through with those crashes in her family. "And you don't have to keep promising."

But he did, because she didn't trust him yet. Smart woman. "We'll just take a short drive to a place you'll like, then."

She glared at him, but only managed to look adorable as she said, "You always get your way, don't you?"

"I try," he said with a grin.

Most people were willing to give him his way. But then, most of them wanted something from him. Whereas from everything he'd seen so far, Harper didn't. In fact, if he let her have her way, she'd be keeping her distance from him rather than letting him come closer.

But he couldn't stand the thought of giving her up. Not when she sparked something inside him that he'd never felt with another woman.

"Come on, Harper," he said in the same voice both he and Jeremy had used on her when they'd wanted her to change her mind. "Say yes."

She sighed, but her lips had curved up at the corners. "All right. A short drive."

* * *

Harper should have made Will take her home, but she'd told Trish she'd be out until ten or ten-thirty, so she figured she had a little time left for a drive.

They hurtled along a two-lane road, the top down, her hair blowing. "I thought you promised not to go too fast." A mesh bar between the head rests kept the rush of air from overpowering their voices.

He slid a lock of her hair back behind her ear, then pointed past her. "I'm going slower than the cars on the freeway."

He was always touching her—a hand at her back as she climbed the stairs, fingers at her elbow as he helped her into the car—his touch making her crazy inside.

Looking out the passenger window gave her an excuse to draw away, far enough to breathe without his scent filling her head. The road paralleled the highway, with lush greenery flashing by on the other side. He was right; the cars up there were traveling considerably faster.

"It's the convertible. It makes everything feel like it's rushing past." He downshifted around a turn, and trees rose up between them and the freeway. "I'm not going to promise never to drive you faster than you want to go, Harper, but I can promise that I'll never let you get hurt."

Her fingers dug into the door's armrest. But it wasn't fear. Far from it.

The wind in her hair, the *shush* of tires on the road, the feel of speed—it was all so exhilarating. She found herself wanting Will to take her faster than she'd ever dared. And she wanted to believe he'd never allow her to be hurt.

He made her feel things, made her want things she shouldn't. Like the moment he'd taken the toasted bread and caviar from her fingers, when she'd wanted to feel the warmth of his mouth and know the taste of his skin. When she'd wanted to bask forever beneath the sensual heat in his eyes.

He was as dangerous as her desire for speed and just as addictive. He had her saying yes when she should say no.

Heck, he even had her asking herself *why* she needed to say no!

As the headlights slashed through the darkness, she couldn't tell how fast they were going. And, at least for the moment, as the moon and the stars shone above and the crisp air moved over her heated skin, she couldn't bring herself to care.

She caught his gaze, and in the moonlight, she swore she could see in him the same wildness that was brimming in her.

He was so far beyond any man she'd dated. Her most serious relationship had been with a middle manager for a company she'd done business with. Kevin owned his own home and was amassing his 401(k), and she'd thought he was a prize until he'd suggested that Harper should send Jeremy to a care facility to live with strangers. But Kevin was like a fly on the wall compared to Will, who wore his power and magnetism as though he'd been born to them. Even though, from what she'd read about him, there was no indication he'd come from any money at all, especially since he was always referred to as a self-made man. She hadn't been sure about much of his past before meeting him and was no clearer after their dinner.

Still, even though he was a mystery—or maybe because of that—she wanted to put her palm over his on the stick shift, mold her fingers around his on the steering wheel. She wanted to touch him, feel the power of the car with him, sense the speed.

Sense *him*.

It was wild. It was crazy. It wasn't like her.

And yet...tonight, it felt right.

More right than anything had in a very long time.

CHAPTER EIGHT

The car rocked through a few ruts until Will stopped beside a chain-link fence. Harper tried to smooth her hair down after the wild ride, even though it had to be a lost cause by now.

"Where are we?" She heard the breathlessness in her voice, a sensual sound no one had ever brought out in her before.

"An old fountain I found while I was out exploring the area after I first moved to California."

Despite the fact that he was a businessman at the very top of his game, she could easily imagine him screaming through the countryside in one of his fancy cars, taking roads no one else would dare try, finding places no one else would go. "How long have you lived here?"

"A little over a decade." Once they'd climbed from the car, he extended his hand to her. "It's locked, but I know a way in."

Of course he did. Something told her Will Franconi knew *exactly* how to get into anything he wanted, whether it was off limits or not.

Even, possibly, a heart like hers that had been shut down for far too long.

She put her hand in his, the contact doing nothing to calm the racing of her heart. He'd touched her way too much already. And she'd not only let him, she'd wanted him to touch even *more* of her, if she were being completely honest with herself.

She'd been worried about Jeremy getting too attached—but wasn't she in just as much danger?

They prowled along the fence for several yards, then Will kicked at a bottom piece until it pushed loose. He let go of her hand to slide through the opening. On the other side, he tangled his fingers in the chain link and pulled it higher, widening the gap for her. "You'll have to bend down a bit."

She was wearing heels. This was crazy. But the whole night was already crazy—a crazy blip away from her usual reality—so she gathered her skirt, crouched down, and shimmied through, sneaking under the chain link like a naughty teenager.

The fence fell back with a metallic clang, and Will took her hand again. This time his grip was tighter, warmer. More possessive, as if he thought he'd already made her his. And at this very moment, she wasn't sure he was wrong, not when she was so aware of him that she could feel her own pulse at her throat, beating faster, rushing like the wind over the car.

"Over here." His deep voice was laced with a hint of excitement. The same excitement she couldn't help but feel herself.

He seemed to have vision like a cat, picking his way through the grass. She could hear water ahead, the crash and babble over rocks. Something dark loomed ahead of them, then formed walls and columns, like a small Greek temple.

Will pulled her up to the edge, a parapet overlooking a dark hole through which the water rushed. "It's part of an old aqueduct. Crystal Springs Reservoir is just down the road."

Water crashed beneath them, and no grate covered the hole. If she leaned too far, she'd fall right in. But Will's hand kept her steady. Steady and safe, even though she knew that what she was beginning to feel for him was the most dangerous thing imaginable.

The scent of the water was clean and fresh, as though the river below had come straight from the mountains. Cool air blew up, pushing through her hair, caressing her like fingers. Like Will's touch.

The noise all around, the darkness, her hand in his, the closeness of his body, his thigh pressed to hers, his heat—it was too much. Too good. Too mesmerizing.

Something was burning inside her, a secret need that she'd worked so hard to push down for so many years. It had begun with dinner, when they'd taken the caviar from each other's fingers, then sizzled in the car as they'd sped through the night. And now, as they explored a secret, off-limits place together, she was simply burning up inside.

He turned to her then, and if he'd said something, anything, she might have found some control. But when he simply *looked*, with something sparkling in his eyes that felt like longing and desire entwined, Harper was lost.

She had to taste him, had to see if his kiss would be as good as the fast ride he'd just given her in his car.

Her fingers fisted in his shirt, and she yanked him close, chest to chest. Then she was up on her tippy toes, wrapping her arms around his neck, bringing his mouth down to hers. Angling her head, she licked along his lips, savoring him just as she had the caviar.

But it was the moan she couldn't keep inside that truly set everything in motion. An instant later, Will was holding her tighter and lifting her off the ground. His mouth came down hard against hers and she had to cling to his arms to steady herself. Seating her on the edge of the parapet, he cupped her face in his big hands and devoured her.

Just the same way she was devouring him.

She couldn't get enough—the hard, strong length of him as he stood between her legs, the headiness of his kiss. In a matter of moments, he had taken control of the kiss she'd initiated, and she was stunned to realize that she loved the way he played with her, sweeping in, stealing her breath, then backing off to take her lips at another angle, before going deep again.

He wooed her passion out and out and out, until it was inextricably tangled up with his. The stone was cold beneath her, a delicious contrast to the burning heat inside and the warmth of his mouth on hers.

No one had ever kissed her like this— taking, demanding absolutely everything she had to give. Kissing had been a prelude with other men, but Will made it seem like kissing her was exactly what he'd been dying for, precisely what he'd dreamed of.

And Harper realized she'd been dreaming about it all along, too. From the moment he'd stepped out of his car beside the hangar, she'd been hurtling toward this moment without even knowing it.

He skimmed his fingers down her arms. "Hold on to me," he murmured against her lips, bringing her hands up around his shoulders.

 His mouth consumed her all over again, his hands on the move, leaving trails of heat. His thumbs grazed the sides of her breasts, setting fire to all her nerve endings. Harper couldn't breathe. She could only *want.* Could only *need* as his mouth owned her and his hands promised pleasures beyond her wildest dreams.

Teetering on the edge, she knew she was going to fall. Not into the water, but into something far deeper. Right into Will. Into anything he wanted, right here, right now, with the water raging below them and the midnight sky burning above.

And then nothing would ever be the same again.

She suddenly pushed at him, slamming the brakes on with a squeal of her heart. "Wait, wait, wait."

She needed to stop, needed to breathe, needed to try and think straight. This was going too fast. Way too fast.

All she'd wanted was a test drive. All she'd wanted was to see if he kissed the way he drove.

But it turned out that kissing Will Franconi was a million times better than any fast ride could ever be.

She never, ever took her eye off the ball. Never for one second forgot that her focus needed to be on taking care of her brother, with everything else coming a distant second. But tonight, for a few heady moments in Will's arms, she'd forgotten.

Forgotten so easily that it terrified her.

"You okay?" he asked. His breathing wasn't so steady, either, but that was no consolation.

"I need a minute, just a minute."

But the truth was that she needed way more than that, needed to find a way to clear her head, her body, of everything Will had just done to her with only one hot kiss.

"I got carried away." There was a raw huskiness in his voice, and the moonlight was bright enough that she could see the pulse beating hard and fast at his throat. "Forgive me, Harper."

But Will didn't need to be forgiven for anything. *She* was the one who had just lost her mind over his kiss, while making the extremely troubling discovery that nothing had ever given her as much pleasure as going fast with him just had.

Which was especially crazy given that caution was her watchword where men were concerned. Sure, she knew it was a world where people jumped into bed on first dates, but that wasn't what she did. And not with someone like Will Franconi. Not with a fast man who owned a whole bunch of fast cars. If she were stupid enough to jump into his bed, she couldn't also be stupid enough not to expect him to drive right on past her as soon as they were through.

"I'm the one who should be apologizing," she told him. "I shouldn't have kissed—"

He put a palm to her cheek and his thumb on her lips to halt the rest of her words. "Yes, you definitely should have." Then he added, his mouth only a kiss away, "Your kiss was better than the richest caviar I've ever tasted. You taste better than *anything* I've ever tasted, Harper."

She was stunned at how he simply seemed to accept that they'd gone too fast and pushed past her comfort zone, rather than being angry with her for slamming the brakes on a super hot kiss. A kiss that *she* had been the one to initiate.

Harper needed to make it clear to him that there wasn't going to be another kiss between them, but the words wouldn't come. "I should go," was all she could manage. Although the truth was that it was probably all she needed to say, since she couldn't imagine he'd want to see her again. Why would a gorgeous billionaire who could have anyone want a woman with whom he always had to try so hard? Even just to set up a date? "I don't want to keep Trish out late."

Will slowly backed off, his hands trailing down her arms, leaving thrill bumps in their wake. Holding her at the waist, he helped her down from the parapet, then took her hand in his and led her back across the grass to the hole in the fence. She walked on the balls of her feet so her heels wouldn't sink into the grass.

Back in the car, she asked him to put the top up. "It's getting cold." She touched her hair. "And my hair is already enough of a mess."

"Your hair is gorgeous."

Of course he'd say that. He always had the perfect words. And it wasn't truly her hair that worried her. She was afraid the speed would turn her into a wild thing again, and she might actually throw herself at him while he was driving.

Slow, steady, rational—that was what had worked for Harper and Jeremy for the past several years, and she couldn't risk messing up anything for the two of them. Especially not with a man like Will, whom she sincerely doubted had the long haul on his mind.

It all made perfect sense in her head. Unfortunately, however, neither *perfect sense* nor the much slower ride back down the peninsula to her house did a darned thing to help quench her thirst for more of Will.

CHAPTER NINE

Other than a text saying how much he'd enjoyed their date, Will deliberately left Harper alone for a few days to think things through. She'd told him she wanted time. So he forced himself to give it to her, even though the need to hear her voice was like an ache inside him.

As for Jeremy, Will didn't want her brother to think he'd been forgotten, so they'd talked cars over Skype a couple of times, and had emailed, as well. Will figured that Harper must be reading his emails because she'd said Jeremy sometimes needed help with the computer. He didn't use big words, but everything was spelled correctly, as though Harper had made him run spell check before hitting Send. Will enjoyed Jeremy's emails. He was always upbeat, always excited about whatever car picture or information Will sent him.

What a way to live, seeing only the good.

Needing to wait a few more minutes until midnight to make his call to Italy, Will spent the time thinking about Harper, a pastime that had become almost like breathing. She'd been perfect on their date, from beginning to end. She'd looked—and tasted—like a fantasy. He knew he could have pushed for more in the wake of their kiss, could have stripped her bare in the moonlight, could have tasted her soft skin everywhere and taken her straight to heaven. But despite how much he'd wanted to do just that, he'd also known it meant risking any ground he'd gained with her over dinner.

And even though they'd only just met, he wasn't willing to chance losing Harper.

Instead, he wanted to know her—wanted to know what made her laugh, what made her sigh, what heated her up, and what cooled her down.

Sitting alone in his office, he had to fight the urge to call her. Three days, and he'd missed her like hell. He'd never called a woman just to hear her voice. Will enjoyed women, of course. But it had always seemed that one female was much the same as another.

Until a smile—and a kiss—from Harper had rocked his world.

Lord, he loved the way she'd practically dived on him, with no restraint, no hesitation. He knew her focus was on Jeremy and her job, and that her needs always came second to those. But for a few moments when she'd been in his arms, nothing had held her back.

At least, not until she'd realized how fast they were going, hitting the gas harder than any race car driver ever had. Will loved speed, lived for it, knew he needed the rush to keep his secret darkness from spiraling out of control again the way it had when he was a teenager. But though speed clearly called to Harper, too, she fought like hell against it. He understood her reasons in the wake of her brother's and parents' crashes, and yet he couldn't help but want her to embrace the rush and the thrill again with him. The same way she'd embraced him for those few precious moments by the aqueduct—with nothing held back.

The truth was, however, that Harper wasn't the only one who needed time. Will needed it, as well, to force himself to think through his own intentions from all angles.

He'd never romanced a woman before, never pursued one with unwavering focus. The press assumed it was because he was a player, and thankfully they'd never dug deeply into his reasons for keeping all of his relationships on the surface. He'd never let the women he'd been with before Harper get close enough to find out his real story, either.

But if he pursued Harper—if he romanced her, and also helped her tap into that secret well of wildness and passion that he believed ran deep and true inside of her, the way his every instinct demanded—how long would he be able to keep his past hidden? How fast would she leave him if she ever found out what he was really made of and the sins that tainted his soul?

He wished with everything he was that he could rewind the clock, back to that day with the Road Warriors when everything had spiraled so far out of control. But he couldn't have a do-over. He hadn't saved that kid. He hadn't saved the Road Warriors.

And he sure as hell hadn't saved his own soul.

Will couldn't stand the thought of hurting Harper in any way. He would never forgive himself if he did. And yet, everything inside of him rebelled at the thought of letting her walk permanently out of his life. Somehow, he needed to find a way to get closer to her while still keeping her safe.

He'd walked a lot of fine lines in his life, but he had a feeling this one just might be the trickiest line of all. Not to mention the most important.

Will's computer beeped. Midnight. Time for his call. He clicked it into life and a grizzled face appeared on the screen.

"Mr. Franconi, I hope you are having a pleasant evening. I received your email. And the attachments."

Though he lived in Italy, Rupert Rivoli was French, and his lilting accent had turned to gravel with age and cigars. He could have been anywhere from fifty to eighty. His skin was slightly sallow and dark pouches bloomed beneath his eyes. But he was the best of the best. After getting his contact info from Daniel, Will had researched the man. Rupert had been a master craftsman at Maserati—a miracle worker.

Will had a miracle of his own he wanted the man to perform. "Can it be done, Rupert? Can you make me a Birdcage Maserati kit?"

"Of course it can be done, Mr. Franconi." He sounded almost offended. "It is only a matter of money. And time."

"Money is no object. And I'll pay to have it as quickly as possible."

"You understand I will have to coordinate my work with commissioning the engine, transmission, and other parts. It is not a small undertaking, Mr. Franconi."

"That's why I'll pay you whatever you need to get it done. We can start with the chassis and sheet metal pieces. Then I'll need to lay in all the wiring. You can take longer to get the engine and transmission. Tell your crew I'll give a bonus for early delivery."

The older man wagged his head, staring down at the schematics Will had sent. "These will have to be modified for what you want."

During the past couple of days, Will had combed the Internet for a similar racing model. What he wanted, though, was much more specialized. "You're the only man who can do this." It wasn't flattery, it was true.

"I will try, Mr. Franconi, but my shop has customers."

Rupert's *shop* was damn near a factory. He was the largest employer in his small town. He had a reputation for overseeing every project like a hawk. Will had a feeling the man would be so intrigued by the project that he'd do a lot of the work himself.

"I'm willing to pay to get this design first in line. I'll even pay your customers a wait fee, if that's what it takes."

"You make an offer a man cannot refuse. But what is the penalty if I discover I cannot deliver on time?"

There was always a penalty clause. But Will was asking for a miracle. "No penalty. Just give me your honest estimate, and I'll work with that. Keep in mind that this is a present for a teenage boy. And I don't want him disappointed." Which was why Will would approach Harper about the car after it was a done deal. He didn't want to get Jeremy's hopes up only to crush them later.

Rupert nodded gravely. "Your son is a lucky boy."

"Not my son. A friend."

"Then he is very lucky to have a friend like you. I will do my best. You will hear from me by the end of the week."

Will was the lucky one. For the first time in years, he felt major excitement stirring in his gut. It was partly the new project. It was partly doing something that would mean so much to someone else. It would be the look on Jeremy's face when he invited the kid to help build the Birdcage Maserati.

But most of all, it was *Harper*.

* * *

Working from home, Harper's Thursday morning had been so full with phone interviews and follow-ups for her recruiting company that she hadn't even folded the weekend's laundry. Too often, she didn't finish putting away the previous week's clean clothes before she had to wash the current week's dirty ones.

She pushed her hair out of her face as she stared in dismay at the mess in the family room. On the coffee table, Jeremy's coloring book and crayons were a hodgepodge of color. The kitchen bar was littered with papers, lists, notes, and several days' worth of junk mail. She really needed to weed out the important stuff and toss the rest. But housecleaning was always at the bottom of the to-do list.

This afternoon, she told herself. And this time she meant it.

Now, where was the Gordon resume? She could have sworn it was on the dining table, which served as her desk. Back in the dining room, she sat down at her computer to reprint the resume.

She hadn't been quite this disorganized in the past when she'd gone into an office every day, but at home things sometimes got away from her. Jeremy often dropped his notebook on top of her work, and he'd been known to accidentally grab her papers along with his homework. He'd also been using the computer to email Will, who had come up with the brilliant idea to use Skype, too.

Will.

He always told Jeremy to tell her he said hi, but Harper hadn't spoken directly to Will since their dinner at Cannelli's. Not since she'd thrown herself at him by the water temple...and then completely freaked out.

She was still embarrassed at the way she'd acted on their first—and only—date. Throwing herself at a man, and then flip-flopping back to being stone cold, wasn't like her at all. She wanted to apologize for her behavior at the same time that she wished she could forget all about it.

In any case, it was very nice of Will to continue corresponding with Jeremy even though he didn't want to go out with her again. And it was all for the best that they didn't become more deeply involved, of course. It was taking everything she had to keep her and Jeremy's life together as it was. She didn't need to add a complication like Will Franconi to her personal life.

Unfortunately, just because she didn't *need* something didn't mean she didn't *want* it...

"Okay, stop thinking." Especially when her thoughts were going round and round in circles about a man she could never have. "You've got work to do."

She'd just found the resume buried deep in her email inbox and was about to print it out again when the doorbell rang. She glanced at her watch. Had she forgotten an appointment? Or maybe it was Trish?

Harper opened the door to find Will standing there, beyond scrumptious in a dark suit, charcoal shirt, and black tie. He had been mouthwatering in jeans, but in a suit and tie...*oh my*...he was downright edible. She felt the impact, and the heat of him, low in her belly.

Like a match striking to life with a sizzle and a hiss.

CHAPTER TEN

"What are you doing here?" Harper realized how rude it sounded as soon as the words came out, but fortunately Will didn't seem at all put off.

"I was on my way to a meeting. But I wanted to talk to you about a new project first."

"A new project?"

"It's for Jeremy."

"Jeremy," she echoed, still feeling totally off balance at his unexpected visit.

"May I come in?"

She hesitated, glancing over her shoulder. The house. The mess. She was about to be a *whole* lot more embarrassed in a minute. But Will's visit was about Jeremy, so she couldn't leave him standing outside.

"Of course." She opened the door wide, gesturing him inside.

The foyer was a muddle of sneakers. She made Jeremy remove his shoes when he came in, and he never seemed to wear the same pair until several were scattered about. To the right of the front hall, the dining room table held its usual clutter.

She caught sight of herself in the hall mirror. Her hair was brushed, thank God, but she hadn't put on a speck of makeup, and she'd dressed in leggings, an oversized green sweater that hung to her thighs, and very unsexy striped toe socks.

"Sorry, I was working," she said to try to explain away the piles of folders and papers. "Can I get you some coffee?" Too late, after he nodded, she realized she couldn't take him back there, with the overflowing laundry, the upended box of crayons, the untidy breakfast bar. And the full kitchen sink. "I'll be back in a minute. Why don't you have a seat in the living room?" It was the only neat room in the house because she and Jeremy never used it.

"You don't have to bring it to me," Will said. "I can pour." And when he followed her down the hall, there was no way to stop him other than throwing herself at him again...a thought that was *far* too tempting.

"Sorry," she felt compelled to say again as she spread her arms to encompass the whole misbegotten family room. "I'm not usually this messy."

"I meant it when I said that you don't have to keep apologizing to me. Not for anything." He put a finger to her lips, zinging her with an electric jolt of awareness that stopped her breath right in her chest. "If you don't stop apologizing soon, I promise I'm going to have to find another way to make you stop."

She knew she shouldn't do it, shouldn't push him to see if he meant it, shouldn't do anything to encourage his interest in her...but just as she hadn't been able to say no to a dinner with him, now she couldn't keep the word "Sorry," from leaving her lips.

Saying the word again was a dare, one he immediately rose to, as he pressed his mouth to hers for one perfect second. "Like I said, I always keep my promises." She was still trying to find her breath when he asked, "Mugs?"

With her brain still muddled from the teeny, tiny little kiss he'd just given her, she somehow managed to send a signal to her hands to point to the cupboard. Will pulled down one flowered mug and one with black and white stripes.

He filled the flowery mug with coffee from the pot on her counter, then stared into the other one. "There's something in this cup."

"It's a zebra." By the time she came around him and reached into the cupboard, her synapses were firing again, thank God. Though she still didn't understand why he'd kissed her if he was only here to discuss something that concerned her brother. "There's also a giraffe, an elephant, and a tiger." She pulled down the mugs to show him the ceramic creatures in each. "Jeremy likes the surprise at the bottom of the cup. I have to admit I like them, too."

"I'd rather be the tiger," Will said with complete seriousness, and poured into that mug instead.

She laughed, and when he grinned with her, a great deal of the tension she'd been feeling since she'd opened the door and found him standing there vanished. Especially when he said, "I like your brother a lot."

"Me, too." *And I also like you,* she couldn't help but add silently.

Will leaned back against the counter. "So here's what I propose. I finished the Cobra several months ago, and I'm ready to build a new car. I'm getting a Maserati kit, and I'd like Jeremy to help me with it, if that's okay with you."

Her mouth dropped open before she could stop it. "You mean a Birdcage Maserati? The one he's been dying for?"

"That's the one."

"But you said they don't make kits like that."

He shrugged. "I found someone who can pull it all together for me."

He made it sound so easy, but she knew it couldn't be. "That must cost a fortune. I can't let you spend that kind of money on my brother."

"I don't waste my money," he told her, "but I do like knowing I have it to spend on things that are important to me. The fact that this kit car is important to Jeremy, too, makes it worth even more. I wanted to talk to you about it before I mentioned it to him, though."

Harper knew how thrilled Jeremy was with this new friendship. Will was his first real male friend, not someone Harper had brought home. They didn't just talk about cars, but sometimes veered off into other guy things, like sports and action movies. She couldn't count the number of times she'd heard her brother invoke Will's name over the last few days.

"Look, that's very nice of you, but—" She put her mug down, stepped back, and forced herself to forget that she was talking to a powerful billionaire who was so sexy he made her knees weak. She needed to be totally honest right now. "My brother really likes you. And when you get tired of him, he's going to be hurt."

Will's expression was unreadable as he repeated, "When I get tired of him?"

"Talking to him on Skype. Buying a car to work on together. That's the kind of thing a father does. Or a brother. But you're neither of those things. And I know there must be a thousand other important things that you could be doing instead of hanging out with him. So since I don't understand your intentions, how can I not worry that he'll end up hurt?"

Will set down the tiger mug and held her gaze. "First of all, when Jeremy wrote to me, his enthusiasm came through loud and clear on the page. His attitude is refreshing and like I said, I like him." He moved in on her, one step, then two. "So where Jeremy is concerned, I don't have any intentions except to build a car I believe he'd enjoy helping me with." One more step, and he had her backed up against the breakfast bar.

"But with you?" He gently cupped her jaw, stroking it with his thumb, which left a trail of sparks in its wake. "I have a hell of a lot of intentions for you, Harper. So many you wouldn't believe it. So many I've been going crazy giving you that time you said you needed after our first date."

Her heart stuttered and stopped, then beat as wildly as it had speeding along in his car with the top down. As crazily as it had the moment she'd grabbed his shirt and dragged his mouth down to hers.

"I *intend* to touch you." He slid his hand lower to bracket her throat loosely, his fingers a light caress that turned her skin hot. "I *intend* to make you moan with pleasure."

She leaned back, gripping the counter behind her. Her legs seemed so weak that she was barely able to stay upright as he bent his head until his lips were only a breath away.

"I *intend* to kiss you so slowly, so thoroughly, that you'll be begging me to never, ever stop."

Didn't he know every inch of her already burned for him, inside and out? He was a master of the slow, agonizing caress, and everything inside seemed to be melting, every part of her burning up.

She felt the moistness of his breath along the shell of her ear. He inhaled slowly, scenting her, his chest rising, but he didn't press against her, didn't let her feel the rest of his body, which somehow made it all the more sensual and erotic.

"And I *intend* for you to have your taste of me, too." Those wicked hands of his skimmed down her sides, barely touching but laying down fiery tracks of heat nonetheless. "As much of me as you want, Harper. As much of me as you need."

She almost whimpered, almost said yes.

Yes, please.

She had to hold onto the breakfast bar behind her for dear life...otherwise she was in danger of leaping on him and begging for everything he promised.

She wanted him now. Needed him now. Was crazy for him *now*. And all she had to do was take—put her hands on him and take.

But right then, he stepped back, giving her room to breathe again.

Barely.

"Now you know my intentions for both of you." His voice was low, intense. He backed up two more steps, then added, "As for Jeremy, I'm guessing he might learn some new skills. It could be good for him to have a man around. I should have the first shipment of parts a week from Saturday."

When he put it that way, she felt churlish for saying no. Especially when she knew he was right, that working on the kit car together could be good for Jeremy. Her brother had blossomed around Will, even if it was only chatting on Skype in the evenings. Did she have the right to deny him this opportunity? She wanted to watch out for him, but she didn't mean to stifle him, too.

Harper took a deep breath, one that didn't give her nearly enough oxygen to make up for all that Will's hot words had just stolen from her. "Okay, I'll let you work with Jeremy on the car. I know he'll be ecstatic when you tell him. But as for you and me..." She licked her lips and, despite the desperate need racing through her, forced herself to tell him, "I know I might have given you some mixed signals the other night—" *And again today when I all but dared you to kiss me.* "—and I regret doing that, but I still can't date you."

"Can't?" He raised an eyebrow, the dark heat still in his eyes. "Or won't?"

She raised an eyebrow right back at him, even though she wasn't doing a good job tamping down the heat glowing inside her. "Is there a difference?"

"*Can't* means you're already with another guy and aren't available to date me. *Won't* means you still don't trust me enough to let me take you out again."

"We had a nice dinner, and you've been very sweet to my brother, but I don't know you, Will. All I know are your *intentions.*" Very wicked ones, at that. Deliciously wicked, some might say.

"I'm not asking you to decide about us today, but I am asking you to give me another chance before you make up your mind about whether to shut me down or not."

He held her gaze for another long moment, letting her see his desire—and something more. Something she couldn't quite define, but that touched her all the same. Maybe because it mirrored the longing for him she couldn't figure out how to stop feeling.

"I like you, Harper. I like how straightforward you are. I like how smart you are. I like how you care so deeply for your brother."

She was nearly speechless from all the wonderful things he'd just said about her. Had any other man ever noticed—or appreciated— so much about her? Or thrown her quite so far off her game all at the same time?

"And I sure as hell like kissing you and holding you in my arms." With that, he pushed away from the kitchen counter and said, "I'd like to tell Jeremy about the Maserati kit when he calls tonight, if that's all right with you."

Even if she knew that she needed to say no on her own account, she couldn't say no for her brother. "That's fine with me."

"And will you be able to bring him over the Saturday after next to start the work?"

"Yes."

But she honestly wasn't sure whether she was saying *yes* for Jeremy.

Or for herself.

* * *

Will punched the gas and veered around a slow car in the fast lane as he headed away from Harper's house and to his office. The Lamborghini shot ahead, and the burst of speed was a rush.

But it wasn't anywhere close to the rush he'd felt with Harper.

She'd had every right to call him on his intentions with Jeremy. But he still wasn't sure she understood that the cost of the Maserati kit was nothing compared to what Will would get out of it. Jeremy made him feel like he had a second chance to make up for the worst of the things he'd done when he was a kid.

And Harper simply made him *feel*.

He'd been charmed by the animal mugs, and her endearingly messy house, so in contrast with the professional façade she wore. On the surface, she was polite and polished, but after seeing her at home, he now believed more than ever that there was a wild—and delightfully unruly—woman inside of her dying to break out.

She was so strong as she'd peppered him with her questions—and so sexy that he'd been *this close* to pushing for everything he wanted, right there in her kitchen. But he'd only let himself push a little bit. Only let himself tease her with words and brief touches until they were both panting with need.

Sweet Lord, had she ever been heaven against him. The leggings had revealed every gorgeous contour of her legs, while the sweater had made him desperate to uncover the rest of her sweetness. Even the striped toe socks had kicked his heart into high gear. She'd smelled delicious, like fruity shampoo and shower gel and lotion, and without makeup, her skin had been peaches-and-cream smooth.

In the end, though it had nearly killed him to push away from her and walk out of that kitchen knowing he wouldn't see her again for nearly a week and half, the big tease had been perfect. Because they'd been riding the edge together. Soon, he'd push them both over.

Until then? Will knew he'd be going crazy with anticipation.

And if he'd played his cards right in her kitchen, hopefully Harper would be going more than a little crazy, too.

CHAPTER ELEVEN

As the Saturday of their next visit to Will's garage finally dawned and Jeremy's enthusiasm knew no bounds, Harper tried to keep her anticipation at seeing Will again at bay.

Jeremy had been so excited when Will told him about the Maserati kit and had asked her to take him out to purchase a new notebook in which he'd written furiously and also pasted numerous pictures. Making notes, he'd said, but they were a secret. Just for Will and him. Still, even if she couldn't help but worry about Jeremy, she also couldn't bring herself to crush his enjoyment.

As for herself...she shook her head as she put on the brakes for a stoplight in the thick Saturday traffic. She'd never been the kind of woman to go all gooey just from thinking about a guy. But every time she thought about Will, both her brain and her body went topsy-turvy.

"I like Will," Jeremy said from the passenger seat with his usual big-hearted cheerfulness.

Harper couldn't deny the truth. "I like him, too."

And it wasn't just Will's sex appeal that drew her to him like moth to flame. It was all the little things that added up—his patience with Jeremy, the tin of caviar he'd given Mama Cannelli, and the genuine empathy on his face and in his touch when she'd told him about the car crash, the rich teen getting away with near murder, and then their parents' passing.

"I brought drinks and sandwiches for when we get hungry." She didn't want to assume that Will would feed them. "Your favorite, PB and J."

"I can't wait to get there!" Jeremy said. "This is going to be the best day ever."

Jeremy had clearly been swept away by Will. And the problem was, no matter how much she'd tried to deny it over the past ten days, Harper kept secretly fantasizing about being swept away by him, too. Will had an irresistible magnetism, much as she'd been reminding herself that she *had* to resist.

The way he'd turned her inside out in her kitchen with nothing but words was something her body couldn't forget. Not when deep inside, she knew how good—how *amazing*—it would feel to be taken by him.

I intend to kiss you so slowly, so thoroughly, that you'll be begging me to never, ever stop.

All of his sexy, crazy, wild intentions came back to her deep in the middle of the night when she couldn't sleep. They were *why* she couldn't sleep. Because she wanted so badly everything he was offering.

But again and again over the past few days, she'd wondered—what if she took her eye off the ball in her quest for even a small, but heady, taste of wildness, and something happened to her brother? What if she went in for a few perfect gulps of the thrills that Will was offering her and ended up putting the safe little life she'd created for herself and Jeremy at risk? Especially when, despite how kind Will had been to both of them so far, she didn't know very much about him at all. He hadn't shared anything about who he was or where he'd come from. In fact, he'd skillfully avoided revealing himself.

They pulled up at the top of the driveway, and as she came to a stop, Jeremy all but threw himself out of the car when Will appeared in one of the open roll-up doors. Harper opted for a more reasonable pace, yet her heart was beating wildly. God only knew why, since Will was covered in the long white overalls she'd seen hanging in the garage.

How can a man look that sexy in overalls?

"Where is it, Will?" Jeremy asked in an excited voice.

"Up in the barn." Will pointed to the hill beyond the garages. "That's my workshop for major projects." He gestured to the two garage buildings where they were standing. "This place is just for tune-ups, oil changes, and regular maintenance."

Stepping back into the garage, he reached for a pair of blue overalls. "Better put these on, Jeremy, or your sister will have my head for creating more laundry." From the curve of his lips as he said it, she knew he was remembering the baskets of unfolded clothing in the family room.

She blushed as he tossed the overalls to Jeremy. Who missed.

Her brother scrambled to grab them up off the concrete. "Do I have to take my clothes off?"

Will shook his head. "Nope. The legs should be wide enough to fit over your sneakers and jeans."

Harper liked that he didn't make a big deal out of Jeremy not knowing what to do.

"Okay. I have to sit down." Jeremy sat on the concrete and tried stuffing his feet into the legs.

Will didn't help him, and Harper liked that, too, since she tried not to let herself help Jeremy unless he asked for it.

Still fighting the overalls onto his legs, rolling onto his back and pulling at them, her brother called, "Doesn't Harper need these, too?"

Will eyed her, giving her a long, slow look—which Jeremy was too involved with his overalls to notice. The heat in Will's gaze told her he'd taken in her tank top and capris. And liked what he saw. "Oh no. I want Harper just the way she is."

Even if he couldn't possibly mean that the way it sounded, it still managed to be the sweetest thing any man had ever said to her.

Jeremy finally got the blue overalls on his legs, then scooched his bottom to pull them over his hips. Rolling to his hands and knees, he pushed himself up. While her brother put on the overalls, Will had reduced the distance between himself and Harper to two steps.

He was close enough to touch her now, but he didn't. That in itself was another tease, something that Will was just too good at.

"Ready?" Will directed the question to Jeremy, who'd finally zipped up his overalls.

"Yes!" her brother yelled.

Then Will finally did what she'd been secretly dying for. He put his hand on her bare back between the straps of her tank top, guiding her toward the garage, making her acutely aware of him with the caress of his fingers above the line of the tank.

And, even if she shouldn't, she couldn't help but love every second of it.

* * *

Harper had pulled her hair up into a sexy, messy knot held by a butterfly clip. Loose tendrils flirted with her seductively bare shoulders. But it was the silver toe ring on the middle toe of her right foot that really got Will going.

It should have been unexpected. To anyone else, it might even seem out of character. But not to him. Because he already knew about the secret wildness inside her that was practically bursting to come out. Even if she clearly thought she needed to keep it firmly tamped down.

"Pile in." He pointed to the golf cart parked just inside the roll-up door.

"Cool, I can't believe we're going to ride in that!" Everything excited Jeremy, from overalls to golf carts.

"Makes it easier to come back down the hill if I need something here." Although Will had outfitted the barn with everything he could possibly need when he was building the Cobra, the golf cart and the path he'd built made it easier to travel back and forth.

"I almost forgot." Harper backed off so that his hand fell away from the heat of her skin. "I brought lunch. And drinks. I hope you like peanut butter and jelly."

He'd planned on having his housekeeper, Mrs. Taylor, bring up a tray around noon, but it was sweet that Harper had planned ahead. "My favorite," he told her. He hadn't eaten a peanut butter and jelly sandwich since Susan made them for lunch every day when she'd sent them all off to school, but back then it really had been his favorite. At least, when he hadn't been getting into too much trouble to eat lunch.

"Climb into the backseat," he told Jeremy, then jetted the golf cart out to Harper, swinging it around so that she could climb in beside him.

She carried a six-pack of water bottles and an insulated lunch bag. As soon as she was seated, he couldn't resist reaching out to brush away a lock of hair from her gorgeous mouth. Once the strand was gone, however, he let his hand linger on her soft skin, appreciating the way her eyes dilated slightly with an awareness she couldn't hide.

"Thank you for taking care of us, Harper. Guys working on cars don't think to stop and eat. But we're going to need our sustenance." Then he added over his shoulder, "Isn't that right, Jeremy?"

"Right, Will."

He moved his hand from her cheek to rest lightly over hers as he whisked them up the hill, feeling Harper's gaze on him.

"Stop teasing," she said softly.

"Teasing?" He lifted one eyebrow. "I'm perfectly serious."

And he was. He intended to make her crazy. As crazy for him as he already was for her. The prospect already had his blood rushing.

She tried to look stern. "You know what I mean."

He knew *exactly* what she meant. And he had a lot more planned for her. Touching, teasing, flirting—anything that would remind her of every single wicked intention he'd whispered against her skin in her kitchen a week and a half ago.

He wanted the woman who'd grabbed his shirt and dragged his mouth down to hers out by the old aqueduct. And since something told him she was secretly dying for that, too, he'd do whatever he could to bring out that thrill-seeking side of her again.

* * *

With each zing of Will's fingers on her arm and her shoulder and her back, Harper felt a little crazier. Resisting him was the rational choice—the safe choice—but staying rational around Will was one of the hardest things she'd ever tried to do.

"You've got quite a setup here," she said, attempting to divert her focus away from how much she wanted him.

"I converted the barn when I was building the Cobra."

The barn floor had been filled in with concrete and covered with black and white checkerboard squares. A car lift was central to the huge workspace, and above was a suspension system that Will explained could be used to lower the engine block and transmission into place, and even the fiberglass car body. Ringing the floor space were rolling tool chests, workbenches, an air compressor, a welding machine, bins of rivets, pins, nuts, bolts, and screws, along with racks of drills, electric screwdrivers, and other tools, all in pristine condition.

The second they stepped inside, Jeremy ran around asking Will what everything was. Will not only patiently answered Jeremy's questions, but he actually seemed to enjoy explaining. It was another big point for him in the plus column, at least where her brother was concerned.

Will turned to the covered item centered over the lift. "And here is the object of our desire."

He stood so close that their arms brushed. Thrill bumps rose along with the fine, nearly invisible hairs on her forearms, like a static shock from too much friction. His mouth curved as he glanced down at her, knowing full well what he was doing with his double entendres. No question about it, he enjoyed teasing her way too much. But the secret truth was that she enjoyed it, too, even if she shouldn't.

When she was with Will, Harper felt young and sexy and giddy for the first time in a very, very long time.

Will whipped away the tarp, and Jeremy said, "*Wow*," on a soft note of awe.

"That's exactly what I said when I first saw it," Will said with equal reverence.

"What is it?" Harper asked as she stared at the contraption.

It looked like a twisted metal cage. Or a complicated set of monkey bars on a playground. Rods were stuck together seemingly every which way, but also with a synergistic sense of purpose she couldn't fathom.

"It's the frame of the car," Will explained.

"How could you have had this made in less than two weeks?" Suddenly, she felt the awe. For Will and what he could accomplish.

"I offered a bonus so the factory would work around the clock." He said it matter-of-factly, as if it hadn't cost a staggering amount.

All Will had to do was snap his fingers, and poof, there was a complex car frame sitting in his retrofitted barn. She knew he was rich, but this was the power to have anything he wanted. Anything at all.

And he'd said he wanted *her*.

A hot shiver shot through her body...along with a healthy dose of tension as she reminded herself that rich men played by their own rules.

By now, she knew that Will was nothing like the man who'd paid her parents to make his son's car accident go away. But at the same time, no matter how nice Will seemed, she and Jeremy lived in a *very* different world. Harper wasn't intimidated by much anymore, but she wasn't going to lie and say that Will's world of infinite luxury and power wasn't overwhelming.

"It's called a space frame," Will told them. "Or a tube frame." He trailed a finger down a metal pipe, and Harper felt it as though he'd run that finger down her arm.

"We're going to attach the sheet metal and just about every single part somewhere on this frame." He signaled Jeremy closer. Harper leaned in, too. "Each tube is for something specific." He pointed. "This is where we'll attach the firewall between the engine and the cockpit." He patted the air over where she assumed the driver would sit. "Here is where we'll put the floor panels." His words drew a picture, and Harper could almost see the leather seats. "Those are the pieces we've got for the time being. The rest will be here next Friday."

He wrapped his hand around Harper's, and with her fingers engulfed in his, he took her back for the larger view. Jeremy followed suit. Together, the three of them stared at the hunk of metal.

Suddenly she saw it. "It's like a bird cage surrounding the driver." No wonder they called it the Birdcage Maserati.

"All we have to do is put her parts together, shape her, and bring her to life. With loving hands."

Though they were talking about a car, with her hand in his and his heated gaze burning up every inch of her skin, Harper felt as though he was slowly bringing her to life, too...patiently working to uncover and unleash the sensual woman hidden inside of her with every word, every look, and every touch.

CHAPTER TWELVE

Will grabbed his camera off the workbench. "We need to document our work progress as we go along." He snapped a couple of shots of the bare frame, then waved Harper into the picture.

"It should be Jeremy in the photo," she protested, hanging back. "Not me."

"Sorry, but he's not the hot babe we need for our hot car shots."

She glared at his teasing use of the term *hot babe,* and he wanted to kiss the disapproval right off her pretty lips.

Will took her hand again, her skin smooth and warm as he brought her over to the frame. Had she figured out that while he was teasing her, he was working himself up, too? He enjoyed her wide blue eyes, the puffs of breath that signaled her arousal—or anger—and the way she bit her lip without even being aware of it.

"We need you in the picture to show proportion," he explained. "And you, too, Jeremy."

Jeremy needed no further prodding to jump into the photo. Will didn't always require human subjects, but he wanted them. This was a joint project. Plus, he had a major desire to see Harper on camera.

"Act like a model showing off the car," he directed, watching her on the digital screen.

He thought she might be shy, but she surprised him by throwing her hands out, cocking her hip, and pointing one toe on the concrete in a ballet pose. Her hair swirled around her shoulders, and her pink lipstick glistened. An ache grew low in his gut, and he swallowed hard.

Watching her was addictive.

Beside her, Jeremy was a surprising ham, striking one ridiculous pose after another, and Will wondered when the last time had been that he'd had fun like this.

Finally, Harper stepped out of the camera frame and held out her palm. "Okay, give it to me. We need some of you and Jeremy, since you two are building this thing."

He relinquished the camera, but not before making sure his hand lingered on hers. She met his gaze, pursed her lips, and shook her head. "Stop being bad."

"You have no idea how bad I can be," he said in a soft voice. And he couldn't wait to show her.

He caught the way her eyes flared with heat right before she rolled them, and then she gestured for him to move toward Jeremy and the metal frame. He'd raised it off the floor with four jack stands, to which he'd added small pieces of cloth so they didn't scratch the frame's paint. He'd enjoyed their reaction. When the crate arrived yesterday, he'd considered the best presentation. In the end, he'd uncrated it, used the suspension crane to place it on the jack stands, and covered it with the tarp so he could whisk it aside to reveal the masterpiece. The effect was perfect. Even Harper had been impressed.

He put his arm around the boy, and felt damn near fatherly, something he'd never even thought of before.

After Harper took a dozen or so shots, Jeremy said, "Now we need you and Harper." He obviously didn't want to be left out of the picture-taking.

"You two don't need me in more pictures," Harper objected again.

"Come on, Harper," Jeremy begged.

Of course she gave in to her brother, pointing to the button he should push to take the photo. And of course Will wasn't about to waste the opportunity to pull her in front of him and set his hands on her hips until she nestled back against him.

The scent of her hair tantalized him. The heat of her body against his started the mercury rising in his thermometer. She was just the right height, and he was in just the right position, to snake an arm around her stomach and pull her tight against him.

She tipped her head back to whisper, "What are you doing?"

"Taking advantage of a perfect opportunity to hold you close."

Meanwhile, Jeremy had his tongue stuck between his teeth and was busy centering the camera, moving a step one way, then the other, angling, holding his arms straight out, then pulling them in slowly. Will didn't think he'd even pushed the button yet.

His heart was beating hard. Could she sense the faster rhythm between her shoulder blades? Did she know the effect she had on him? Holding her in his arms was so damn good that he closed his eyes, breathed her in, and let his fantasies spin out...until a voice blew his fantasies to hell.

"If I'd known you were doing a photo shoot, I'd have brought Whitney." Evan Collins stood in the open barn door.

Harper immediately jumped away from Will, and Jeremy started, fumbling the camera. Will saw it tumble to the floor, with no way to reach out before it landed with a crack.

For one long moment, everyone stared. Then Jeremy began to splutter. "I'm sorry. I'm sorry. Don't be mad, Will. Please don't be mad. I didn't mean to." The boy's face had crumpled, and his eyes were tearing up.

Harper leaped to him, bending to retrieve the camera. "It wasn't your fault, Jeremy. I should have put the strap over your head." She looked at the crack in the view screen and grimaced at Will. "We'll replace it."

"It's just a cheap model," Will said as he crossed to her side. An image of his shoes filled the viewfinder, and the crack was a short diagonal line across the upper right corner.

"Don't make me go home, Will. I'm sorry. I won't touch anything else. Promise." Jeremy crossed his heart.

Will put a hand on the boy's shoulder and made sure he was looking straight into his eyes as he said, "It's okay, Jeremy. It was an accident."

A tear slid down Jeremy's cheek, and Will felt a rip in his heart. How many times had the kid been punished for accidents that weren't his fault? Never by Harper, he knew, but it was a cruel world out there, with little tolerance for people who didn't measure up. And Will should know, since he hadn't always been tolerant, hadn't always been kind. And others had paid the price.

Will took the camera, switched it to display mode, then clicked on the last photo to show it to Jeremy and Harper. Her brother had captured a shot with Will's arm locked across Harper's waist, her hand over his as if she were holding him there. It hinted at an intimacy he craved to make real.

But this moment was about Jeremy, so Will told him, "See, it still works."

Beside him, Harper sighed with relief. He gave her the camera as Jeremy whispered, "You're not mad?"

"Of course I'm not mad. We're buddies. Buddies don't get mad at stupid stuff." Which brought him back to Evan, who was still standing in the open barn door. "You certainly know how to make an entrance."

His friend raised his palms in surrender, a manila envelope in his right hand. "I didn't mean to surprise everyone."

They'd been friends since the sixth grade, when they'd first become the Mavericks. Evan had been a fifth grader, along with Matt, while Sebastian, Daniel, and Will were a year older. Evan's brains were huge, and as a kid, people had called him a nerd. Though with his broad, muscular frame, he now looked more like a professional athlete rather than the financial wizard behind the Mavericks.

Evan gave Jeremy a lopsided grin. "Sorry I scared you. I'm Evan Collins."

"Hi." Jeremy's voice was overly loud in the barn. "I'm Jeremy."

Evan switched the envelope to his left hand and shook Jeremy's. Then he swiveled his gaze to Harper, clear male appreciation lighting his eyes. "And you are?"

"Harper Newman." She put her hand out, too, and shook his. "Jeremy's my brother."

Will didn't like seeing Evan's hand curve around Harper's. Not because he thought Evan was going to try to swoop in and claim her, given that his friend had a wife to whom he was one hundred percent faithful. No, it was simply that Will wasn't ready to share Harper yet, not even with his friends, who would be full of raised eyebrows and silent questions, just like Evan was right now.

What's more, he didn't want any of them to remind him that he had no business romancing a nice girl like her. Not when he was already well aware of that fact. And not when he'd already spent sleepless nights torn between wanting to do the right thing...and just plain *wanting* her.

"Nice meeting both of you," Evan said, his voice low and powerful, a Maverick through and through.

"What do you need?" Will knew he was being abrupt, but his friend had just caused Harper to jump out of his arms, and he hadn't yet forgiven Evan for it.

"I brought the Link contract for your signature."

While each of the Mavericks had their own enterprises, they often entered joint ventures. This new agreement would fund Link Labs, a startup for a state-of-the-art, and affordable, personal robot. Matt, being the robotics guy in their group, saw huge potential in the field, and they'd all bought into it.

"Thanks, but you didn't need to bring it by personally."

Evan shrugged. "I felt like a drive."

Figuring there was trouble in paradise, but that his friend wouldn't want to talk about it around Harper and Jeremy, Will headed to the workbench and pulled out the document to scan it quickly before initialing the changes. He knew Evan was meticulous and didn't make mistakes. Not with business matters, anyway.

"So what's going on here?" Evan gestured toward the frame.

"Will and I are building a Birdcage Maserati." Jeremy skittered across the floor to the front end, his enthusiasm back, the incident with the camera thankfully forgotten. "It was my idea, and Will agreed."

"And you're supervising?" Evan asked Harper.

Obviously catching the way his friend's eyes moved between her and Will, her mouth tightened slightly. She put her arm around Jeremy, who quickly squirmed away as if it was too childish. "Jeremy recently wrote Mr. Franconi asking if he could see the car collection."

Mr. Franconi? What was up with that?

"And Mr. Franconi was gracious enough to invite us to participate in his car project."

If she said *Mr.* a third time, he wouldn't be responsible for his actions. She was obviously trying to act like the only thing between them was a business arrangement. Anything but a relationship. But as much as he didn't want Evan's questions right now—and as much as he was trying to be careful not to push her too fast—Will sure as hell wasn't going back to being *Mr. Franconi.*

He scrawled his signature and shoved the agreement back into the envelope, then stalked the few paces to Harper's side, where he draped his arm across her shoulders and pulled her into him.

"Here you go." He handed the envelope to Evan with one hand and played with the ends of Harper's hair with the other. "We're going to start punching holes in the sheet metal. Want to help?"

He was sure Evan would rather watch the endless loop of a ticker tape. Cars didn't interest his friend. Evan drove a luxury vehicle for the roominess and the comfort—and because Whitney liked to travel in style—but otherwise, he couldn't care less.

True to form, he said, "Thanks for the offer, but I've got to drop in on Sebastian for the last signature. Nice to meet both of you. I hope I'll see you again."

"'Bye, Evan." Jeremy waved big, his whole body getting into the action.

Just as Evan was engulfed by the bright sunshine, Harper elbowed Will in the ribs. Oh yeah, there'd be hell to pay for his little stunt.

But as long as it was Harper dishing it out, he'd look forward to every second.

CHAPTER THIRTEEN

What was that about?

Harper glared at Will. He'd deliberately made it appear as though they were a lot more than acquaintances in front of his friend and fellow Maverick. Evan was a very good-looking man, but even so, Harper thought he didn't hold a candle to Will.

"I think you'd better start punching your holes," she said flatly. Or she might punch him.

He was barely stifling a grin and she knew for sure that he'd been showing off to his friend. Or staking a claim. And she'd felt...

"All right, Jeremy, time to get started." Will reached into a large wooden crate set against the wall. "We'll work on the firewall first. That's the panel protecting the cockpit."

"I remember, Will." Jeremy followed him back to the workbench, where the long piece of metal was laid out, its top curved.

What *had* she felt?

Harper thought of Will's teasing and the feel of his body against her back. Every hard inch of it. His nearness had turned her insides to liquid. The final photo Jeremy snapped had exposed a woman flushed with desire. She'd looked—and felt—wanton. Sexual. Wild. And very willing. Way too willing, especially since she hadn't even decided yet whether to let him make good on any of his wicked intentions.

The possessive arm Will had put around her after he'd signed the contract had clearly stated that he knew how tempted she was. And he'd had no qualms about letting his friend know it, too—as if she were some sort of conquest.

God. She must seem so easy to him. To both of them. Take her to dinner, flash around a little money, throw out a few sexy caresses—and she was about to cave.

"This is a fan spacer." Will laid the accordion-style metal tool against the edge of a ruler he'd placed along the sheet's edge. "We use it to make sure the rivet holes are equally spaced." He fanned the spacer, a series of crisscrossed metal strips that could be adjusted, with a small hole at the end of each piece. As Will pulled, the spacers widened. "That measures one inch. Now we use a spring-loaded punch to mark where we're going to drill. Like this." Jeremy craned to watch as Will punched a small, sharp tool through each of the equidistant spacers.

Still fuming, Harper clicked off a shot of the work in progress as Jeremy happily wrote it down in his journal. Even though her brother was with them, she pulled a stool away from the wall near the workbench, and asked, "Did your friend Evan get whatever message you were trying to send him?" Fortunately, Jeremy was too interested in what he was doing to pay attention.

Will looked up at her, his eyes far more guileless than they deserved to be. She and Will had seen each other only a handful of times, yet she already *knew* that look. His lips curved up slightly, and he had a knowing spark in his eye.

"What message was that?" Before she could answer, he handed Jeremy the sharp tool, which resembled a skinny screwdriver. "You try now."

Jeremy bit his lip, concentrating hard as he took over the task. "Yeah, just like that, you've got it," Will praised him. "All we're doing right now is marking with a little hole. Then we'll drill."

She took another picture, determined not to let Will off the hook just because he was so sweet with her brother. "When you put your arm around me and started playing with my hair."

Will didn't look at all apologetic as he said, "He wasn't the one I was trying to send a message to."

His bold words—words that all but screamed how much he wanted her—shouldn't have sent heat rushing through her. But they did. Crazy heat. Just the way all of his bold *intentions* had in her kitchen.

She could feel herself flushing as Will focused on the car again and said to her brother, "We're going to move the spacer along now and make our marks all the way to the end."

A short while later, Jeremy held the press tool high in the air like an athlete who'd just run a marathon, and said, "I'm done."

Will inspected the work. "A perfect job. I couldn't have done better myself."

Jeremy did a happy dance and emotion blossomed in her heart. No matter how conflicted Will might make her feel, he was good for Jeremy.

Her brother suddenly said, "I gotta pee."

"Down there." Will hooked a thumb past a long row of shelves and cupboards, and Jeremy raced to the bathroom as if he'd suddenly realized he might not make it in time.

Literally the second the door closed behind him, Will was standing right in front of her, pulling her up, pushing the stool she sat on back against the wall, and framing her head with his hands. His he-man act shot a forbidden thrill right through her—the same forbidden thrill she felt with him every single time, whether it was smart of her or not.

Her mouth was suddenly dry as she looked up at him, her breath coming fast.

"You don't like it when I touch you in front of anyone else?" He dipped his face into the crook of her neck, his breath warm on her skin. "You don't like them thinking you're mine?"

Oh God. She could barely process what he was saying when he was this close to her, not quite kissing her, but heating her up all over just the same. "I'm—" She worked to gather enough oxygen, and brain cells, to be able to tell him, "I'm not yours."

He pulled back slowly, his hair brushing along her cheek. It was incredibly soft. And he smelled so good as he said, "Not yet," his low voice humming along her nerve endings. "Soon."

She knew what she should be doing. She should be pushing him away and making it clear to him—yet again—that their kiss by the aqueduct had been nothing more than a crazy whim. But when he slipped to the other side of her face and sensually nipped at her earlobe, she forgot where they were, she forgot Jeremy, she forgot about his friend seeing them together, she even forgot her name. As if they didn't even belong to her, her hands reached up, nearly taking hold of his shirt.

The toilet flushed at the other end of the barn and she felt the rumble of Will's low—and clearly frustrated—laugh against her throat. "Very soon we'll both have what we want," he promised her as he slowly pushed away from the wall, then turned around to focus once again on her brother and the car.

* * *

By the end of the afternoon, Will was so keyed up from wanting Harper, he was ready to blast past every last wall that she was still trying to hold up. But rushing her wasn't part of his game plan. She had to be ready. More than ready—he wanted her desperate and wild, the way she'd been that night at the deserted fountain.

They'd left an hour ago, without his securing another date with Harper. In fact, for the rest of the afternoon, though she'd been involved in taking pictures of their progress— and she'd been perfectly polite—he could easily guess that she was stewing on everything that had happened between them. And everything he'd said.

Soon we'll both have what we want.

Will wasn't a man who waited for what he wanted. And he wanted her badly enough that he'd been sorely tempted to ask them to come back tomorrow. But he'd corralled every ounce of his self-control and had, instead, let her go with the promise that she and Jeremy would return the following Saturday. When they'd do the dance all over again.

Until Harper wanted him as badly as he wanted her—and no longer thought she needed to keep fighting the inevitable. Because if there was one thing Will knew for sure, it was that the sparks between him and Harper wouldn't be nearly so hot if they weren't supposed to come together.

His cell rang beside him on the arm of his chair, signaling that his favorite person in Chicago was calling. "So," Susan said after his warm greeting, "I hear you have some new friends."

He choked out a laugh. "Evan gossips like an old woman. It's only been six hours since he met Harper and Jeremy."

"You know he always checks in with us on Saturday."

Evan tended to be driven by routine. Will, on the other hand, called Susan and Bob a couple of times a week without any set schedule.

"He's still a gossip," he said without rancor.

Susan was the closest thing Will had to a mother. He barely remembered his real mom. And it was Susan, along with Bob, who had helped Will become the man he was, instead of the man his father would have turned him into. Susan had been a waitress and Bob a baggage handler at the airport, even after he'd injured his back. They hadn't had much money, but they'd taken in each and every one of the Mavericks. Loved them. And treated them like their own.

Will would do anything for them. And the other Mavericks felt exactly the same. Their bond was stronger than any blood tie could have been.

"How's Bob doing?" Will asked before Susan could start peppering him with questions.

"You know him." He could hear the smile in her voice. "He's got to be out there helping the contractor put the new deck in. Can't just sit and watch."

The first thing the Mavericks had done when the money started rolling in was to get Bob the back surgery he'd badly needed. He'd still stubbornly continued to work long after Daniel or any one of the Mavericks could have supported both him and Susan. It had taken years to convince him that a less physically demanding desk job might not be as bad as he thought. Then finally, last year, he'd agreed to retire and start enjoying life. But he wasn't yet sixty and no one was putting him out to pasture, as he loved to say. He worked on the house and the yard, and volunteered with Habitat for Humanity.

"So are you going to tell me about her, honey?" Susan wasn't going to let Will avoid the reason for her call.

"I met Harper through her brother. He was hit by a car when he was seven. He worked through the physical issues, but he acts younger than he is."

"I'm so sorry." She hated it when kids got hurt. So did Will.

"He's a great kid. Enthusiastic. Positive. He loves cars so I bought another kit car, and he's going to help me build it."

"You sound happy. Helping him is going to be good for you, I can tell."

Happy was as good a word as any to describe what he'd felt as he helped Jeremy mark the sheet metal. For the last few months, even longer than that, he'd been running on empty. But Harper and Jeremy seemed to be filling him up again.

"And his sister, Harper? Is she someone special?"

He didn't even have to think about it. "Very." He'd known from that first day in the hangar that Harper was special. And good. Too good for him.

"You have no idea how glad I am to hear you say that, Will. I want my boys happy. And you deserve a good woman."

Susan didn't see him shake his head. She really did love all of her boys, so much that Will knew she let herself forget where—and who— he came from. Forget who he *was.*

If Harper knew what he'd been like as a kid, all the crimes he'd committed for his dad, the hellraiser he'd been even after the asshole went to prison and he'd moved in with the Spencers—would she ever trust him with her brother? Would she ever trust him with herself? She already doubted his motives with Jeremy. If she knew the guy Will was on the inside, all the lies he'd told, all the houses he'd broken into for his dad, all the cars he'd stolen, and then what had finally gone down with the Road Warriors...

He ran a harsh hand through his hair, knowing Harper would run a mile to get away from him if she ever found out. And she'd take Jeremy, too.

Because the hard truth was that with his father's blood flowing through his veins, no matter how far he'd come, Will would never completely be able to outrun the things he'd done.

CHAPTER FOURTEEN

On Wednesday morning, the Mavericks gathered around the boardroom table in the main conference room of their headquarters in Palo Alto, near the Google campus. They'd be moving in the late fall, when Sebastian Montgomery's new high-rise production studio in San Francisco was completed.

On the face of it, Sebastian was a self-help guru with a charismatic personality; a tall, muscular frame; and celebrity good looks that he'd channeled into a media empire. He spoke to vast audiences on anything from creating money in your life to finding your true destiny.

Sebastian had achieved every goal he'd set the day they'd made their pact to get out of Chicago. But Will wasn't so sure happiness had been one of those objectives, except in terms of Sebastian being in control of his own destiny after being so out of control as a kid.

For today's meeting, they presented a united front, all dressed accordingly in suit and tie—even Daniel, who was video conferencing from New York, where he was negotiating the site for another grand opening in his home improvement chain.

They came together as the Maverick Group on various investment opportunities, had even financed movies, their latest being with Smith Sullivan. And of course, there was the Link Labs endeavor. Matt Tremont, the Mavericks' electronics genius, had brought them the prospect, since his interest lay in robotics. The group was also involved in real estate—selling, buying, renovating, developing—which was why they were all meeting today.

"Ray's been waiting since ten o'clock." Will flipped his arm to reveal his watch. "Only ten minutes." They should have let the man stew for an hour. "Remember, I want to be the one to fire his ass." Because he'd been the one to hire him. It had seemed like a good choice at the time, but a year ago, Ray Passal's work ethic had nosedived. In the worst possible way.

"I know you're pissed. I am, too," Daniel said, his voice as crystal clear as his image on their state-of-the-art conferencing equipment. For the meeting, he'd tamed his unruly wavy hair and donned a suit jacket over his big shoulders. "But we don't want to deal with the lawsuit if you beat the crap out of him. Even though he definitely deserves it."

"Spoilsport," Sebastian said, lounging in his chair.

"Personally," Matt said, "I'm willing to pay for a ringside seat."

They all knew Will had been the fighter, even if he hadn't had a physical knockdown since he was sixteen, and he had to admit his blood was up today, itching to pound Ray into the plush conference-room carpet.

Instead, he asked Evan, "What's the latest report?"

A couple of days ago, Evan had discovered that the majority of the deals Ray was claiming commission on weren't Ray's at all—at least, not for the past year. He was stealing sales from the people who worked for him. More specifically, he was bullying his sales guys into splitting commissions and giving him credit for their work.

"I've identified eight deals in the last year. Nothing prior to that." Evan had meticulously checked every project Ray had been involved in. "Carstairs reported working with Martin on the Castaway Ridge project. Hanson dealt with Barry on Midland." The list was long, all major multimillion-dollar deals. "And of course, there was Headley on La Verne. He worked with Drucker."

The La Verne transaction had been Evan's first discovery when he'd spoken with Headley, who'd offhandedly mentioned he'd never met Ray Passal, despite the fact that Ray's signature was on the paperwork. He'd dealt exclusively with Drucker and was so impressed with the young sales guy's abilities that he'd told Evan the man deserved a bonus. When Drucker was questioned, he'd said Passal had made him sign a contract the first day of his employment, splitting all commissions fifty-fifty with Ray because, supposedly, all the leads came from him. It was take it or leave it, sign or lose the job.

That was total bull. None of the Mavericks had ever approved such a contract. And the leads hadn't come from Ray. He was a bully with a pen and an authority complex.

Which pushed all Will's buttons.

Will had taken a short, fast ride in his Lamborghini Miura this morning to work out his tension before the confrontation, but his gut was still simmering with anger. He'd wanted to see Harper, drink in her sweet scent, steep himself in her like a balm. But he knew he couldn't let her see him like that, all keyed up and ready to rumble. He couldn't let her guess at the Road Warrior still lurking inside.

Yet somehow, just the thought of her eased the churning in him. Enough for him to breathe, to close his eyes a single moment, and feel the touch of her hand on his arm. And help him calm down enough to act rather than react.

"We'll start with Headley, Drucker, and the La Verne deal," he said.

Sebastian grinned, but it was a smile that promised retribution. "Since we've got a fox in the henhouse, let's play cock of the walk with him."

Will hit a button on the intercom, buzzing their executive assistant to usher Ray in. The man who entered was forty-five, but today he looked ten years older, his jowls sagging with the extra pounds he'd put on.

"Hey, Will." His gaze jittered nervously around the room and up to Daniel's face on the video screen. "I didn't realize everyone would be here."

"It's an executive meeting. That means all of us." Daniel hard-eyed the guy with a laser-sharp gaze.

"Sit," Will commanded.

There was only one chair on the opposite side of the table. Sebastian had lowered it so that when Ray faced them, he looked like an overgrown kid in a child's seat. He couldn't even rest his elbows on the table.

"What's up, guys?" Ray was trying for friendly, but Will could hear his fingernails tapping on the arm of his chair.

Will simply said, "La Verne."

Evan opened a folder in front of him, withdrew a stapled sheaf of papers, and shot the package across the table. "The contract."

Ray barely caught it before it hit him in the chest.

"Your signature is on the last page," Daniel said, his crisp voice echoing out of the screen.

"Ah, yes," Ray said slowly, hesitantly, his face reddening.

"And you took half the commission," Matt added, specifically avoiding the word *earned*.

"Funny thing." Will kept his tone mild. "Headley never talked to you. Only Drucker. And he was impressed with the kid." He paused two beats. "He never even met with you."

"Well, no, that's, uh…" Ray started to splutter, then he sucked in a huge breath that made his shirt buttons look like they'd pop. "It's how I train my people, hands on, right from the get-go. We strategize together. I write the sales script for them. I monitor their progress every step of the way. The only thing they do at this point is the talking." He stopped to suck in another shirt-busting breath.

"Ray, I have to ask," Sebastian drawled, leaning back in his chair, arms crossed. "Do we look stupid?"

"No," Ray pushed out.

Matt waved a hand. "Why don't we show him the other contract, Evan."

"Sure thing." Evan looked like a big cat ready to pounce on a lizard.

They hadn't scripted the meeting, but the five of them had been together so long, they didn't need a script. Right from the day they'd made their pact, they'd known exactly how to back each other up. Sebastian had gone to LA, where he'd founded a media empire, Matt and Evan had gone to college, Daniel had turned his contractor's license into a billion-dollar home improvement kingdom, and Will had begun importing the right thing at just the right moment. But they'd all been there for one another with exactly what was needed right when it was needed.

This issue with Ray was no different.

Evan withdrew more papers from his magic folder and flicked them across the table.

Ray missed and it slid to the carpet. His chair was so low, he disappeared for a moment to retrieve it from beneath the table. The only sound was the rustle of paper and his harsh breathing.

His face was even redder when he popped back up like a buoy in the water. "What's this?" But he already knew.

Matt stared the man down. The kid he'd been at ten was a distant memory. At thirty-four, Matt was formidable. "Drucker gave it to us."

A drop of sweat rolled down from Ray's sideburns. "He couldn't have."

"Did you really think you had the only copy?" Will asked.

Ray's eyes flitted back and forth as if searching for a way out. Then, suddenly, he crushed the two-page contract in his hand. "This is standard operating procedure. I bring in the leads. I teach them the ropes. In fact, I'm devoting all my time to them rather than following the leads myself, which I could very well do. I'm actually the one sharing with them, not the other way around."

Will leaned forward. "One—" He tapped his index finger on the table. "—we give you the leads. Two—" He tapped his middle finger. "—it isn't *our* standard operating procedure to let anyone skim off half of someone else's commission unless they actually do half the work. Which brings me to three." He brought his hand down on the table. "You're fired."

"But I've got debts!"

Ah, so it was debts that had turned him away from being hardworking and honest? Even so, Will didn't give a damn why Ray had turned rotten. He still wanted to grind the man down for taking advantage of kids fresh out of college who didn't know better.

Will had seen it over and over again with his father and with the Road Warriors as they picked on the weak. It wasn't just a way of life for them, it was sport—and how they made themselves feel bigger than they were. And Will had been one of them until he was sixteen and had tried to leave all that behind.

Now, faced with a bully like Ray Passal, Will felt the anger boil up all over again, the need to use his fists. "Get your things, Ray, and get the hell out. *Now.*"

Before Will let anything else boil over.

"But what am I supposed to do?" Ray whined.

Will stared him down. "How about thanking your lucky stars that we're not asking you to pay back the commissions you stole?"

Ray blinked, swallowed, looked at the floor. Then, as if he saw it written down there how much worse things could get, he looked up and said two very simple words, "Thank you."

It was only after the door closed behind the now shrunken and sweaty man that Will thought again of Harper. Finally, his fists relaxed. He hadn't pounded on the guy. He hadn't even humiliated him. He'd simply pointed out the facts.

It was a far cry from the boy he'd once been.

Sebastian slapped him on the back as he rose to pour himself a cup of coffee from the pot no one had touched yet. "Something tells me that's the last we'll ever hear from Ray. He won't want to have to slink back around any of us with his tail between his legs. Good job, guys. We were brilliant."

"Right," Evan said. "Brilliant like all the crap we used to pull when we were teenagers."

"Speak for yourself," Sebastian shot back. But Evan was right; they'd all had their less than stellar moments back then. Though Will's were worse than the rest.

"And you—" Sebastian nodded at Will. "—didn't even tear him to pieces with your bare hands."

It was meant as a joke, but Will felt the truth of it. That was how he used to do things. Talked with his fists. Back when he was a kid, he'd thought that was how he'd always be. But he'd held it together today—kept things above board rather than dragging his ex-employee into the back alley and teaching him a lesson street-style.

"No Road Warrior justice today, I guess." Even from the video screen, Daniel's smile was wide, as he put into words what Will had just been thinking.

"Come to think of it," Matt said, as the one who knew best what Will was capable of, "I can't actually remember you knocking anyone's block off in twenty years."

For all his fears, Will was surprised to realize Matt was right. Even though fighting had once been all Will knew, he *hadn't* resorted to violence in two decades. He'd actually kept his cool with Ray today. And while that had felt pretty damn good—if something ever happened to Harper or Jeremy, Will couldn't imagine how he'd be able to keep from tearing apart the people who had hurt them...

The guys all razzed him about the Road Warriors, but they'd each had their own way of dealing with the old neighborhood. Evan hid out with the library computers, sucked into his circle of numbers and equations. Matt loved his universe of books and gadgets. Sebastian got by on the power of persuasion and charm. And Daniel used his hands, not to fight, but to build things.

Will was the only one who'd chosen a gang. Even after Susan and Bob had taken him in, he had still straddled those two worlds for years. The Mavericks versus the Road Warriors. He'd thought the gang was his family—at least, as long as he stole cars, won drag races, used his fists—and kept his mouth shut when they did stuff he hated. *Don't step into the middle of someone else's business.* He'd understood their rules and he knew where he fit in—the kid with the good eye who wasn't afraid to go really fast. But with the Spencers and his new non–Road Warrior friends...

He hadn't been able to believe a *good* family could actually want him. So he'd kept screwing up, and screwing up, and screwing up. Until one screwup had been bad enough to finally set him straight. Or at least as straight as it could, when fighting his way out of problems was still fundamentally in his bones.

"You were different today." Evan caught the mug of coffee Sebastian slid across the table to him. "It's Harper, isn't it?"

It was the very thought of Harper that had helped him keep himself in check.

"You've been holding out on us," Daniel added from the other side of the country. "Evan tells us there's a new lady in your life."

Will had never had a lady in his life. He'd had women he dated, women he slept with. But there'd never been anyone like Harper.

The Mavericks knew everything about him, from the day they'd met when he was in the sixth grade to the time he moved in with Susan and Bob at thirteen, to the night the Road Warriors imploded. They'd been there for everything in between and all the changes that had come in the two years after that. The truth was that they'd become his family in a way the Road Warriors had never been.

Which was why, even though Will hadn't yet gotten used to the idea of not only wanting Harper, but *needing* her, too, in a way he'd never needed anyone else, he found himself telling his closest friends the same thing he'd told Susan.

"She's special."

So special that even if he didn't deserve her...he still couldn't make himself walk away.

CHAPTER FIFTEEN

Harper's nerves were at an all-time high the following Saturday as she drove up Will's driveway with Jeremy grinning like crazy in the passenger seat.

"I've been waiting all week to come back here," he said.

And the problem was, so had she. Because Will had gotten under her skin. Big time.

All week long, Harper had tried to convince herself that she should be glad she hadn't heard from him since the previous Saturday. He'd talked with Jeremy over Skype about the car, but he hadn't asked for her. And she hadn't asked for him, either. Instead, she'd told herself a thousand times that she shouldn't let Will pull her in, shouldn't risk giving herself a taste of the pleasure he was promising her.

She knew what he was trying to do with all that talk of his intentions, with the way he'd said *Soon we'll both have want we want* right after he made her forget everything but how much she wanted his almost-touches and almost-kisses. He was trying to get her so worked up that she couldn't think straight, couldn't remember all her good reasons to steer clear of him.

Knowing precisely what he was trying to do should have made her even more firm in her plan to keep things purely friendly for Jeremy's sake. She didn't want to shake up their lives. But even as she tried to convince herself that staying clear of Will was the only reasonable course of action, the truth was that she'd been feeling less and less reasonable as each day of that long week passed.

And she couldn't stop wondering—if she didn't take this chance with Will, would she always regret it?

As she stepped out of the car, she could see the gleam in Will's eyes, a wicked heat full of so many *intentions* that her heart felt as if it were about to race right out of her chest. And he hadn't even touched her yet.

How was she going to keep resisting him? She had all her good, practical, sensible reasons laid out, yet whenever he came near...

Fortunately, just as he came into touching range, her phone rang. She grabbed it from her bag and when she saw it was one of her clients, she leapt on it. "Sorry, it's work." She waved her phone at him as if it were a shield blocking his progress toward her. "Excuse me."

She all but ran around the corner of the big barn, close enough that she could still hear Will's and Jeremy's voices as they got to work on the Maserati, but far enough away that she couldn't make out what they were saying.

And it was a good thing she'd been looking for a big distraction, because the negotiation ended up being a long one. Over an hour, in fact, by the time she'd talked to both the employer and the new hire and achieved agreement on salary, benefits, and bonus.

After she hung up, she spent a few moments working to center herself. She knew she was acting crazy. Which was silly, because *crazy* was the very last thing Harper had ever let herself be. This time, she decided firmly, she would keep it together. Will was just a guy. She could handle spending a little time around him on the weekends while her brother worked on the car.

Taking a deep breath, she put a smile on her face, then returned to the barn. "How's the work coming along?"

Jeremy leaped forward to grab her hand. "Look what we got done." He brought her over to a line of sheet metal parts laid out on a tarp. "We have to number each panel," he explained. "Then we put the same number on the frame. And then we know where everything will fit." He pointed to a piece. "See that one?" He raced to the metal carcass. "We put it here." He stopped, stared. "Wait. I think—" He frowned. "Will?"

Will was there quickly, putting his hand on Jeremy's shoulder. "It goes there."

Jeremy's brightness immediately returned. "Right. There. See, Harper?" Her brother smiled at Will. "Thanks. You're so cool."

Will smiled at Jeremy with the light of affection in his eyes as he said, "You're cool, too."

Harper instantly melted. Not from the naughty thoughts she'd been having about Will all week...but from the kind, friendly look on his face. And suddenly, in the face of his kindness to her brother—kindness that had been utterly lacking in every man she'd been with before him—all those reasons for distancing herself from Will didn't seem quite so important anymore.

Because for the first time in her adult life, Harper desperately wanted to take a risk with an incredibly hot guy, one who wanted her in a way no one else ever had. That freedom she'd tasted during their dinner at Cannelli's and the drive to the aqueduct had her longing to unfurl her wings. Wings that felt as if they'd been clipped long ago.

Somewhere between a deep craving for a few thrilling flights outside her normal life and Will's whispering those deliciously naughty *intentions* to her, she couldn't help but wonder if hot sex with him might not be the end of the world. At least, as long as she didn't get overly emotional and involved.

Holding onto as much of her sanity as possible—while always remembering that Will was just a short-term pleasure—would be the key to the whole equation. Even if his friends found out, well...she didn't care what they thought, right? Not if, for once, she was going to do something entirely for *herself.*

Something totally wild and crazy like seducing Will Franconi.

She wasn't so far gone that she thought it would mean anything more to him than dinner, drinks, and sex—and she wouldn't let herself get attached. She'd be cool, calm, and collected. At least, she'd be calm and cool until he touched her...or she touched him.

Then she'd let loose the wild woman inside her.

Only, she couldn't possibly seduce him in what she was wearing—jeans and a T-shirt with a plain white cotton bra and panties beneath. She needed new lingerie. She needed new clothes.

She needed new *everything*.

"You guys look like you're doing great," she said in an overly bright voice. "You don't mind if I head out for a bit and let you work, do you?"

"I'm good with Will," Jeremy said, turning back to the car, clearly having already forgotten her.

But Will didn't look at all happy about it. "Are you sure you can't stay?"

"No, I really can't." Because if she actually went forward with her plan to seduce him, she was going to do it right. "I'll be back as soon as I can."

His dark eyes held hers for a long moment, somehow seeming to pull her straight to him. "We'll miss you."

She almost reached for him then, almost blurted out that she'd made up her mind to give his *intentions* a whirl. But she still felt like a butterfly wrapped in its safe little cocoon.

By the time she returned to him this afternoon, she planned to have her brightly colored wings unfurled.

* * *

Harper was on the run, damn it!

Will had driven himself nuts thinking about her all week, planning the ways he'd tease her today. Fool that he was, he'd thought giving her some space to relive their crazy chemistry over and over would make her wild and crazy for him, too, when she finally saw him again.

Instead, she'd taken a business call, then rushed off.

Will was used to people wanting something from him, especially women. But Harper didn't seem to want anything. Not even the things he was dying to give her. Just the opposite—he had to cajole and seduce her every step of the way, whether it was about the Maserati or a date...or to get his hands on her.

So today it was just Jeremy and him. Not that working with Jeremy didn't have its own rewards. The kid was intelligent, he just had trouble with bigger concepts. But he followed instructions well. They worked companionably all day, continuing to number the shipment of sheet metal panels that had arrived on Friday.

"Great teamwork," he said when they broke for the roast beef sandwiches Mrs. Taylor brought. She'd included milk and cookies as if they were kids.

"Thanks, Mrs. Taylor." Jeremy's voice was loud in the barn. He used a big voice when he was excited. Or when he met new people. Just as he had last weekend with Evan.

"You're very welcome." A short, rotund widow with white hair, Mrs. Taylor had been Will's housekeeper for five years, moving with him from his previous house in San Mateo. She fixed meals when he was at home, did the cleaning, the shopping, laundry, household errands. Once a month, Will had a service come in to do all the heavy work, saving Mrs. Taylor's back.

"I like her," Jeremy confided after Mrs. Taylor had returned to the house in a golf cart. "She makes really good sandwiches."

"She does." There wasn't much not to like about Mrs. Taylor.

Jeremy talked with his mouth full. "When are you going to take Harper out again?"

Will, in the middle of swallowing, almost lost his roast beef. "Do you want me to take your sister out again?"

Jeremy nodded vigorously. "I like you." He chomped off a bite of cookie even though he hadn't finished his sandwich yet. "You're a lot nicer than the other guys she goes out with."

Jealousy hit Will like he was a crash test dummy, straight in the chest, at the thought of Harper with another man. But he wouldn't use Jeremy to get information about Harper, so he didn't ask any questions. He merely said, "I like you, too, Jeremy. And I like Harper."

Jeremy beamed, his eyes aglow. "Then it's a deal. You take her out."

"I have to ask Harper first."

"She'll say yes. She likes you. She always comes into the room to listen when we use Skype."

"Maybe she's just checking up on me."

Jeremy shook his head, turning all the way to the right, then the left in an exaggerated movement. "Nuh-uh. She *likes* you. I know. Whenever I talk about you, she gets this funny look in her eyes. Like she's dreaming even though she's awake."

Again, though Will loved getting this inside scoop on the woman he couldn't stop thinking about, he wouldn't allow himself to pry any more information out of Jeremy. "Let's just wait until she gets here, okay?"

Which meant, unfortunately, that he'd have to dig deeper into his reserves of patience. Reserves that were running *really* thin where Harper was concerned.

But it wasn't only patience Will was nearly out of by the time Harper finally returned—it was also self-control.

When she left, she'd been wearing jeans. Now she wore a gorgeous dress that skimmed her curves and flowed down in long lines to her calves. Her sandals laced up over her ankles and met the bottom of the dress, looking like something a gladiator would wear. And what made Will's self-control nearly snap completely was his realization that the gauzy material of the dress was almost see-through in the light from the open barn door behind her.

The faint outline of long legs made his mouth dry up. The neckline dipped low, cushioning a teardrop necklace between her breasts. A hint of lace peeked out. The sun was a halo around her hair, a gentle breeze lifting the locks, and her lips were the luscious shade of ripe plums, a deeper color than the usual pink she wore.

She stole his breath.

She made his jaw hit the floor.

She drove him crazy.

Which was exactly where Will wanted to go with Harper—utterly crazy.

* * *

The look on Will's face was worth every single penny she'd spent. He seemed stunned, unable to speak, unable to move, able only to look.

And to want her in the same way she'd been wanting him.

Oh yes, *definitely* worth it. What's more, she felt sexy and desirable, from the new makeup to the new sandals to the new dress. And everything new underneath. It had been a really long time since she'd treated herself...and she wondered suddenly why she'd waited so long.

"We had a good day," he told her. "Got a lot accomplished."

"We even marked a bunch more panels that we still have to match up," Jeremy rushed to add.

"That's great." She beamed at them both, easily able to see how happy they were with the day's work. Two peas in a pod...who would have thought? The billionaire and her brother.

She was still marveling at that when she realized Will was saying, "Jeremy has given me his permission to take you out to dinner tonight."

"He has?" She felt a kick in her pulse, as if he'd stepped on the accelerator. All afternoon, she'd been trying to figure out how to make her move. The problem was that she'd never made a move on anyone before, so she didn't have the first clue how to do it. But now, thankfully, that problem might very well be solved for her.

Will and Jeremy both nodded. "We were thinking he could stay with Mrs. Taylor." Will patted Jeremy's shoulder. "And you're excited about streaming any movie you like, aren't you? Action. Comedy. Animated."

"Will has *everything*." Jeremy widened his arms to encompass the enormous expanse of Will's streaming library. "And me and Mrs. Taylor can have pizza. Will says she makes the best one ever in his pizza oven."

"As long as you don't mind Jeremy having pizza and watching a movie," Will added.

"Pizza's fine," Harper said with a smile she knew must be bordering on giddy. "And so is a movie. Or three."

She didn't care if Will had talked Jeremy into staying with Mrs. Taylor, or that he seemed to have it all mapped out as if she were an opponent whose every objection he had to overcome.

All she cared about was being alone with him tonight.

"So is that a yes?"

She was surprised to realize that the powerful billionaire standing in front of her actually seemed a little nervous as he waited for her answer. She had assumed she'd always be the nervous one, not he. And she'd certainly never thought that she could hold the power in a relationship with a man like him. But while she knew that might be a huge stretch, at the very least, it was lovely to be wanted. *Beyond* lovely, actually.

"Yes, I'd love to go out with you tonight, Will."

For a moment, she thought he might kiss her right then and there in front of her brother. Instead, he simply stroked her cheek with the back of his hand and looked at her as if she were the most beautiful woman he'd ever seen. She knew that couldn't possibly be true, but she didn't care.

The three of them took the golf cart down the hill, both men still in their overalls. Once in the house, Will led them along a back hall past the kitchen, laundry room, and a bedroom, which she assumed was used by Mrs. Taylor.

"Make yourselves at home," Will told them as he pushed through a swing door that led into the main house. "I won't be long." He disappeared up a wide staircase. It wasn't a second floor, but another level sitting on the rise of the hill on which the house was built.

Harper took a few minutes to appreciate Will's beautiful home. The open floor plan consisted of a dining area on one side of a long marble floor that ended at the double front doors, with a massive living room on the other side. Picture windows faced the driveway and rock garden, then flowed around into a huge wall of windows overlooking the infinity pool and a valley below it all. And what she'd thought was a putting green was actually a small golf course.

"Wow," Jeremy said at her side.

The view was magnificent, but the living room itself took her breath away. Curved couches in black leather surrounded a sunken fire pit ringed in slate. A round, burnished metal flue hung over the center of the fire grates to draw up the smoke. On the wall beside the stairs, a long wet bar featured every kind of alcohol imaginable and every shape of glass, from tumblers to martini glasses to champagne flutes. A stocked wine refrigerator stood floor to ceiling.

With three different chair groupings, it was a room for entertaining. Double sliding glass doors opened to flagstone steps leading down to the pool deck. In the summer, with the doors wide, the party could flow easily from inside to outdoors.

She'd been thinking about wild sex with an incredibly hot guy. She'd thought she'd already come to terms with his wealth. But this was something more. Will was an incredibly hot *super rich* guy. Of course she already knew that he was a billionaire, but the fact kept hitting her over and over again.

Caviar worth thousands that he gave away to a friend.

A Maserati kit car he conjured up with a snap of his fingers.

A golf course in his backyard.

A fire pit in his sunken living room.

"He needs a Ping-Pong table," Jeremy said matter-of-factly.

She slung her arm around his shoulders and laughed, glad that her brother could always pull her from her spinning thoughts. Thoughts about just how far out of her depth she was with Will. "He probably has a game room somewhere."

Will's voice carried across the immense room. "Indeed I do. And it's right under here." He tapped the floor with his foot.

His newly washed hair was so dark it gleamed with blue highlights in the late sun falling through the tall windows. He was delicious in black jeans and a dark blue shirt, its sleeves rolled up his forearms. So delicious that the sight of him sent another flush of heat rushing over her skin.

"There's a pool table and some pinball machines down there as well," he told Jeremy. "You can get to it from the pool patio. Or there's a set of stairs from up here." He pointed behind the first staircase leading to the second level. "The media room is down there, too."

"A media room?" Harper echoed, even though at this point she shouldn't be surprised by anything in this magnificent house.

"It's got a projection TV. Like a small movie screen."

"Cool," Jeremy said, and then he kissed Harper on the cheek, yelled "'Bye!" and raced down the stairs to check it all out.

As soon as her brother was out of sight, Will moved close. He put his hand on Harper's arm and skimmed his fingers down until he clasped her hand in his. His thumb stroked a slow rhythm against her skin.

"Feel like a drive to Pacifica for dinner? There's a great place right on the ocean."

God, yes. She'd go anywhere with him tonight. Absolutely *anywhere.*

Smiling up at him, she let her inner vixen shine through. "Sounds good, especially if you can get us there fast."

As the word *fast* registered, his eyes dilated nearly to black as he understood that she was up for another wild ride—in every sense of the phrase. For one breathless moment, Harper wasn't sure they'd even make it out of his house. Especially when he leaned in close and said, "I'll take you as fast, and as wild, as you want." His mouth was close enough that she could almost taste him as he added, "As many times as you want."

But then, instead of kissing her, he drew out the tease by merely putting his hand on the small of her back. And as they headed for the door, Harper realized that a person really *could* go weak in the knees.

Because she just had.

CHAPTER SIXTEEN

Throughout dinner, Will barely tasted the food, though he assumed it was good. He didn't care about what he ate or the view from the restaurant's tall windows overlooking the ocean. He cared only about watching Harper. Touching Harper. He'd kept her close beside him in the booth, her thigh against his, the friction of their bodies like jolts of electricity.

She seemed excited tonight—which he understood, because he felt exactly the same way—and he was glad to see that she wasn't trying to hide her innate sensuality anymore. But at the same time, she seemed a little nervous. As if she couldn't quite believe she was wearing that super-sexy dress while out on a date with him.

Now, as they got back into his car, he asked her, "Do you want the top up or down?"

It was cool out, and her dress didn't have sleeves. But she surprised him by saying, "Top down. Heater up."

They flew down the coast road. The mesh deflector behind the seats reduced the noise and wind. Despite the stick shift between them, he kept her close with a hand over hers. She'd half-turned toward him, her head resting on the seat back, one knee bent, the hem of the dress rising higher. The night sky above was bright with stars and moonlight, everything reflected in her eyes. Her hair blew around her face in lazy tendrils. He didn't want to scare her away, but he needed to touch her, so he moved his hand to her knee and stroked her bare skin in small circles.

Hell. It took serious effort to keep his focus on driving. He damn well might get them into an accident at this rate.

Will made the turn off the coast road onto Highway 92, which crossed over the mountains, back to the San Francisco Peninsula, then said, "How fast do you want to go tonight, Harper?" He wanted her—wanted her so badly that he needed to make absolutely sure he wasn't the only one feeling this crazy. Or wanting this badly.

It was too dark to see the color of her skin clearly, but he could have sworn she blushed as she said, "Fast." Her voice was husky and more than a little breathless as she put her hand over his on her knee and added, "I'm ready for you to go really fast. As fast as you've ever gone."

He felt the hum of her words in his chest. Hell, he felt it *everywhere*. He could tell she wasn't normally this bold with men, and he loved that she wanted to be bold with him. He was supposed to be the seducer, she the seduced. But she was reversing roles on him, and he liked it.

Liked it a hell of a lot.

He wanted his hands on her, his lips tasting hers. He wanted to feel her skin, hold her close, rub his body against hers. And fill her with everything he had.

But at the same time, he didn't want tonight to be the beginning and end. Which meant he'd have to make it so good she couldn't help but come back for more...

* * *

The speedometer climbed, and Harper held onto Will's arm as they took the corners. It was late, the road empty as the headlights cut a path through the dark. It felt so sexy to be cocooned in the car with him, the wind whipping over the top of the convertible, leaving them virtually untouched.

She'd never been this bold before, had never asked for what she wanted from a man. But no man had ever made her feel this hungry, this greedy, this desperate before.

"*Faster,*" she whispered. All the times in her life she'd wished for speed, then forced herself to shove those wishes aside, felt like they were flying away on the wind.

His capable hands gripped the wheel, kept them true. But, oh, how she wanted his hands on *her*.

She was done waiting, not just for Will, but for this rush. The rush of speed and joy and *pleasure*.

She'd had just enough wine at dinner to give her courage. The new lingerie gave her the nerve. The speed did the rest.

She didn't want him to slam on the brakes, didn't want to be the one to slam on the brakes, either. She wanted both of them to drive each other fast and furious.

As fast and furious as they could go.

"Will," she said. Just his name. It felt loud in the small cockpit of his sporty car.

They'd come off the other side of the mountain, and he downshifted to take the entrance ramp. When he was at freeway speed, she took his hand off the stick shift and put it on her knee, where the dress had pulled high enough to reveal a little bare flesh.

His hand slid beneath the dress, gliding halfway up her thigh. Then he trailed his fingers back down. Her pulse pounded in the wake of his touch.

She'd thought about having him all week. Longer than that—since the first time she'd set eyes on him, if she was being totally honest with herself. She wanted him. If there were consequences, she'd worry about those later. Not now. Not tonight, when she was so close to finally having what she wanted.

What she *needed.*

She'd always been a good girl, playing by the rules. Yes, she'd had sex, but she didn't invite men into her bed when her brother was home, and she'd never before thought of buying lingerie to seduce a man.

But with Will, everything was different.

And now she wanted to be wild.

* * *

It was the longest drive of Will's life, and it nearly killed him not to be able to give Harper his undivided attention. At long last, he saw the lights lining his driveway and the sports car purred up the hill. He pressed the garage opener under the dash, and they glided inside.

A second later, he had his seatbelt undone and he was already reaching for her when she grabbed his shirt and pulled him down to her mouth. The kiss was long and deep. He couldn't get enough of her. The stick shift dug into his thigh, but he didn't pull away. He let her take him, eat him up. She tasted sweet, like the raspberry tart she'd had for dessert, warm and sweet and rich. He slid his hands through her hair, pushing her back against the seat. Angling his head, he licked her lips, and she pulled him back for more, their mouths melding.

He could feel his heart hammering and the answering beat of hers against his chest. "I love the way you taste. And I want more. So much more, Harper. But not in a sports car." He wanted to enjoy her, take his time discovering—and pleasuring—every inch of her body, which was why he hadn't gone any further in the car during the drive home.

After climbing out, he rounded the hood and held out his hand to her. Her mouth was bare of lipstick and seductively kiss-swollen, and his heart rolled over in his chest just looking at her.

She was so beautiful, so damn sexy, yet somehow she retained the sweetness of the all-American girl next door. She was the kind of woman he'd never dreamed he could have. The good girl. The nice girl. The smart girl. The *forever* girl.

She didn't want his money or his fame or to hang on his arm while photographers snapped her picture. She was fresh and sweet and sexy as all-get-out.

He'd never be good enough for her. But he couldn't let himself think about that tonight. Instead, he'd let all his bad deeds be erased by her beauty and her sweetness.

But instead of heading for the house, and his bed, she pushed the remote button under the dash, and the garage door slid soundlessly closed. He could see the nerves still simmering away in her eyes as she turned back to him. But those nerves didn't stop her from saying, "I've never been naughty in a car." Her hands flat on his chest, she went up on her toes, her lips a breath away. "And I've never done anything naughty on the *hood* of a car before, either."

* * *

Harper couldn't believe what she was saying, could hardly believe how fearless she felt. But the bars she'd been confined by for so long seemed to have burst wide open tonight. And she knew she had to race to enjoy every last second of her freedom before they closed down around her again.

"Here?" Will asked in a voice heavy with desire. "Do you want me to take you right here, Harper?"

"Unless," she said in a husky voice, "you're afraid it'll muss up the paint job."

"I don't give a damn if it does." He lifted her as though she weighed nothing. Setting her on the hood, he slid his hands up her thighs, pushing the dress high, and stepped between her legs. "Tell me what you want me to do to you."

Everything. She wanted to feel his skin against hers, his body deep inside her. "Touch me," she whispered. "Touch me like you almost did in the car. I bought satin and lace for you today, and I want you to see it. *Now.*"

"Satin and lace?" She'd never seen such hunger on a man's face. "I want to see it. I want to see *you.*" He lightly stroked both hands up and down her legs, enough to make her skin hot and her body buzz, before his voice dropped to a sexy growl. "Undo the dress for me."

Reaching behind with less than steady hands, she drew the zipper down, then slid her arms free, letting the bodice of the dress fall to her lap.

"*Jesus*," he whispered. "You're so beautiful."

He swept his thumbs along the underside of the bra cups, up the sides, tracing the thin shoulder straps. His fingers were feather light on the swell of her breasts, leaving sparks that shimmied through her body all the way to her toes. Then his mouth was on hers, consuming her as his hands explored every inch of satin, every scrap of lace.

She was already mindless with need and he hadn't even undone her bra.

"I need to know how the rest of you tastes," he whispered against her lips. "I've been dying to know. Dying to get my hands and mouth on you. *All* of you."

His hands slipping down to her waist, he pushed her flat onto the warm hood of the car and came down over her. He was deliciously hard where his body rubbed against the apex of her thighs, creating friction with the bulge of his jeans. Pulling the bra aside, he trailed kisses over her breasts. Then his lips closed over her and Harper moaned, biting her lip. His touch was sensual, reverent. *Wild.* He licked, sucked, nipped, until she felt a jolt straight down to her center.

"Oh baby, you're so sweet. You taste like cherries."

Her nerves slipped back through as she said, "I do not. No one does."

"Cherries," he insisted, raising his head. His lips were wet, and she was half naked, one breast still covered. The decadent sight spiked her desire. "Your lips are like cherries, too," he said.

Then he kissed her again, and she tasted the slight saltiness of her own skin. Holding her head, he moved his mouth on hers, licking, biting, just the way he'd taken her breast. Then he went deep, his tongue sweet and hot, his body bearing down on her.

No man had ever played with her like this, teased her, taken her over. She wrapped her arms around his neck, lifting her head slightly to kiss him as passionately as he kissed her, fully open to him.

"So sweet."

Reaching between them, he effortlessly popped the front clasp of her bra. He closed one hand over her breast, molding her flesh with his fingers before flicking his thumb over the peaked nub. And then he put his lips over her once more and sucked hard, making her arch and moan against him.

"So pretty."

She raised her legs and wrapped them around his hips to hold him tight, intensifying the sensations. Gripping her thigh, he held her leg high, squeezing her bottom as he drove her mad with his mouth. He turned to her other breast, giving it the same sweet treatment.

He didn't rush—he savored.

"So perfect."

He seduced her with his words as much as with his body. And tonight, she wouldn't let herself think about the other women he might have said these same things to. She wouldn't think about her real life that was waiting for her just around the corner.

For a few precious moments, it was enough that he was lavishing attention on her, worshipping her body as if he couldn't get enough.

He trailed kisses down her abdomen, licking her navel. Then he bunched her dress and pushed it up until it was just a ribbon around her waist.

The garage lights were bright overhead. He'd see everything. Touch everything. Taste everything. She closed her eyes and felt the rush of speed again, flying along the highway in his fast car with his fast hands on her skin.

Harper wanted all of it—Will's mouth, his hands, his desire, his laughter, his intensity.

Everything.

CHAPTER SEVENTEEN

Harper was like the finest whiskey, the sweetest of late harvest wines. She reacted so beautifully to each touch, each word, as her sensuality took her over, opening her up to pleasure for pleasure's sake.

"You're so damn sexy. Look at all that see-through lace. You make me crazy with all your naughty lingerie. I want to see you in it and nothing else. And then?" He paused, made them both wait. "And then I want to see you out of it. Just you, Harper. I want to see *you*."

She ran her hands through his hair. *"Please."*

The one word sounded so breathless that he was tempted just to tear everything off her. But he wanted to give Harper more. So much more. Enough to drive her crazy. Enough to drive them both crazy.

He pulled the bunched dress down. "Lift up."

She flattened her hands on the hood and levered herself up. Will tugged the material down, then stepped back to slide it over her legs, and tossed it on the hood of the car, next to her head.

Every coherent thought fled as he took in the creamy satin bra with pink lace, her breasts wet from his tongue. And then there was the hint of flesh and other delights through the lacy panel of the endlessly sexy panties.

Leaning over her, he trailed both hands from her breasts to her belly to the scrap of satin and lace at her apex. He took her lips at the same time he slid beneath the fabric and took her with his fingers. Harper moaned against him, then opened her mouth, her kiss wild, her nails scoring furrows through his hair. She bucked up against him, wanting more.

He went slowly, stroking, teasing, loving the way her body moved beneath his. "Remember what I said?" he murmured against her mouth.

She shook her head. "No. I can't even think right now."

Neither could he, but Lord, he was trying the best he could. "I told you I'd make you scream with pleasure."

"Oh God." It was almost as if the memory of his saying that was too much for her right now. "Do it, Will. Do it *now.*"

The desperation in her voice made him nuts, too. It wasn't for his money or his power or his position or the things he could give her. It was for his hands and his mouth, his touch. It was for *him*. And he craved that.

Just as much as he craved her.

Will had developed incredible self-control as an adult. But now, with Harper, he couldn't hold back one more second from giving her what she wanted. What they both wanted, as he kissed his way down her body. Her limbs quaked, and her hot, sexy sounds filled the garage like music. Hooking his thumbs in the elastic, he tugged her panties down, needing all of her.

Needing *everything*.

"Mine," he said softly, tossing the lacy confection onto the dress beside her. Then he cupped her hips, shoved her higher up on the hood, and put his mouth to her.

He relished her, loving her taste on his tongue, loving the way she gasped and moaned and cried out his name, writhing beneath him. "*Oh God, oh God*," she chanted, a quivering mass of sensation. But he wanted to push her higher. Higher than she'd ever thought she could go.

He repeated the wicked pattern of his tongue sliding over her and his fingers sliding into her. Again and again and again until he felt the orgasm begin in her contracting muscles. She rocked, rolled, shuddered, and finally screamed out his name. It was long—it was loud.

And it was the most beautiful sound he'd ever heard.

* * *

Nothing had ever felt like that. She'd been a mass of vibrating nerve endings, her skin fiery to the touch, explosions of color before her eyes, his mouth magic on her.

"I want you. I need you. Now. Right now, damn it. But protection is in the bedroom." Will leaned over her, murmuring words it took her a moment to understand. "I hadn't planned on seducing you out here."

"I seduced you." Maybe she should have been shocked that she'd told him to drive her fast, fast, faster. Begged him to touch her right here in the garage. But there wasn't any room for shock amid all the glorious pleasure.

He touched his lips to the pulse beating at her throat, as if he needed to feel the racing of her heart. "You had me seduced at day one."

Before she could react to his surprisingly beautiful words, he took her with a mind-blowing kiss. It was sexy, decadent, exceptionally naughty, and she closed her eyes and arched up into his body, loving the hard press of him along her entire length. "I have protection." She wouldn't let herself feel shy again. Not yet. Not when she had *intentions*. Just as he had. "In my bag. In the car."

He moved so quickly to get her bag, she almost laughed out loud. When he handed it to her, she snapped open the clutch and produced a small box of condoms.

"I love a woman who plans ahead." He gave her a swoon-worthy smile.

But she was too focused on having him—*all* of him—to notice anything now but the fact that he still had all his clothes on. And she wanted them off.

"I want to touch you." A wild thrill coursed through her as she gave in to the urge to grab the open neck of his shirt and give it a hard yank with both hands. The buttons popped free, scattering across the concrete.

"Oh my God." Her hands stilled, holding the edges of his shirt. "You're so beautiful."

His chest had a dusting of dark hair across his pectorals and around his nipples, arrowing down to his jeans. Her skin was pale against the darker tones of his rippling muscles. But even this wasn't enough. She wanted to hold onto his bare shoulders, wanted to strip him the way he'd stripped her.

She started to drag the shirt off his shoulders, but before she could, he leaned over to trap her wrists against the hood.

"Not as pretty as you are." Holding her down with one hand, he ran his fingers between her breasts at the same time that he shifted his hips between hers.

He was all sexy male and hard flesh, and she needed him to finish what he'd started. What *she'd* started. Pulling her hands free of his hold, she pushed herself to a sitting position between his legs and tugged on his belt. She wanted to play, tease, see if she could make him as crazy as she felt. After unzipping him, she shoved her thumbs into the waistband at the sides and slowly slid the denim and cotton down until all that hot, hard, gorgeous flesh was in her hands. She felt him throb against her palm, and her breath hitched with the thought of how he'd feel inside her.

"Don't tease." His eyes were dark and fathomless.

A shiver of need ran through her as she whispered, "I thought you liked to tease?"

"I do," he said with a wolfish smile that made her core clench tight and hot. "But I need to be inside you. *Right. This. Minute.*"

There was something in his hoarse words that made her tremble. She had never felt so desired in her life. No one had *needed* her in quite this way.

"Yes," she answered softly as they sheathed him together. "Right this minute."

He pulled her legs around his waist. "Don't let go. Hold me tight."

She had no choice. Holding him tight was the only thing she could do.

The only thing she wanted to do.

But instead of just taking her, he braced himself on the hood and pushed her flat against the mctal. Stroking between her legs with his hard heat, he played her in slow, mesmerizing circles. Harper closed her eyes and let sensation take over the rising pulse of her body. She locked her legs around his waist the same way her arms imprisoned his neck and rose up to meet his touch, rolling with his rhythm.

"That's it, baby, just like that." Leaning close, he finally moved with a faster pace. "I want you right on the edge when I finally take you."

His words were as potent as his touch, and she shuddered. Her breath puffed with sounds she barely recognized as her own, and her skin heated.

"Oh God." She arched her neck. *Almost there.* One more second. Just one more...

"Now." He plunged deep.

And she shattered.

* * *

"Harper."

The way she came apart for him, not holding anything back, giving him all of her pleasure, was enough to make him lose everything right then. But he wanted more. Wanted to see her, to drink in every detail of her pleasure.

She was beautiful in her bliss, her breath coming fast as she arched her neck. The long column of her throat begged for his mouth, but he kept up the slow plunge inside her, forcing her to ride the edge. Her eyelashes fluttered, and sexy little cries fell from her lips.

She grabbed his forearms, her nails digging in with the most delicious pain he'd ever felt. "I don't... I've never..."

"You will," he promised her. "Take me, baby." He needed to get as close to her as he could, needing to erase any distance that remained between them. "Please take me. All of me."

He'd think about the meaning of his words later, but for now, he moved faster, stroked harder, went deeper. So deep he could lose himself in her. Become one with her.

With a soft cry, she anchored herself to him, her arms around his neck, her body hugging him, her legs tight at his waist.

"Yes, yes, yes," she panted. "That feels so good. Will...please...*more.*"

He took her completely then, with everything in him. Pounding hard, his blood racing, his mind fogging to anything but the feel of her hot skin, her breath on his throat, her silky hair against his cheek.

He felt her next orgasm begin in the quiver of her limbs. Moments later, he was looking into her blue eyes and calling out her name. And as he gave her everything—and she did, too—he had the strangest sense of being *owned*.

No one had ever owned him. Not since he was a kid, when it felt like his father had wrapped a tight and jagged chain around him.

But when he was with Harper, it was as though something eased inside him.

Like a sweet refrain telling him everything was—finally—all right.

* * *

Harper couldn't let go. Didn't want to. Not when letting go meant returning to the world.

To reality.

She felt so wonderfully engulfed by Will, his skin warm, his muscles hard and hot. She wanted to stay like this, without thinking or questioning, just indulging her senses a while longer before they let reality seep back in.

Only...all the things she'd done with Will were the wild and crazy acts of another woman. A sexy siren. But she was so *not* that. And already the jittery nerves were rising again.

He'd called her *baby*. And in the moment, it had sounded so sweet, almost gut-wrenching. But she knew she needed to be honest with herself about the fact that it was a pet name most men used for casual sex buddies. Which should be fine, since that's exactly what this was. She had to keep that firmly in her mind.

"Making love with you was absolutely perfect," he murmured into her hair.

Again, though they were easy words, it felt like Will was infusing them with so much emotion, almost as though he was saying it had been more than just sex for him. Which, of course, he wasn't. This had just been weeks of teasing, some really hot pheromones swirling in the air, and a fast ride in—and on top of—his sexy sports car.

She needed to remember that's all it was.

Still, she wanted a few more moments in his arms. Just a few more and then real life could start up again.

"I must be crushing you," he finally said, but he rose slowly, swiping his tongue over her shoulder. She'd never known a man like him before, such an innately sensual creature, always touching, licking, kissing. As he eased away from her, he trailed a hand over her skin and said, "The things you do to me."

Except for her bra, she was naked on top of his car, her body still glistening with desire. And when he went to toss the condom, it was cold without him. Cold and exposed. So even though her limbs still felt boneless, she found her panties and dress on the hood beside her, tucked herself back into her bra, then slid off the hood of his expensive car and stepped into the dress.

A few moments later, he was beside her again, his hand warm on her back. "I'll help you." He did her up with a slow slide of the zipper, the brush of his fingers teasing her skin. "Taking you out here wasn't exactly what I had planned for our first time." He was nuzzling her neck, and it did things to her insides all over again. He bit the soft flesh between her shoulder and neck, sending shivers of delight through her. "But it was so damned sexy, Harper. *You're* so damned sexy."

She'd bought pretty lingerie, a new dress, and made a trip to the drugstore, all in the name of seducing him. She'd had *intentions*. And now she'd just had the most amazing sex of her life. She would not ruin everything because she couldn't stop thinking of all the other women before her to whom he'd likely said the exact same thing.

She turned in his arms, looped hers around his neck, and said, "It was perfect."

Her voice was too high and bright, overenthusiastic, like Jeremy's. She needed to bring herself under control. The problem with Will was that he could make a girl lose her head.

But Harper couldn't afford that.

* * *

Will changed his torn shirt while Harper corralled her brother. As soon as Jeremy climbed into the passenger seat of her car, he nodded off.

"You two should spend the night." Reluctant to take his arm from around her waist, Will herded her a few feet away so Jeremy wouldn't overhear their conversation, just in case he woke up.

"No." Harper shook her head.

She could be stubborn, Will realized. And the truth was that one of the things he appreciated about her was her iron will. No one would ever hurt Jeremy while she was on watch. She would be the same way about her kids, he knew—protecting them with her life.

"We need to get home," she told him. "Thank you for giving him a fabulous day. And," she added with another one of those pretty blushes, "for the fabulous evening I had, too."

Fabulous didn't even begin to cover it. And even though he wasn't nearly ready for the evening to be over, it was easy to guess that she didn't want to sleep with him when Jeremy was in the house.

"I have several guest rooms. You don't need to sleep in my bed."

"Jeremy's better with his routines at home."

Clearly, Will wasn't going to sway her. But he was going to leave his stamp on her one way or another, damn it, so he crushed her into his arms and took her mouth hard and fast. "Do you want to know my next *intention*?" he asked a beat later, his lips still touching hers. He could feel the rapid tattoo of her heartbeat against his chest. Her breath was fast against his mouth. She wasn't unaffected—nowhere near.

"Will...tonight was a great break from reality, but it was—"

"*Not* a one-time thing." It never had been, not for him, not when it was Harper in his arms. "I don't want to lie to you. Not now, not ever. So you need to know I intend to do that again. Over and over. Every single delirious moment. And more. Whether you spend the night or not. Whether it's in a bed or not."

Then he kissed her one last time for the evening, a lingering moment of pure bliss that he hoped would make her long for him in the middle of the night as much as he'd be longing for her.

CHAPTER EIGHTEEN

Will called early on Sunday morning, just after eight, but Harper was already up. "You and Jeremy want to come over for a little work on the car?"

God, how she wanted to. Inside, she wanted nothing more than to run to him. Being with him was so good but so dangerous. Too much of a good thing got you hooked. Besides, she didn't want Jeremy to get too dependent on Will.

"Thanks, that's nice of you, but we've got chores."

He was silent for a moment, one in which she knew he wasn't at all happy with her answer. But instead of pushing her, he said, "All right. But if you need anything—" He lingered on the word *anything*. "—don't hesitate to call."

He couldn't possibly know how badly she wanted to say yes to his offer. But she shouldn't do it. Not so soon after losing herself in his arms last night. And not so soon after he'd made his next round of *intentions* perfectly clear.

All night long in her dreams, his voice had echoed in her ears: *I intend to do that again. Over and over. Every single delirious moment. And more.*

"Thanks." The fact that the word came out sounding a little breathless only solidified her decision to put some space between them, giving her time to recover from last night's wonderland. She put on her best breezy and independent voice as she said, "Talk to you later."

Because, for all that she worried about her brother, *she* was the one who could become dependent on Will if she wasn't careful. Good sex was like chocolate truffles. Every so often, you gave yourself one as a treat. And she knew darn well that if she saw Will today, he'd manage to get her into bed. Or onto the workbench in the garage while he sent Jeremy off to have lunch with Mrs. Taylor. And then she'd end up even more deeply under his spell...

No, she couldn't let herself forget that what she was doing with Will only worked as long as she didn't let herself get too emotional or too involved. Short-term pleasure, that's all this was. And when it hit its inevitable end, she needed to be absolutely sure that she could walk away with her head held high and no regrets.

* * *

Harper should have known better than to think Will would simply back off. On Monday, he wanted to talk to her while he was on Skype with Jeremy, but she told her brother she was too busy. A few minutes later, however, she had to step away to answer the doorbell...only to find a flower delivery guy waiting with a huge bouquet that Jeremy couldn't stop marveling over. She might have done more than her fair share of marveling, too, when her brother's back was turned.

On Tuesday, he had a gourmet lunch sent to her office, complete with chocolate and a split of champagne. She'd saved that for later when she got home.

The man was relentless. Which was probably why he was as rich as Midas. But she'd determined that she wouldn't see him until Saturday. A week seemed appropriate. It kept things casual. At least, that was what she told herself during the day when she was rational.

But then there were the nights. When she was alone in bed and her body was screaming for his touch. She only had to close her eyes to feel his mouth on her...and those memories of their lovemaking only got better by the night.

On Wednesday morning, she didn't hear the alarm clock, mostly due to the fact that the night had been filled with erotic dreams about Will. She had to rush through her shower and barely got Jeremy out the door in time to catch his bus.

He took a special bus to school and in the afternoons they dropped him off at the grocery store where he worked bagging groceries. She picked him up on her way home from work.

The doorbell rang and she wondered what Jeremy had forgotten, not even considering until she opened the door that Jeremy wouldn't have used the bell. Which meant...

It was Will. He was to-die-for in a black suit and crisp white shirt that looked yummy against his tanned skin. On the other hand, her hair was still wet, she wore no makeup, and her robe was soft but well worn.

"Will?" His name was barely out of her mouth when she realized that she wanted him so badly she actually ached for his touch.

"You didn't call me." He stepped inside and closed the door behind him. "You haven't let me see you."

Intensity burned in his eyes—a look that closely mirrored her own longing every time she'd caught her reflection over the past few days, thinking of him, missing him.

Before she could blink or breathe or say anything more, his hands were in her hair and he was kissing her. Devouring her. Utterly.

It was so much more than her dreams. So much better even than her memories of Saturday night. She simply melted against him. She wanted to touch him, but her hands were trapped between them. There was something so elemental about a man holding you still for his kiss, just his mouth taking you as though he could never get enough.

Finally, he pulled back, his eyes closed, a deep satisfying breath filling his lungs. "There. That's better." Then he gave her one of his gorgeous grins. "I couldn't start the day any other way."

"You're crazy." Her mind dazed, she could barely muster more than a whisper.

His desire was addictive. If she wasn't careful, she could want it, start to need it, until she couldn't live without it. He played havoc with the meaning of *casual*.

"Crazy for you," he said. "Is Jeremy at school?"

Guessing there was only one reason he would ask that, she knew she should force herself to stick to her need-a-week-off plan. But with his hands on her and her mouth still tingling from his kiss, it was frankly impossible to corral her own desire. She had no willpower whatsoever.

Willpower. She almost laughed at the realization that Will definitely had all the power right then.

As soon as she nodded, he reached down to the belt of her robe. "I want to make you come. I want to *hear* you come. I want to *feel* you come. I want to *watch* you come."

Just as he hadn't asked permission to walk inside, or to kiss her, or to undress her, he didn't ask permission to pick her up, hoisting her high on his body. Harper wrapped her legs around him. His mouth unerringly found her breast, and the pleasure was so intensely connected to all her other intimate places that she couldn't help leaning back in his arms and locking her ankles. She gripped him hard in the circle of her legs to intensify the sensations zipping through her body.

"You're irresistible when you're all heated up." His voice was a low purr vibrating right into her. "Hell, you're *always* irresistible." He carried her through to the living room, set her down on the couch, then pushed the coffee table back with his foot.

Her robe fell open around her, and Will looked incredibly pleased about it. "I've always been known for my timing, but it's never been better than right now, coming here and finding you all naked and pretty for me."

She loved the way he said hot, sexy things all the time. "I just got out of the shower."

He removed his jacket and tossed it on the other end of the couch. "Then my timing wasn't so impeccable after all, was it? A few minutes earlier, and I could have stepped under the water with you."

The idea of him taking her with his pristine shirt and tie on was exciting. So exciting that it was almost impossible to remind herself—and him—that there needed to be boundaries to what they were doing. Whatever the heck it was.

"You shouldn't be here. We shouldn't be doing this."

He came down on one knee between her legs. "Give me a good reason why not."

The problem was that when he touched her, Harper couldn't think of any reasons at all. Nothing more than a simple, "Because."

"That's not a reason," he said with a smile. One full of anticipation. As much as she was feeling herself. "It's just a word."

He moved his fingers over her, and Harper felt her temperature rising, a flush of heat coloring her skin. "Someone might see."

Will glanced to the window, then back to her with a quirk of his mouth that said it all. Because of course her mother's lace curtains would hide them from prying eyes.

"Try harder," he said. But he was the one trying harder, finding just the right rhythm with his hands, his wonderfully talented fingers, to make her toes curl.

"Because it's morning. And it's not the weekend. And I have to get to work. I've got appointments. So do you." There. All good reasons. But his touch was magic.

"Then you'd better come quickly."

Only, she didn't want to come quickly. She wanted to savor his touch. She tugged him down by his tie and was surprised to find a challenge on her own lips. "Make me."

He laughed, a heady masculine sound filled with desire and delight, just before his lips met hers. It wasn't like the fast, wild kisses on Saturday night. This was slow and delicious. He licked her lips, nibbled on the lower one. He kissed her lightly, turning one way, then angling the other. She laced her fingers through his thick hair and held him closer, opened her mouth for him. All the while, he did amazing things with his hands. She gasped as his tongue took hers, a particularly sweet shaft of pleasure rolling through her. She deepened the kiss, raising her head off the cushions. He was all minty toothpaste and hot male.

Then she couldn't concentrate anymore. There was just his hand and the sweet, hot build of tension as he kissed and caressed her. She squeezed her eyes shut and her hips rolled to his movements.

"That's it, baby. Come for me. Fast and hot, just the way we both love it."

She panted, soft moans rising in her throat, knowing she was going to do just what he wanted as a hot spike of pleasure shot down to her center and exploded. She cried out—maybe it was his name, she couldn't be sure. Her body bowed, and she clutched his shoulders, then wrapped her arms around his neck, holding him tight as the waves of pleasure swept through her.

And after, she was clinging and knew she ought to let go, but as she floated down from that blissful place, she felt so good in his arms. So complete.

There was no way she could bear to let him go.

"Definitely the perfect way to start the day," he said into her hair.

Despite the hint of arrogance in his tone, she couldn't deny that she'd never had a more perfect wakeup call.

He gave her one more kiss, then drew back. "I hate to leave you, but you're right that both of us have meetings to go to."

Her eyes snapped open. "But you haven't—"

He cut her off with another kiss, then pulled back slowly. "The next time I take you for a ride in my fast car, I will. And so will you. Again and again and again."

Grabbing his suit jacket off the couch, he shrugged into it. After straightening his tie, he held out his hand. Harper took it and let him pull her to her feet. Will tugged the robe over her breasts, his large hands gliding possessively across her flesh before he tied the belt.

He was always fully clothed while she was exposed. It was yet another way he used his power. Yet another thing she liked despite herself—though she still desperately wanted him to be naked, too.

He led her to the door, opened it, then demanded in a low voice, "One more kiss before I go."

She wanted so badly to kiss him again. She wanted him as crazy and out of control as she was. Wanted him to want her so badly that he couldn't walk away. Her body was still humming with the things he'd done to her on the couch. He wasn't like any man she'd ever known. She'd talked herself into having burning-hot sex with a sizzling-hot guy. And she'd gotten way more than she'd asked for. Maybe she'd even gotten more than she could handle. Because now she didn't think she could wait until the weekend.

He'd stepped on her accelerator and she was ready to race. Only, she'd promised herself that she'd stay in control, that she'd let herself have fun, but wouldn't make the mistake of reading too much into any of this. Suddenly, however, she wasn't feeling casual at all. She was starting to want a whole lot more. Whereas he seemed perfectly happy to drop by, make her come, then head out for his meetings. Check, check, check—all part of a billionaire's day. As if he were used to doing things like this all the time, making women crazy for him, getting them to fall in a hot, senseless rush, while he kept everything seamlessly compartmentalized.

After all, who had the still perfectly pressed suit and tie?

And who had the sex-hair and barely closed robe?

Somehow, some way, she needed to grab the control she'd just lost. Which meant that instead of kissing him again the way he'd just commanded, there was only one way to reassert the control she'd given him from the moment he'd stepped inside without an invitation.

Harper smiled, held onto the doorknob, and said, "Have a great day, Will," then closed the door with a soft, but final, click.

She barely breathed as she waited for the sound of his footsteps that would let her know he was heading back down her front path toward his car. None sounded for several long moments—moments where she knew he must be trying to decide whether to let her win this round or not.

Finally, he walked away, and her held breath left her in a hard *whoosh* as she heard him start up his engine and drive away. She tried to return to her day as if nothing out of the ordinary had happened, tried telling herself that she was just as much in control of her life, and her emotions, as ever.

But all the while, she couldn't help but wonder if the feel of his kisses still lingering on her skin revealed the true story: that where Will was concerned, she wasn't in control of anything at all.

CHAPTER NINETEEN

"No, Miss Newman," Harper's client said to her over the phone the following afternoon, "there's no way I can get there earlier. My son is sick, so I couldn't take him to day care. But my husband will be home by five, and it will only take me fifteen minutes to get to your office."

Harper breathed deeply, then calmly replied, "That's fine. These things happen, and I hope your son feels better soon." Hadn't she run into the same problem when Jeremy wasn't well? Illness was the bane of the working parent's existence.

But the meeting delay left her in a real bind. She was supposed to pick up Jeremy from his after-school job at the grocery store at five. Finding someone to take over the task with two hours' notice late on a Thursday afternoon would be difficult. There was no way she could make it to the store, then back to the office that quickly in rush-hour traffic. And she couldn't postpone the meeting, either. Not when she had a position open that Carol's resume indicated she'd be perfect for, and the first-round interviews shut down tomorrow.

She called Trish, who didn't answer, probably because she was in class. After leaving a message, Harper mentally tapped her fingers waiting for a return call, but when it didn't come after twenty minutes, she knew she had to find an alternative.

For some crazy reason, the first person she thought of was Will.

Actually, it wasn't all that crazy, given that she hadn't stopped thinking about him since Wednesday morning. To be honest...she hadn't actually been able to stop thinking about him since the day he'd raced into their lives a month ago.

He'd told her to call if she needed anything. *Had he meant it?*

She picked up the receiver on her land line, holding it to her chest a moment, the dial tone vibrating against her as she thought about Will's promise on Wednesday morning—that he was saving up his fully unleashed passion for her and the next fast ride they took together. She didn't care that some might say it lacked the romance of moonlight and rose petals on a big, soft bed. Sex in a car, the almost clandestine nature of it, actually excited her more. As had the quickie in her living room, which had taken her to a level of heat she'd never experienced before.

Even after kicking him out to prove the point that he didn't hold *all* the power, she'd still ended up working in a dreamy daze all day. He'd made their quickie on her couch all about her. What kind of man put his own pleasure second? Could it possibly be the kind of man who would help her out of a tight bind that had nothing whatsoever to do with sex?

She punched in his cell number, and he answered on the second ring. "Harper, I was just thinking about you."

All he had to do was say her name in that sexy drawl and she melted like an ice cube in the summertime. It suddenly occurred to her that he might have picked up the call assuming she had something sexy to say to him. But since he knew how important her brother was to her, she hoped he wouldn't be too surprised when she said, "I have a huge favor to ask. I'm supposed to pick Jeremy up by five at the grocery store where he works, but I've got a meeting I can't miss."

"I'll get him."

Just that quickly, her heart swelled in her chest, the same way it had last Saturday when he'd been so kind to Jeremy while working on the Maserati. His sweetness had prompted her instant decision to take a risk by spending a few hot nights with him. It meant a great deal to her that Will didn't ask questions, didn't make excuses. He simply offered to help.

At the same time, however, she knew running a billion-dollar corporation couldn't be at all easy. And he'd already given her and Jeremy so much of his limited free time. "I thought you might have a driver? Or that maybe Mrs. Taylor could do it? I'm sure you're probably still up in the city and I know how busy you are."

"I'm happy to do it, Harper."

She'd called him to ask for help, and now that he was giving it so freely—and she needed it so badly—she stopped trying to talk him out of it. "Thank you. I really appreciate it." He had no idea how much. Not since her parents died had she been able to pick up the phone and call someone who would bail her out so quickly and easily. Not until Will.

He was too good, a dream come true. She didn't have anything to offer in return. Except for sex. It shouldn't make her smile to think of paying off her debts in his bed, but lately, everything about Will made her smile. "If you can drop him off at the house, I should be home by six-thirty. He'll be fine until then."

"No, I'll stay until you get home. I know you don't like him to be alone. Don't worry about a thing tonight. I've got it covered."

And maybe, she found herself hoping, even though she'd already had far more than a sensible quota of him for the week, he was also staying so that he could spend time with her, too. "Thank you," she said again. "You're sweet."

He gave a burst of incredulous laughter. "No one has ever called me *sweet* in my entire life."

"But you are."

"Believe me," he said in a voice that was suddenly serious, "I'm *not* sweet. But I promise I'll always do whatever I can for you and Jeremy."

Will made a lot of promises. And though Harper was still wary of letting Jeremy—or herself—get hurt, Will hadn't broken a single one yet.

* * *

The grocery store was only a ten-minute walk from Harper's house. Will figured Jeremy could probably have handled it just fine, but he knew Harper would have worried the whole time. It wasn't Will's business to say anything about how she handled her brother. Besides, hearing her voice over the phone had been the best thing that had happened to him all day, and even if he'd just blown off several meetings, he wanted to see her more than he wanted to sit in on a conference call. Not to mention the fact that he'd been able to hear her desperation when she'd asked him for the favor...along with a note in her voice that told him she'd expected him to say no.

Will loved surprising Harper. In fact, his plan was to keep surprising her over and over again, in the best possible ways.

Seeing Harper once a week wasn't nearly enough. And he wasn't just thinking about the hot sex they'd had in his garage after their date. He missed her laughter, her innate spark. He grinned every time he thought about the way she'd kicked him out of her house Wednesday morning, loving the way she could be so soft and pliable one moment, then strong and determined the next.

Both Harper and Jeremy added something to his life, something he couldn't define, but that he now realized had been missing for quite a while. It had been in that strange weariness he'd felt in the months before meeting them, a sense that all the wealth and all the changes he'd made in his life were no longer enough.

The traffic was bad, but fortunately Will arrived at the grocery store before Jeremy's shift was over. The place was a madhouse, with working moms rushing in and out, men with nothing but frozen dinners in their carts, and teenagers holding six-packs of soda. Though all the checkstands were open, the lines still snaked down the aisles.

He spotted Harper's brother three checkstands away, loading a vast expanse of groceries into reusable shopping bags. The mother had a child in the cart and two more were milling around Jeremy's legs. His tongue between his lips in concentration, Jeremy was trying to stack food carefully in the bags, but the kids kept screaming and jumping, bumping into him and knocking him off his rhythm. The mother shook her head, glaring at Jeremy with her mouth pursed.

Will headed down to them, his immediate thought being to intercede, or even help pack the groceries. Until he thought about the humiliation factor. Will didn't want Jeremy to think he couldn't handle the job. Here he'd just been thinking that Harper didn't always give Jeremy enough credit, like being able to walk home by himself, but rushing to her brother's rescue now would be exactly the same thing.

By that point, the checker, a stout woman with frizzy red hair, was furiously loading goods into plastic bags as well, tossing them at Jeremy and pointing to the cart. "Come on, come on," she practically yelled at him.

There was too much confusion, too many people waiting. And the customer was doing absolutely nothing to control her kids. A cantaloupe rolled down, and Jeremy stuffed it into the last bag.

"Do you need help out to your car, ma'am?" he asked politely.

"No, I do not." The woman snapped her fingers, and the two kids ran like furies out the door while the one in the cart screeched at an earsplitting volume.

Not wanting to blow Jeremy's concentration, Will was about to back off and let him finish his shift. Until he heard the checker say, "You put that cantaloupe on top of her eggs. Can't you do anything right?"

"I'm sorry," Jeremy said. "I didn't mean to mess up."

"I don't know why they hire people like you. You're so slow. You and your pea-sized brain. *Idiot.*"

"I'm really sorry," Jeremy said again, his face now completely red.

"If she complains, I'm gonna tell the management it's your fault for being the worst bagger we've ever had."

Rage welled up in Will. His hands fisted until his knuckles turned stark white. If Jeremy hadn't been there as witness...if the clerk had so much as laid a hand on him...if Will hadn't damn near annihilated the Road Warrior inside him...

Will reached Jeremy's side just as she issued the last threat. He flayed the woman with a look that could shred flesh. "Don't ever talk to Jeremy that way again. Apologize to him. Now."

The checker's hands stopped moving over the scanner, where she was holding a can of green beans. She stared at Will, openmouthed. Finally, she muttered, "I'm sorry."

"Say his name when you apologize to him." Will hadn't raised his voice, but his intent to tear her apart with his bare hands if she didn't fix things was crystal clear nonetheless.

"His name?" Her face screwed up. "I don't know."

"Didn't you just say you work with him all the time? How can you not know his name?"

Fixing her stare on Jeremy, she opened her mouth, and by her narrowed eyes, Will was sure something merciless was about to spew out. Until she looked back at him, took in the steely set of his mouth—and the silent threat in his eyes—and swallowed hard. "I think it's Jeremy."

"Apologize again. Properly."

"I'm sorry, Jeremy."

"It's okay." Jeremy's face was still beet red.

Will gave her one last look that personified the expression *if looks could kill*. And the clerk clearly recognized it. "There are no idiots here." Except her. "And I will know if you use that word to speak to anyone here again. Ever." He turned to Jeremy. "Ten minutes left on your shift, buddy. I'll wait for you over there." He crooked his chin toward the door, where the checker would be in his sights.

"Okay, Will," Jeremy said, his voice too quiet.

Watching from his spot over by the doorway, Will was afraid he'd make Jeremy nervous. On the other hand, there was no way he'd let anyone have another crack at Harper's brother. But Jeremy did well, with no more cantaloupe-versus-eggs incidents. He even helped an old lady out with her groceries. She winked as she passed Will. "You did good, sonny. That woman's always been a nasty piece of work."

Of course, the checker was as sweet as apple pie for the rest of the time that Will watched. Then it was five, and Jeremy ran to clock out. When he returned, Will slung an arm around his shoulder as he removed his store apron. "You did real good in there."

"I didn't. I put the melon on the eggs."

"They probably didn't break. And even if they did, it was just a mistake. We all make mistakes sometimes." As Jeremy climbed into the BMW, Will wished he'd had one of his fun cars for the kid to enjoy. "Is it always like that in there?"

"Like what?"

"Busy. Crazy." With nasty women calling him nasty names. Will's jaw tensed again thinking about the madness that had almost taken over when he'd seen Jeremy being bullied.

"Just at the end," Jeremy confessed. "Most of the time it's fine. But around five, it's really busy."

Will didn't like it. The boy had to put up with that every single damn day. How many times had someone called him an idiot? Will's hands were fists on the steering wheel. For so many reasons, nothing bothered him more than watching people being bullied. "That woman shouldn't be working there." His voice was a growl.

Jeremy fluttered his hands in the air. "Sadie didn't mean it. It's just that her mom's sick and she's going to die soon."

He wanted to say that was no excuse for being a total jerk. Sometimes, he knew, there were reasons why a person lost control. Not an excuse, just a reason. But he still couldn't quite squash the desire to flatten the woman with a cast iron skillet versus a fly swatter.

Will had tried to tell himself he didn't solve things with his fists anymore, but in that grocery store, he'd been ready to run down anything in his path. It was the part of himself he still feared lurked inside him, even after all the years since he'd ditched the gang.

"Jeremy—"

"Are you going to get her fired, Will? 'Cause I'd feel really bad if you did." The plea appeared as two big furrows across Jeremy's brow and a moist sheen in his eyes.

Will didn't want to let the woman off the hook, but for Jeremy he'd make an exception. "I'll give her one more chance. But if she treats you like that again, I need to know about it. Okay?"

"Okay." Jeremy nodded vigorously.

It was time to lighten the mood. Jeremy needed to move on even if Will's nerves were still firing like a racing engine. "Now, what do you say we order some Chinese? I know a great place."

"Yay." Jeremy clapped, his enthusiastic self again, as if he'd forgotten the whole thing.

Will could only hope that he had.

CHAPTER TWENTY

"I'll be back in the office tomorrow morning," Will told Maya, his Human Resources director. It was after seven and he'd had to call her at home. "Thanks for rescheduling our meeting." Ending the call, Will turned to Jeremy. "Enjoying dinner?"

Jeremy nodded exuberantly. Seated at the breakfast bar in Harper's kitchen, he was chowing down on yet another helping of sweet-and-sour pork.

"I've got another question for you," Will said. "How would you feel about a new job?"

"For me?" Jeremy asked, his mouth full. Harper likely wouldn't be pleased with the lack of manners, but Will felt it meant that Jeremy's guard was down with him. More like a person was with family.

"Yeah. A job for you."

He wanted to make things better for Jeremy. Will hated it when the big fish picked on the little ones.

Mostly because at one time he'd been the big fish. But that had ended with the Mavericks. It had taken a few years before he'd believed that he truly belonged with them, but they became his brothers. And even if he hadn't been as careful with other people as he should have been, he'd always fought for the Mavericks and protected them when they needed it.

But it had been a long, long time since anyone had needed him like that. Until Jeremy and Harper.

"What kind of job?" There was a piece of rice on Jeremy's shirt, which Will flicked onto the bar top.

He'd come by the idea somewhere between ordering the Chinese food and the delivery person's dropping it off: If Jeremy worked for him, he would no longer be a victim of sharp-tongued checkers. Or anyone else, for that matter. No one at Franconi Imports would dare to call him names. He would be treated with respect, Will would make sure of that. There would be no late-afternoon customer rush to confuse him, either. Sure, the tasks would be new to him, but they'd teach him new skills without the stress of too many people coming all at once. Anyone would have a problem with the environment he'd been in.

"How about working in my mailroom?" Will said. "You can deliver mail, pick up packages."

Jeremy's eyes glowed. "You mean like a postman?"

Will nodded, smiling. "A postman for my employees."

"Wow. Cool." Jeremy bit off half his spring roll and chewed, his eyes wide.

"You can also pick up people's papers to put through the shredder, and run office errands, and deliver supplies." The more he thought about it, the more tasks came to mind that Jeremy could easily handle. "What do you think? Would you like to try it?"

Jeremy nodded eagerly. "I do!"

Harper's brother was so exuberant about everything that sometimes it was hard to tell if he actually wanted to do something or he merely thought he needed to play the yes man. Which was why Will asked, "Will you miss your friends at the grocery store?"

"Yes, but that's okay. I like making new friends." Jeremy shoveled more food into his mouth.

"Great. We'll talk to Harper and see what she thinks."

"Okay, Will."

She opened the front door almost as Will said her name—and he got that special little kick under his ribs when he saw her. Her lipstick had worn off as though she'd been biting her lips on the way home, her suit jacket was crumpled in her hand, and she was clutching a grocery bag that looked ready to topple.

She'd never looked more gorgeous.

Will moved quickly toward her, grabbing the sack before it fell. And then, without a word of greeting, he planted his mouth on hers. The kiss was sweet and closemouthed in front of her brother, but it still made his heart beat faster. Especially when she leaned into him, as though she was glad that he was there to put his arms around her.

"Sorry I'm late," she said as she drew back. "I forgot we needed milk. The lines at the store were atrocious."

"I want to talk to you about that. But later. Right now, you need sustenance."

He took her jacket, laying it over the back of the sofa. Then he stashed the milk in the fridge and pulled out the wine he'd been chilling.

"Oh my God." She stopped dead in the kitchen. "You did the dishes. But how?"

"Believe it or not, I've loaded a dishwasher and washed dishes plenty of times," he said wryly. She seemed to have the mistaken notion that he'd been brought up privileged. Then again, he hadn't exactly shared the truth about his childhood with her, had he? So why would she think any differently?

"I helped," her brother piped up.

"That's great, Jeremy, thank you," she said. But she was glancing warily at the dishwasher.

"Don't worry," Will said. "I also know the dry soap goes in the machine and the liquid is for the hand-washing."

"I didn't mean to doubt your dishwashing prowess...it's just that you've already gone to so much trouble tonight." She rubbed a hand over her eyes. "I'm sorry. I didn't even think about what the house looked like when I sent you over or that you'd need to do the dishes so that you could have plates to eat with."

"I told you not to worry about anything tonight, Harper. And I meant it." He held up the bottle of Riesling he'd picked up. "I'll pour a glass of wine and fix you a plate."

"You don't have to." She clearly wasn't used to having anyone take care of her.

He pointed to the couch and put on his best boss voice. "Sit."

She shook her head at his tone, but he caught the way her lips were curving up as she relaxed into one end of the sofa. Slipping off her high heels, she leaned back with a sigh, obviously admiring the newly tidied room.

They'd also cleaned up in there, sorting Jeremy's crayons by color into the huge box. Will had learned that coloring was homework, likely a hand-eye coordination exercise.

"Can I watch *Animal Planet*?" Jeremy dashed across the room and picked up the remote, but stood motionless, his finger on the button, until Harper nodded. Then he plopped down on the carpet in front of the TV and started flipping channels.

"Not so close, please," Harper chided.

As Jeremy spider-walked backward, Will poured her wine. Between them, he and Jeremy had unloaded the dishwasher, found where everything went, and stacked all the dirty dishes in the machine. Which meant that Will not only knew where her wineglasses were, he also knew that she had too many cans of baked beans and an empty peanut butter jar, as if she always forgot to make a grocery list and couldn't remember what she needed when she got to the store. He'd also found the bag of white chocolate truffles in the cupboard next to the fridge, probably the only treat she let herself indulge in.

But most of all, he loved that her house was clearly a *home,* full of warmth and messes and laughter and love. His own spectacular compound seemed cold by comparison.

"This should ease the day's tension." He handed her the glass of wine.

She sipped gratefully, closing her eyes to savor either the flavor or the relaxing effects. "This is just what I needed. Thank you." She glanced up. "This is the same wine I had at Cannelli's."

"I remembered you liked it."

"You're too good to be true," she said softly, and something tightened in his gut. The same tightening that occurred when she'd called him *sweet* over the phone. Because if she knew the truth about the things he'd done...

Forcing the thought aside, just as he had so many times before with her, he plated a portion for her from each carton and finished off with a spring roll covered in sweet-and-sour sauce.

"Aren't you eating?" she asked when he sat on the couch empty handed.

"Jeremy wouldn't eat unless I did, too. And since I wasn't sure when you'd make it back—"

"I'm really sorry."

"Stop apologizing. In fact, as I recall, I promised that if you did it again—"

Will took her mouth in a second kiss that was a heck of a lot less sweet and soft than the first of the night had been. Jeremy might still be in the same room with them, but he was glued to the TV and wasn't paying any attention to them at all.

Forcing himself to draw back before he got completely carried away, Will said, "I enjoyed your brother's company. I always do."

"Am I allowed to say thank you for getting dinner and picking Jeremy up?" She gave him a cheeky smile. "Or do I say thank you too much, as well?"

"I love it when you're polite," he said as he curled a lock of her hair around his finger. Then he lowered his voice and added, "So polite one moment, and then so wild the next." He was close enough to appreciate the sound of her breath hitching in her throat at his suggestive words.

He drank from her glass of wine, then stole a cashew off her plate. It was another intimacy he enjoyed, just like playing with her hair. From the first day they'd met, he'd had a need to touch her in small ways as well as big. It didn't always have to be about sex—in fact, these little touches seemed to heighten their intimacy in a way simple sexual contact didn't. He'd never been like this with another woman, never so much as thought about becoming intimate with one of them beyond a few hours in the bedroom.

But Harper was different. She was important to him.

So important that he hoped the wine had mellowed her. She'd already had a harried day, and he didn't want to make things worse. But he didn't feel right trying to seduce her before he'd talked with her about what had happened at the grocery store.

"There was an issue at the store when I arrived."

She glanced at Jeremy, a deep line forming immediately between her brows. "What happened?" she asked in a low voice.

Will looked at Jeremy, too. Thankfully, the leopard cubs reigned over his attention. "He didn't do anything. It was busy. Like it always is at the end of the work day," Will added to bring home his point. "He wasn't bagging fast enough for the checker or the customer, and he didn't pack the groceries correctly. A cantaloupe on top of eggs."

She waited, an expectant *and* on her pursed lips.

"And," he said in a voice low enough that only she could hear, "the checker called him an idiot in front of the customers. Among other insults."

Her gaze shot to Jeremy again, her eyes darkened with worry. And a deep sorrow that Will wished he could erase permanently. "Is he okay?"

"He's fine. Your brother is resilient. Compassionate, too. He actually asked me not to have the woman fired, because she's got a sick mother."

Leaning forward, she slid her plate onto the coffee table, and somehow, when she sat back, she seemed farther away from him. "Why did he think you were going to have the woman fired?"

"I made her apologize. In front of everyone who had just witnessed her acting like such a jerk." He shook his head. "I know I'm always telling you not to apologize, but when people do something they *know* is wrong, they need to apologize for their actions."

He was one to talk, wasn't he, considering he could never say he was sorry for all the things he'd done in the past. Still, that didn't mean he would allow Jeremy to be denigrated.

"Do you know what it's like in that store at that time of day?" he asked.

She frowned again. "I know it's busy. I just never thought—"

Belatedly realizing his question might have sounded too harsh, he touched her hair again, drawing her back in. "What I'm trying to say is that I'm not so sure it's the best place for him. It's too chaotic."

Her jaw tensed as though she was clenching her teeth. "It gives him purpose. He's always said he likes it." Once again, her gaze shifted to Jeremy.

This was Will's chance to make a difference for them. "I've got a better idea. I talked to my people and I found him a place in my mailroom."

Her nostrils twitched. Like a mother rabbit sensing danger to her young. Yet again, she reminded him of Susan, who had taken better care of him than anyone in the world. Better care than he'd ever thought anyone would.

"You work in the city," Harper said. "He has school until noon, and the bus drops him off at the store. I can't get him all the way up to your office."

"I have a driver who can pick him up after school. And I can bring him home at the end of the day."

"I see you've thought everything through."

Yes, he'd considered the proposal from every angle. That's what he did: analyzed each scenario and conquered every possible problem that could arise. "I'll make it good for him,

Harper. And he told me he'd like to do it, that he won't miss his job at the grocery store."

In a heartbeat, she went as cold as a Chicago night in winter. "You already told him about this? Without discussing it with me first?"

He felt the stillness settle around them. The TV played on, and so did the leopard cubs, while a chilly silence dropped over Harper and him.

And that was when Will realized, far too late, that he'd just made a *huge* tactical mistake with the woman who had already become the most important person in his life.

CHAPTER TWENTY-ONE

"Jeremy, don't you have some homework for tomorrow?" Harper heard the snap in her voice, but she wasn't able to moderate it just yet.

Her brother looked at her over his shoulder. "Uh-huh."

"Then you'd better go do it." She heard a sound in her head like rocks grinding. It was her teeth. "And say thank you to Will for dinner."

"Thanks, Will."

As Jeremy turned off the TV and headed for his room, Harper continued to feel like the breath had been knocked out of her. Her brother had been verbally abused at work. And she shouldn't have had to hear it from Will. She should have known, should have been checking in with Jeremy to make sure everything was okay at the store every day. But every evening when she picked him up, he came bounding out full of stories about anything and everything.

She'd told herself that must mean things were okay.

How could she have been so careless?

She stood and grabbed her plate of food, which was growing more unappealing by the second.

"Harper," Will said, but she stalked out of the room without answering.

Will had figured out how to fix the situation. How to fix her failure. How to fix the fact that she was a rotten sister and a terrible guardian. She thought she'd been doing everything for her brother, but had she really, when all Will had to do was walk into the grocery store and spot all the problems in a second?

"Harper," Will said again, following her into the kitchen.

She almost slammed the plate down on the counter. The immaculate counter. He'd even cleaned up after her like she couldn't take care of her house. Like she couldn't take care of Jeremy. If she hadn't folded the laundry last night, he probably would have done that, too, showing what a mess she was. And look—he'd even cleaned up Jeremy's crayons.

Damn it, she thought as frustration ate her up from the inside, *I'm doing the best I can.*

But clearly it wasn't good enough.

"How could you tell Jeremy without even talking to me first?"

"I wanted to gauge his reaction. If he wasn't interested, the new position wasn't something I would have pursued."

"You should have gauged *my* reaction first."

"I see that now, and I'm sorry."

"Don't apologize," she snapped, because he kept saying the same to her. "Just stop imposing your will on us."

"I wasn't trying to impose my will."

Will. *His* will. His name said it all. Didn't he get what would happen down the road? "Look, when this car project is over—" *And you've moved on to another pet project.* "—Jeremy will be out of a job. He won't have anything."

"The car won't be finished for months. Besides, the Maserati has nothing to do with his working in my mailroom."

"So you'll just keep on sending your driver to pick him up?"

He shrugged, shook his head slightly, like she wasn't even making sense. "If that's what it takes, that's what we'll do."

Did she really have to spell it out for him? "What about when you get tired of doing all this for him?" *And what about when you get tired of me?* "Buying a Maserati because Jeremy wants it. Dreaming up a job for him. In a few weeks or even months, if you get bored with the whole thing, where will that leave Jeremy? Out in the cold. He's not going to understand. I've seen this happen before. I've dated men who befriend him. Then they're gone. And I don't want to see Jeremy get hurt like that again."

"I've already told you this, and I'll keep saying it until you believe me—I'm not going to hurt your brother. I promise."

"Right." She was on a roll and couldn't seem to stop. "And I'm just supposed to take your word on that."

Something changed in him then. After she'd freaked out, he'd been on the defensive, trying to explain himself, trying to get her to understand that he'd meant no harm. But now, it looked like she'd managed to wound him.

"My word means everything. I do not break it." He held her gaze. "I'm not like the men you've dated, Harper. And don't forget, I met Jeremy first, not you. He wrote to me. I liked what I read. So what's between you and me has nothing to do with him." Will held up his hands. "You're right that I should have talked to you first. But I wouldn't have given him the job if I didn't think it would be something new and different for him to try. He can stretch himself. He might even be fine for a few hours by himself. You've got to see that he's capable of pushing himself to do more. Is there something you're afraid of, Harper? Something I haven't figured out yet? You know your brother a hell of a lot better than I do. What am I not seeing?"

He sounded so reasonable and his explanations so good. Which made her feel churlish on top of everything else. He had a way of making her feel totally out of control, whether it was over Jeremy, or on the hood of his car, or while practically naked on her living room sofa.

Honestly, at this point, she wasn't sure there was much Will wasn't seeing. Not when it sometimes felt as though his dark eyes could see all the way through every wall she'd built up.

Finally, she told him, "I'm just afraid of seeing Jeremy hurt."

And yet she hadn't been there to rescue her brother today. Will had done that. And then he'd come up with a solution. One that she knew she had to consider, especially if there was a chance that what he offered might truly be the best thing for Jeremy.

Harper had always been afraid change wasn't good for her brother. But what if she was wrong about what Jeremy needed? And what if the problem was more that she wasn't fond of change herself? Especially after all that had happened in the wake of his accident and then their parents' deaths.

She worked to swallow the emotions threatening to rise up in her throat and strangle her. And as her head of steam finally began to peter out, she realized the injustice of what she'd been saying. Will had only ever been good to Jeremy. He was endlessly patient as he showed her brother how to do each new task on the car. He was never short with him on Skype. He was always considerate of his feelings. And he was the one who'd discovered the problem at the store.

That was why she'd gone off on him. Not just because he'd screwed up by not checking with her first about the new job, but because she was so damned guilty over her own failures. It was humbling to realize she needed to put her own ego aside—the decision had to be about what was best for Jeremy, nothing else.

"I might have been a bit hasty just now," she admitted. "You're right that a new job might be good for him. And that it might expand his horizons." But she'd still ask if Jeremy wanted the job as badly as Will needed to give it to him.

"It might be good for you, too, Harper." He came close again, his body heat enveloping her. Cupping her face in his hands, he held her steady, captured her with that dark, commanding gaze. Mesmerized her. "Your brother has you to protect him. But who looks out for you?"

"I do." But she honestly didn't know if she was any better at that than she was at taking care of Jeremy.

"Let me help." His voice was just short of a whisper.

She felt herself weakening, bending, needing, *longing*. But if she allowed Will to take over even a little, what if she lost herself completely?

And then, when he was gone, what if she couldn't manage to find her way back?

"You're doing enough already for Jeremy," she said softly. She had to draw on the iron will she'd developed over the past few years to force herself to step out of his arms. "Thank you for picking him up and feeding both of us. Thanks for cleaning up my house, too. You went above and beyond tonight, Will, and I appreciate it. But it's been a long day, so..."

He stared at her for a long moment, one where she got the sense he was trying to decide between kissing her—or letting her kick him out again. She knew it was bad that she was secretly hoping for the former...and that she was so disappointed when he chose the latter.

"Say good-night to Jeremy for me."

"I will."

"You won't be coming to work on the car this weekend, will you?"

How could she when she desperately needed to take a long, hard look at what she was doing? Because it was one thing to tell herself she was having a fun, sexy affair—and that she deserved to have something so delicious for once in her life. But it was another thing entirely to watch how easily Will could take over if she wasn't careful. Especially when the only thing that had held Harper and Jeremy together for the past several years had been her tight grip on their lives.

"I think it would be best if we skipped this weekend."

Will's eyes were as dark and intense as she'd ever seen them. Full of disappointment, and something that looked like regret, too. "I know I screwed up," he said softly, "and I'll do whatever it takes to make it up to you."

Before her conflicted brain could even try to think of a reply, he was gone.

CHAPTER TWENTY-TWO

Will didn't blame Harper for pulling back to reassess things—he had completely screwed up by forgetting that she was the boss when it came to her brother. Will might be able to make suggestions, but he'd never again make the mistake of taking decisions out of Harper's hands. She was too strong, too smart, for that kind of behavior. He knew he had a lot to prove, and a lot of ground to make up, but he wasn't giving up.

They quickly established a routine over the next few days. His driver Benny picked up Jeremy from school, and Will drove him home. Fortunately, Harper's brother loved his new job and he also loved the people he worked with. Will checked several times each day to make sure his employees were treating Jeremy right. He'd promised Harper he wouldn't let anything hurt her brother, and he would die before he broke that vow.

The first night, Harper thanked him for bringing Jeremy home—and then shut and locked the door.

The second night, he brought takeout and made sure the bags he was holding at her front door smelled so good that it would be really hard for her stomach, at least, to turn him away. She'd been quiet as they ate together in her kitchen that night, mostly letting him and Jeremy do the talking, but even if it was just a baby step, at least it was one in the right direction.

The third night, while they were eating another takeout meal, he wanted to tell her that she and Jeremy filled up all his empty places. He wanted her to know that he'd drop anything at a moment's notice when one of them called. He wished he could tell her that taking care of them had grown into a need inside him, on a deeper level even than the bond he had with his fellow Mavericks. His friends—his brothers—weren't kids anymore, and they hadn't needed anyone to fight their battles in years. But Jeremy and Harper *needed* him.

Although sometimes he felt like he needed them even more.

By Thursday night, he couldn't stand it any longer and asked her if he could take her out again. She told him she needed to think about it, and he wasn't sure he managed a full breath all the way through until Friday night, when he brought Jeremy home from work again...

...and she finally said *yes.*

Will couldn't remember a time he'd ever been happier, or more relieved, in his life.

Now, with Mrs. Taylor watching Jeremy at home, Will had Harper sitting beside him in his '57 Chevy. Though she was still too quiet, he was content just to be with her. To let her delicious scent wash over him, cleanse him, make him new.

Of course, when he saw an overlook along Skyline Boulevard with a great view, he couldn't resist pushing for more. Because he couldn't resist *her.* She was gorgeous in the moonlight. Stars sparkled in her eyes, and the full moon made her skin glow. There was no wind deflector in the mammoth Chevy and her hair was a mass of sexy tangles.

"Let's park," he said after he'd stopped the car, tugging her gently over to his side of the bench seat.

Thankfully she didn't tense up, but he remained on tenterhooks waiting for it to happen. Waiting for her to pull back. Because they hadn't talked about what had happened last Thursday. He'd wanted to give her time to process, and to forgive. But should he have pushed a little harder to make sure there weren't any lingering mistakes that he still needed to make right?

He'd never been afraid of pushing anyone before. But with Harper, everything was different.

Because he was terrified of losing her.

"Harper." He wanted so badly to reach for her. "Are we good again? Like before? Or are you still upset with me for overstepping my bounds with your brother?"

She looked a little surprised by his question, as if she hadn't expected him to come right out and ask. But also, relieved.

Had she been wanting to clear the air, too?

"To be honest," she said slowly, "those first couple of days, I didn't know exactly how I was feeling. Still a little mad. Still a little guilty. But more and more, as Jeremy came home happier every day, I was able to see just how right you were. He needed this change, needed to get out of that grocery store. I wish I'd been able to see it—"

"You're the best sister in the world. You do so much for him. You can't beat yourself up about this."

"But I did." She took a deep breath. "And now...now I think I'm finally ready to let it go." She looked him in the eyes and held his gaze. "And I'm finally ready to *let go* again, too."

She reached for his hand, and the act felt *huge.* Bigger even than a kiss might have.

"Being with you, being wild and free for a little while—it made me happy, Will. Whereas when I was holding you at bay this week?" She frowned. "I wasn't as happy anymore. Wasn't as free." She threaded her fingers through his. "I'm ready to be free again. Ready to fly fast with you, if you still want me."

"If I still want you?" He didn't even try to keep the incredulous tone from his voice. "All I do all day long, all night long, is want you, Harper."

The smile she gave him was so beautiful, it nearly knocked his heart from his chest. "I want you, too, Will. Just that badly. Only..."

"Anything you want, anything you need, just tell me what it is and I'll make it happen." This was the first real, meaningful relationship he'd ever had with a woman. Whatever Harper needed, he'd give it to her, come hell or high water.

She bit her lip, then let the damp flesh go to say, "You can't make what I want happen tonight, Will. Only I can. Every time we're together, I completely lose control. But you're always so steady. I need to know..." She paused for a moment as if she was deciding whether to finish her sentence or not, and he held his breath until she said, "Tonight I need to know if I can make you as crazy as you make me."

"Crazier, Harper. A thousand times over."

"Let me see it." She leaned forward and whispered against his lips, "I need to see it."

"I'm yours." He now knew that he had been from the first moment he'd set eyes on her. "All yours."

She looked up at him in surprise, as though she hadn't actually expected him to agree to give up his control tonight. And she was right that there was almost no one he would consider doing that with. But she was different. She was special. And he trusted her in a way he didn't trust anyone else.

"Come closer," she said softly.

He immediately moved across the seat. When Harper straddled him, her dress billowing down around them, he couldn't remember ever being happier. She'd forgiven him *and* she wanted to make love with him until he lost his mind.

Was there a luckier guy on the planet?

Summer was just around the corner and a warm breeze rippled through her hair. Stars lit up the sky around her as he thought, *I want you, Harper. I want you like I've never wanted anyone else. I want you more than I can remember ever wanting anyone or anything before in my life.*

He opened his mouth to say the words, but she stole them away. Cupping his face, she kissed him as if she were making love to his mouth, licking him, taking his tongue. Her whole body got into the kiss, swaying and moving on his, her breasts caressing him, her legs tightening along his thighs.

He'd always been the one in control, not just with her, but with all women. He'd always set the pace and the tone, decided where the night began and ended. Even when Harper had kissed him in the garage, he'd taken over, pushing her down on the hood, using his mouth on her because he'd been desperate to taste her. To have her.

Yet now that she was the one controlling his reins, she wasn't rushed. Not at all. Even though he could hardly remember his own name.

"You taste so good," she murmured against his lips. "I wonder how you taste all over." She leaned back to work the buttons of his shirt. When his chest was naked to her touch, and she ran her fingers down his skin, he actually felt a quiver deep in his gut. A part of him worried that she'd want to strip his shirt away completely, and that she'd finally see his tattoo, but even that worry could hardly take hold when she was touching him like this, kissing him like this.

"You have such a magnificent chest." Curling her body, she bent to his nipple. She licked him, sucked him, then bit down lightly. "You like this as much as I do, don't you?" She hummed with pleasure against his chest, the vibrations sending shockwaves through him.

"God, yes, I like it." His voice was hoarse, his hands flexing on her hips, pulling her tighter against him. "You make me crazy."

"Good. Because you make me crazy, too."

When he lost control and went to kiss her, she laughed as she pushed against him. "No, no, no. Tonight, it's my turn to have *you*."

He understood that she was turning the tables, taking charge the way he had that morning in her house. The way he always did.

Who would have guessed that the turnaround would set him on fire like this?

"I'm yours," he said again, something he'd never told another person, but which felt impossibly right with her. "For whatever you want."

She slid farther back so that she could trail kisses down his abdomen. He remembered doing the same to her, her skin smooth and sweet against his lips. He was hard, aching, and only just barely resisting the urge to toss her into the backseat.

The night air was still warm, but his skin was hotter. The sound of an occasional car on the road was far off and muted. They were in a world of their own, and his heart was pounding in his ears as she ran her hand over the rock-hard length of him.

"Holy hell." The words shot out on his exhalation.

"Remember when you said you *intended* to taste me...and that I was going to taste you, too?" She pushed her hand inside the denim of his jeans and wrapped her fingers around him.

"I remember." The words came out a little choked.

"Do you still think we should make good on all those intentions?"

His Adam's apple slid along his throat. He felt like a teenager who had finally managed to make out with the untouchable girl he'd been lusting after. Breathless. Desperate. "Yes."

God, yes.

She touched her lips to his, licked him until he opened for her. But instead of kissing him, she whispered, "Good, because I've decided I want to taste you. All of you."

"Please," he said. He couldn't even come up with a quip or a word of sexy banter.

Each time with Harper was new.

And every time it meant *more*.

* * *

Harper had felt out of control with Will so many times. *Every* time. Tonight, she'd thought the final piece of putting everything back together inside of her would be to turn the tables on him. Yet even as she led their lovemaking tonight, she still felt his power coursing through her body, everywhere she touched him, everywhere he touched her.

By the time she sank down to taste him, she realized that it didn't matter anymore who was in control. All that mattered was the joy—and the pleasure—she felt whenever she was with him.

She used her hands, lips, mouth, tongue on him. He was a savory treat. Better than chocolate. Better than ice cream. She loved the feel of him, the heady scent of his skin, the quake and shiver of his rock hard flesh as she took him deep.

"Harper." He growled her name, and then, a heartbeat later, she was on her back against the

leather seat as he came over her. *"Need. You. Now."* Each word was separate, gasped, harsh. She heard the tear of a condom, felt him between her legs.

When he flipped up her dress and tugged her panties aside, she was just as desperate as he was, miles beyond ready as he pulled her leg high up on his hip and drove into her.

Oh God...being taken hard and fast by Will in the front seat of his car was better than anything she'd ever felt in her life.

"Kiss me, Harper. *Please.*"

He was a dark shadow above her, backlit by stars and moon. She pulled him down, locked her lips to his. His body tensed and flexed inside her as she opened her mouth. She kissed him back as hard as he kissed her, tasting his heat, savoring his need.

With one foot on the floorboard to brace himself, he thrust deeper, and she put a hand on the car door behind her head, pushing to meet each plunge. Hard, delicious, explosive. She dug her fingers into his shoulder as she burst wide open, exploding into a million perfect pieces as he exploded, too, with her name on his lips.

Just as his was on hers.

* * *

Harper snuggled against him as he drove back toward home, one arm thrown around her shoulder, holding her tight.

There was no point in trying to deny anymore that she was in too deep. But honestly, she was having a hard time caring about that, no longer counting down the days until he got tired of her and Jeremy.

Maybe it was stupid. Maybe she would regret it later. But right now she was simply too relaxed—and too full of soul-deep pleasure—to keep shoring up her barriers.

The wind blew through her hair, but with Will's arm around her, she couldn't tell that the night had turned cool. She could only feel his warmth protecting her.

Other men had been after Jeremy's trust fund, or begrudged her the time and energy she gave to her brother, as though it took something from them. But Will didn't need Jeremy's money. And he gave so much of himself to her brother, the car, the new job, driving Jeremy home. Even Jeremy's teacher, Miss Richards, had noticed a marked improvement.

All because of Will.

He slowed for a downhill curve. "I'm having a barbecue on Memorial Day with a few of my friends. I'd like you and Jeremy to come."

"Me? And Jeremy?" She blinked at him. "You want us to come to a barbecue with your friends?"

"Evan met you both, but no one else has yet."

Sex was one thing...but meeting his friends? That felt like something different. Something *more.*

But was it? Or was it just her heart running hopeful because Will Franconi was the most irresistible man she'd ever met?

The night air was suddenly a cool draft down her neck as those worries she thought she'd just buried poked up their heads again. Not only about what Will's wanting her to meet his friends meant about their relationship, but also about whether his friends—aka the Silicon Valley elite—would look down their noses at her and Jeremy.

Will had surprised her, though, hadn't he? All those weeks ago, she'd assumed he would be just a rich man in a fast car, only a slight step up from the father of the teenage boy who'd run Jeremy down. But that wasn't Will at all.

Was it possible that his friends would surprise her, too?

Maybe it was the beautiful night. Maybe it was the beautiful sex. Maybe it was how exhausting it was to keep holding up those heavy walls all the time.

Or maybe it was the way Will looked at her with such hope, as if her attending his party was the most important thing in the world.

Whatever the reason, she suddenly smiled and said, "A Memorial Day barbecue sounds great. I can't wait to meet the rest of your friends."

CHAPTER TWENTY-THREE

Will couldn't stop staring at Harper as she chatted out by the pool with Evan's wife, Whitney, and Whitney's sister Paige. Harper was gorgeous in her bathing suit and matching wrap skirt, but trumping even his need for her was his pleasure at having her there with him and his closest friends.

He wished Evan could feel the same way about his own wife, although that was near impossible when Whitney had been engrossed in her cell phone the entire time she'd been at the barbecue. She had looks that turned most men stupid and as far as Will could tell, she'd been exploiting that her entire life. Her sister, Paige, on the other hand, was the sweet girl next door, the opposite of Whitney in every way, except for the auburn hair. It was hard to believe the two women had been raised by the same parents.

His pulse rate jumped when Harper came to join his conversation with the guys. Well, mostly with Jeremy, who held center stage. Will had to hand it to Harper's brother—he definitely wasn't shy.

"I deliver all the mail." Jeremy mimed pushing the cart. "I stack everyone's mail in order of where they sit on my route. I pass out supplies on my way, too, like pens and Post-its and binder clips and stuff. And I haven't gotten any of the deliveries wrong, have I, Will?"

"You've nailed them all."

"And when there's a big meeting," Jeremy added with a grin, "I make the coffee and go down to the bagel shop. I get a bunch of different bagels and the stuff for the bagels. Like cream cheese."

Harper had been a little worried when she'd first heard about that duty, afraid Jeremy would be in charge of money and have to account for discrepancies. But she'd ended up agreeing that more responsibility was good for her brother, and so far, Jeremy hadn't had any trouble with it.

"Those are really important tasks," Matt said with a seriousness that made Jeremy beam.

Will had known that his friends would see the same things in Jeremy that he did—including his enthusiasm and perpetually upbeat attitude.

"With all those bagels, no wonder Will here is getting fat." Sebastian pushed up his sunglasses and looked at Will's waistline.

"Up yours." Will *thwapped* his towel at him.

Sebastian fended it off and gave him the finger behind his hand so Jeremy wouldn't notice.

"Will's not fat," Jeremy said. "Every day when I get to work, he's just coming out of the gym. We've got machines in the office that anyone can use. It's so cool. I lifted weights there yesterday after lunch."

Will liked Jeremy's use of the word *we*. It meant Jeremy felt like he'd become a part of the place. Which was exactly what Will had hoped for.

Daniel, who had clearly been playing with the power tools his company was famous for, given the new bandage on his hand, cut in. "That's one badass car you're building, too."

"It's the coolest car ever made." Jeremy's mouth was round with pleasure.

All the Mavericks made approving male noises.

Will and Jeremy had conducted a tour earlier. He'd let Jeremy lead the guys through, pointing out critical components. Will had helped a bit and his friends had done the rest by asking the right questions, which fed Jeremy the answers when he couldn't find the words he wanted.

"So this is the intake manifold?" Daniel would ask, and Jeremy would nod heartily.

Harper had stayed by the pool during the tour, watching out for Noah, Matt's kid, who had the same dark hair, blue eyes, and the potential for a frame as tall and broad as his father's. The boy's mother was out of the picture, and at five, the little guy had already gone through six nannies. Will would have razzed Matt about the reasons for his quick nanny turnover rate had he not seen how hard it made things on his friend.

Noah was now playing in the paddling pool Will had installed especially for him. A big plastic ball sailed across the pool deck, and Will stopped it with his foot. "Hey, Noah, I think you might have the makings of a quarterback."

He kicked the ball up and caught it. A few steps from Noah's pool, he gave it a gentle toss and watched the ball plop in the water when Noah missed it. Wading into the pool, Will scooped up the ball again. "Hold up your hands like this." Noah threw out his arms in imitation. "Now get ready. I'm gonna throw it. Wait for it, wait for it—" He leaned forward, getting close, and executed a soft underhand shot right into Noah's hands.

The guys clapped and hooted, especially Matt, who loved his kid to pieces. Harper and Paige clapped, too. Whitney, however, never even glanced up from her phone.

"That was great," Will said. "Now throw it back to me."

The ball flew wild again, though Will wasn't sure exactly how that was possible since he was only two steps away. When the ball rolled over to Harper's feet, she picked it up and tossed it back to them.

Will caught it, but even as he passed it back to Noah, he was drinking Harper in again. She was special. She was perfect. And she was too good for him.

But Will was hoping that he could forget about that last part if he tried hard enough.

* * *

Will was so good with Noah. Just the way he was with Jeremy. Always praising, complimenting, building up rather than tearing down.

He would make an awesome father someday.

Not that she had any business thinking about him that way, of course. But Harper still felt a lump of emotion well up in her throat. Emotion that grew with every kind thing the Mavericks said to Jeremy at the barbecue and the realization that Will's closest friends had gone out of their way to make her and Jeremy feel like part of their family.

They were an amazing group. Will, of course, was totally sexy in a pair of black swim trunks. His black T-shirt emphasized his muscles, the width of his shoulders, and his broad chest. She had to repeatedly remind herself not to drool. Honestly, she was glad he was the only one wearing a shirt by the pool, because if he'd taken his off like the rest of the men, she wasn't sure she'd have been able to control herself around him. *That's* what he did to her—made her lose control again and again and again.

Noah's dad, Matt Tremont, was a leading manufacturer of robotics equipment. He was huge with rippling muscles. And he gazed at his son with such adoration. She couldn't help but wonder where Noah's mother was.

Sebastian Montgomery was the TV media mogul. She'd expected some smooth-talking salesman, but Sebastian slouched in his chair, legs spread as he watched Noah and Will. "If you're going to teach Noah, you gotta learn how to throw right," he called out to Will. He was the tallest of them all, probably six-three, and his sable hair, chocolate-brown eyes, and chiseled features were even more mesmerizing up close than they were on camera. Still, she didn't think he held a candle to Will.

"If you think you can do better, get over here." Will held up the ball while Noah squealed for another free throw.

"There isn't room enough for both of us in that pool," Sebastian shot back.

"You're just worried you won't do any better," Daniel said. He grinned at Harper and told her, "Sebastian always sucked at sports."

Daniel Spencer owned a nationwide chain of home improvement stores and produced a TV show on do-it-yourself remodeling. With dark, wavy hair and some really impressive muscles, Daniel was a mountain-man type. Someone had mentioned during the course of the afternoon that he was building his own cabin near Tahoe.

"I didn't suck," Sebastian said mildly. "I just figured I might as well let you win at *something*."

Daniel laughed, taking the ribbing good naturedly. "Still can't get over that game back in high school where we all piled on you just outside the touchdown zone, can you?"

They called themselves the Mavericks, and they constantly gave each other a hard time. Yet Harper could see the incredibly strong bond between them, along with the way no offense was ever taken. Their connection went right through to the way they all looked after Noah. He wasn't just Matt's son, he was precious to all of them, and she had the sense they would each protect him with their lives.

Evan Collins, however, wasn't quite like the rest. Not that he didn't belong—he was just as handsome and big and strong as the other Mavericks—but he was quieter and didn't always join in the banter. Harper wondered if his wife could be the reason. She'd tried to like Whitney, but it wasn't an easy task. Evan's wife seemed to wear her sunglasses so she wouldn't have to waste time actually looking anyone in the eye, and her mouth didn't seem to be made for smiling. Not even for Noah's super cute antics.

Of course, just as Harper was thinking uncharitable thoughts about her, Whitney made her presence known. Or maybe it was because she hadn't been getting the attention she felt she deserved.

Holding up her glass, she waggled it in the air and called out, "Evan, darling, I need another margarita." She continued texting with one hand.

"I'll get it," Jeremy said.

Just as he did at work, if there was something someone needed, her brother jumped to do it. Whitney was the only one who hadn't said a word to him, so maybe he felt he needed to prove himself to her.

Whitney pulled her sunglasses down to look at Harper over the rims. It was quite possibly the first time the woman had made eye contact with her. "Can he do it?"

Harper tightened her lips for just a second. *Be polite.* "Yes, he's perfectly capable of pouring you a margarita out of a pitcher."

"All right then." Whitney pushed her sunglasses to the bridge of her nose and handed the glass to Jeremy. "Not too much ice," she said with a false note of sweetness in her tone.

But Harper doubted there was an ounce of sweetness in her. Yet there *had* to be a story as to why Evan Collins was even with this woman.

"I put the pitcher of margaritas in the fridge," Evan told Jeremy. It wasn't the first time Whitney had demanded a refresher.

"Thanks, Evan," Jeremy said in his overloud outdoor voice.

Harper felt Will's eyes on her and glanced up to see him smiling at her. The rest of the guys had gone quiet. Even Noah had dropped down on his butt in the water. Almost as if Whitney's voice were a sponge that sucked all the fun out of the air.

Thankfully, conversation resumed as Jeremy skipped to the bar. Sebastian pushed up from his seat and kicked off his deck shoes. He hunkered down at the edge of the kiddie pool and asked Noah, "How about a swim?"

"Yay!" Noah crowed.

Each of the Mavericks had been taking turns throughout the day teaching Noah to swim. He could tread water for at least a minute, and he didn't panic if his head went under. Harper remembered teaching Jeremy to swim when he was a little boy, and she smiled as Will lifted Noah out of the small pool and secured his water wings.

No question about it, he would make an awesome dad. And if she'd been able to pay attention to anything but Will, his laughter, his smile, then maybe she might have noticed

Jeremy returning at a run with Whitney's cocktail in his hand. She looked over at him just as his foot caught on a flagstone, and the tall glass lurched, splashing the contents all over Whitney.

"Look what you did!" Whitney's glare skewered Jeremy. "This swimsuit is one of a kind couture!"

"I'm sorry," Jeremy whispered, clutching the plastic margarita glass to his chest, getting his shirt all wet. He backed away, out of the line of fire.

Whitney turned on Harper. "Sorry isn't good enough."

"It was an accident," Harper said. She wouldn't humiliate Jeremy by apologizing for a simple accident. Though later, when they were alone, she'd remind him about running with anything in his hand. "I'll be happy to pay for it if it's ruined." Even if it was likely worth more than she made in a month.

"You said he could handle it," Whitney snapped.

"Whitney, enough!" Evan stepped in between them. "It was an accident. Jeremy didn't mean any harm. So back off. Now."

Whitney turned her glare on her husband. Her nostrils flared, and her lips turned ugly with tension. "If my own husband could have bothered to get me a drink, then none of this would have happened."

Evan stepped forward, his feet right along the edge of a flagstone as if it were a battle line drawn between them. Paige jumped in before either combatant crossed it.

"It'll wash out, Whit," she said, in a mediator's tone. A psychologist, Paige was pleasant and chatty in a let's-fill-any-awkward-silences kind of way. "I've got that book that tells how to get out just about any stain. Although I don't think margarita mix even stains."

"Fine," Whitney snapped. "You can wash it for me."

"Whitney." Paige said her sister's name softly, but firmly. "I think it's time for us to thank Will for a great barbecue and head home."

Harper itched to take her down a peg—a hundred pegs would be even better—and she was glad to see Paige stand up to her sister.

Anger lines stretched past the frames of Whitney's sunglasses. She tossed her cell phone into the bag beside her chair. "Good idea. I can't wait to clean up and forget about this whole day." Whitney threw on the see-through flowered cover-up that matched her swimsuit and slipped her feet into high-heeled sandals.

Harper glanced over her shoulder, realizing that Will had climbed out of the pool and was now standing close enough to Jeremy to put his hand on his shoulder. Sebastian stood beside Will, holding Noah in his arms. Daniel and Matt flanked Evan. Battle positions.

Evan didn't look at all happy about leaving, with a muscle in his jaw jumping as he stared at his wife. But he was clearly too much of a gentleman to send her home without him. Besides, continuing the fight in front of everyone would put a damper on the whole group, and Evan would care about that, too, Harper was sure.

"All right," Evan said, his voice clipped and tight. "I'll take you home, Whitney. Paige, are you sure you don't want to stay?"

"I can drive you home later," Daniel offered.

But she simply shook her head. For some crazy reason, Harper had the sense that Paige didn't want to leave Evan alone with his own wife. "Thanks for having me, Will. It was great to meet you, Harper and Jeremy."

On his way out, Evan stopped beside Harper and said, "I'm sorry about what happened."

But, honestly, at this point she was the one feeling sorry for him, going home with that woman. How on earth he could ever have wanted to marry her was honestly beyond Harper.

Then again, she knew people's stories weren't exactly linear, were they? Look at hers and Jeremy's, for example. Who could have predicted this would be their life?

Again, she found herself wishing she knew more of Will's story. But though he was always sweet and kind—and so sexy that she could hardly catch her breath around him—he wasn't exactly an open book. She figured he must have his reasons, foremost among them the fact that they were just two people enjoying each other's company for a little while.

"None of that was your fault, Jeremy," Will said to her brother, breaking her out of her musings. "That's just Whitney. Ignore her. We've all learned to do that over the years."

"Whitney's temper tantrums always make me hungry," Daniel said with a hard and fast shake of his head, as if he were literally trying to shake Evan's wife out of his system. "Why don't you start the grill, Will? How do you like your meat done, Jeremy?"

"Rare," Jeremy called out.

Matt grinned at Jeremy. "Jump in the pool and wash that margarita off your shirt. Last one in's a rotten egg," he shouted and landed with a cannonball in the pool, with Daniel right behind him.

Noah squirmed in Sebastian's arms. "Me too! Me too!"

She could have kissed every last one of them. And Evan, too, not just for his simple apology, but also for the way he'd stepped in to end Whitney's harangue before it got even worse.

As Matt joined the others in the pool for a game of Marco Polo, Will held out his hand to her and together they headed over to take care of getting food on for everyone. The barbecue was an entire counter with two grills, one with a curved top, the other a simple metal grill. A pot of water for corn on the cob bubbled on the range. The fridge held steaks, hot dogs, hamburgers, potato salad, green salad, and all the fixings, which was way more food than they could possibly eat, even if Evan, his wife, and Paige had stayed.

"What do you want? Steak, hamburger, or—" He grinned and waggled his eyebrows up and down in an exaggerated fashion. "—hot dog?"

She laughed, glad the sensation washed away a lot of her anger and frustration over what had just happened. As if he could read her mind, he turned serious again.

"I apologize for that, Harper. I should have warned you about Whitney and made sure not to put Jeremy in that position."

"He isn't your responsibility. I should have been watching. And I was the one who said it was okay."

He shushed her with a kiss. "Stop. Evan's wife's attitude isn't your fault."

Finally stopping to take a breath, she realized he was right. Just as he was right about so many things when it came to her brother. She hadn't had anyone to bounce things off in so long. Even though she knew this thing with Will wasn't going to last forever, did that mean she couldn't appreciate him while he was here?

"Is she always like that?"

Will began turning knobs on the grill. "In the beginning of their marriage? Maybe not. At this point, it's pretty hard to remember how things used to be. All I know is that in the past year or so, she's been worse than ever. Honestly, I don't know how he can live with her. Whatever happens between them, though, we've got his back."

She'd seen that—the way the men had surrounded Evan, making it clear that they were there if he needed them.

"We've all known each other a long time," he told her. "Matt and Evan were ten. Daniel, Sebastian, and I a year older. Some bullies were picking on Matt." He shrugged. "Something had to be done."

Harper glanced at the huge muscles in Matt's arms as he chased down Sebastian in the big pool. "*Matt* needed help?"

Will grinned. "He was a scrawny kid."

She had a hard time picturing it. "So you rescued him."

An expression she couldn't quite read flashed across his face, but he wasn't smiling anymore as he said, "Evan ran for the principal."

"Smart boy."

"That's why he's the money man." But his face darkened even further. "We all eventually ended up living with Daniel's parents. Susan and Bob raised us."

"*All* of you?" Wonder laced her voice.

"It wasn't a great neighborhood. Things happened."

His answer was so understated, his features so expressionless, that she felt a little hitch in her chest. She wanted to ask what *things*, but at the same time, she didn't want to make a mistake by pushing too hard. Not when Will had just revealed more to her about his past than he had at any time in all the weeks she'd known him.

"So we stuck together." He blew out a hard breath, and then the cocky grin was back. She'd never been happier to see it. "The Mavericks."

They weren't brothers, not by blood the way she and Jeremy were. Yet she knew they would do anything for each other.

Meeting them shed new light on Will. He'd once said his word was his bond, that he always kept his promises. Seeing him with his closest friends showed her that it was no boast or throwaway phrase. He'd clearly been through hard times with these men, and he was there for them no matter what. Just the way he'd been there for Jeremy time and time again.

And though she kept trying to tell herself that this thing between them was just a casual thrill ride, she couldn't help but hope that he'd be there for her, too.

CHAPTER TWENTY-FOUR

"So," Susan mused on the phone, "I hear things are progressing nicely with you and your new lady." She'd waited a couple of days after the Memorial Day barbecue to call him, but Will had guessed it was coming after every one of the other Mavericks had already weighed in on the subject of Harper.

Evan had called Will first to apologize again for his wife's snapping at Harper and Jeremy. He'd made an excuse about a migraine that Will wasn't buying, but he'd forced himself to let it go. Evan ended the call by telling Will not to screw things up with Harper. Matt was next on the horn to say that Noah kept talking about the pretty lady who had played with him in the pool. The boy had been terribly sad to learn she couldn't be their new nanny because she already had an important job. Then Sebastian claimed he still couldn't get over Will finally dating a woman with looks *and* brains. And finally Daniel had called to say, "You look happy, Will. I like her." Which said it all.

In his high-rise office, Will swiveled his chair to face the San Francisco Bay glittering in the sun. "Who called you this time?"

Susan laughed. That's what he loved best about her: her laughter. She'd never yelled at any of them. Even when he'd been a complete shit, Susan would give him a long look and ask, *"Do you really think that was the right thing to do?"* As if she'd known that he hadn't been thinking, he'd just been doing, reacting, acting out in the wrong way. Somehow Susan always managed to forgive him anyway.

"They *all* told me," she said.

"They're a bunch of freaking busybodies," he grumbled, though it amused him that men in their mid-thirties would rush to their mom with gossipy tidbits.

"How else am I going to be updated? You don't tell me anything unless I drag it out of you."

This was true. He'd talked to Susan several times since Harper and Jeremy had first come to his garage and work had begun on the Maserati, and yet he'd managed to avoid answering nearly all of her questions after that first call.

"You've never introduced your brothers to a woman before," Susan observed. "They say she's lovely."

"She is," he said softly.

"And they all really like her brother, too."

"Jeremy's a great kid."

"We'd love to meet them both. I hope someday you'll bring them to the house."

The Mavericks had planned to buy the Spencers property out in one of the exclusive Chicago suburbs, but Susan and Bob had wanted an average home in an average neighborhood, nothing ostentatious. All they required was something large enough to house all their grandchildren and pseudo-grandchildren. Unfortunately, to date, the Mavericks had done a piss-poor job of filling up those extra rooms, and Daniel's younger sister Lyssa wasn't even close to starting a family.

But Will could easily imagine Harper and Jeremy and a white Christmas in Chicago. Susan would adore them both. She'd fill up the fridge and freezer with baked goods because Jeremy was "a growing boy." And they would both love Susan, too.

"They're good for you, honey, I can tell."

But was he good enough for them?

That's what plagued him. Even in something as simple as that scene by the pool with Whitney. He should have been standing guard over Harper's brother to make sure no harm came to him, just as he'd promised her. But he'd failed. Badly enough that he couldn't stop going over the situation in his head—and also couldn't keep from asking Susan, "Did you hear about Whitney's explosion at the barbecue?"

Susan sighed. She'd obviously been apprised of every nasty detail. "That poor girl. Whitney lost her way after that first miscarriage."

"I'm sorry about that. We all are." Whitney had had three miscarriages in the last two years. It had broken Evan into pieces, especially since he'd been on the road for work each time his wife had miscarried.

"They've been trying so hard for a family," Susan said, "and Whitney's disappointment is coming out in her testiness."

Testiness? Will had a whole other word to describe it. "I know they've been through a lot. But still...Evan's a saint."

"He's a good man. One who bends over backward to handle Whitney's moods because he appreciates how badly she feels about not being able to give him a child."

The Mavericks backed each other up to the ends of the earth, always there when anything bad went down, but they all turned to Susan when they needed to keep their emotional crap from festering inside. She was their sounding board on matters of the heart.

"Trust me, honey," she added, "unfulfilled need can change a woman's entire personality."

He could see that, but the truth was that Whitney had always been more difficult than most. And he knew without a doubt that Harper, in the same situation, wouldn't bust a guy's manhood the way Whitney did.

The thought of Harper with a child, *his* child, growing inside her sent a wave of emotion flowing through him—delight, need, fear, desire. And something that felt giddily like happiness.

"I think that's also why she doesn't pay more attention to Noah," Susan said thoughtfully, as if she'd just considered the point. "It breaks her heart. Hopefully when a baby finally comes, she'll settle down again. Right now, Evan's giving her the supportive environment she needs to try again, and I'll be there for your brother. I know you will, too, all of you. But I also want you to realize that while I understand Whitney's feelings, I'm not making excuses for all her bad behavior. And that incident with your friend..." She didn't finish, and he could almost see the shake of her head.

Her words brought back the ache of guilt. "I shouldn't have let Jeremy get hurt."

"I wish he hadn't been hurt, too. But the truth is that you can't protect everyone all the time. No matter how much you wish you could. Trust me, I should know, with the five of you."

Susan was right. The Mavericks had certainly given Susan and Bob a crazy ride those first few years. But Jeremy was different.

"I wish I could do more than provide a new job for him and work on the car. Harper works so hard to look out for her brother. But every time I offer to help, she insists on doing it all on her own."

"Maybe that's because she thinks she still *is* on her own."

Frustration rose up in Will. "How can I get her to understand that I'm not going anywhere? And that I mean it when I say I won't hurt her or her brother? What else can I do to get through to her?"

"You know how."

No. The reaction was instinctive. Even before Susan continued with exactly what he knew she was going to say.

"Have you told her about your past yet?"

"I rewrote that story already," he said in far too sharp a tone, considering that Susan was only trying to help him. Plus, as soon as the words came out of his mouth, he wasn't actually sure they were true. Sure, he'd rewritten the part where he was poor, but what about the rest? Because he sure as hell had never been able to forget that he came from a worthless thief and bully who hadn't deserved to be called a father. Still, he had to ask Susan, "What's so important about my past that she needs to know?"

"Will." There was a slight note of exasperation in Susan's voice. "She needs to know because you love her. And love means being completely open, even if you're scared."

Will had given Susan and Bob a merry ride, pushed their limits, tested their boundaries. After his dad, he hadn't trusted anyone without proof that they were worth it. Susan and Bob had passed with flying colors in the end, and he'd do anything for them.

But Susan saw right to Will's core—so deep that there was no point in even trying to deny what he was feeling. Not any of it.

"I think I've been in love with her from the first moment I saw her standing outside my hangar with her brother, so protective, so beautiful, so strong." And then so free and passionate during their first fast ride. His heart brimmed over with all that he felt for Harper. "I admire everything about her. But if she knew about me—"

"You were a child, Will. Your father made you do those things for him." Susan, God love her, made excuses for everyone, even him.

"I kept doing them even when I got older. After he went to prison."

"It was all you knew. All you had to go on. But then you learned what was wrong, you learned what was right, and you never mixed up the two again."

"I learned those things from you," he said softly, remembering her never-ending patience. And loving her for it.

"Does it matter where or how or from whom you learned it? *You* made yourself into the man you are. That's why I've always said you don't need to wear that tattoo as some sort of reminder about your father and the life he forced you to be a part of. You're your own man, not the least bit tainted by him in any way. And I'm so proud of you, honey."

He could hear the tears in her voice. Susan rarely cried when she was upset. She cried when she was happy. "If you reveal who you are, I know she'll love you as much as I do. How could she not?"

But unlike Susan and Bob and the rest of the Mavericks, Harper hadn't lived not knowing where her next meal would come from and had no idea of the depths to which people could sink. She hadn't known men like Will's father. She'd never stolen or lied simply because someone ordered her to.

What if she didn't understand that sometimes you became exactly like the very person you hated because that reflection in the mirror was the only thing you knew how to see?

"I can't tell her, Susan."

"Listen to me—I'm proud of you because I *know* what you went through. Because you rose above it. I've never known better men than any of my boys. And that most definitely includes you."

Her words humbled him.

"Tell me something, Will. Do you think Harper is worthy of love? And happiness?"

"Of course she is. The biggest love. The most happiness."

"Is she worthy of your trust?"

"Without a doubt. She'd never lie or cheat or steal." *Not like me.*

"Neither would you. Not now. Not ever."

Again, it was as though Susan was right there inside his head, hearing all the voices that had never gone away. The ones that said he didn't deserve any of this. Not the success. Not the money. Definitely not love. And certainly not Harper.

But three days ago he hadn't told Harper the whole story about the day he'd met the Mavericks. Despite the sun and the pool, he'd kept his T-shirt on to hide the Road Warrior tattoo. And he hadn't told her the full truth about those bullies who had gone after Matt. Nor had he told her anything about that terrible day when he was sixteen...and he'd made the worst mistake of his life.

"If you truly trust her, then let *her* decide whether you're worthy. Don't choose for her." Susan paused. "Trust her to realize that you're a man of your word, not a product of your father."

That was the question, the one he couldn't see a straight answer for, not anymore. Was he his father's son?

Or was he a man worthy of Harper's love?

"She needs to know how you feel. Trust her with your secrets, Will."

"And if she walks away?"

"Believe me, honey, if you refuse to let her in, she'll leave anyway."

CHAPTER TWENTY-FIVE

"You got tickets to *Wicked*?" Harper looked up with surprise into the face of the most beautiful man on the planet. A man who was giving her one of those slow, sexy smiles that always made her dizzy with desire.

"Friday night. Dinner in San Francisco. Then a private box for the show."

It was a lovely Wednesday evening, the air cooling down after the heat of the day. Once Memorial Day was over, summer hit with temperatures that baked concrete. She and Will were taking a leisurely stroll through her modest Palo Alto neighborhood while Jeremy stayed home building a Lego kit. It wasn't just putting blocks together anymore. There were complicated instructions, and Miss Richards felt the toy would stretch his capabilities.

When Will had brought Jeremy home after work that evening, he'd removed his suit jacket and thrown his tie over the back of the sofa, but he was still tempting in a striped dress shirt. His hand over hers felt divine. And yet, even though it felt as though they were a couple—a real one—Harper kept reminding herself to stay in the moment. It was enough just to appreciate being here with him now. Which meant she needed to stop thinking about *more.* Especially since he'd already given her more happiness—and pleasure—than she'd ever thought to have.

He slipped the tickets back into the breast pocket of his shirt. "After the show," he said, "we'll check to make sure that Jeremy is doing fine staying the night at my house with Mrs. Taylor. And then I'm going to take you to my flat in the city and have my way with you." He dragged his gaze down her body until she was hot all over. "All night long." He drew out the words.

All night long.

They'd never spent the whole night together. In fact, they'd never even been completely naked together. Everything was always fast and hot, ripping clothes off and devouring each other. Or getting *her* naked.

But now he wanted all night.

It suddenly felt hard to breathe, in both a bad *and* a good way. Because God, yes, she wanted a night with Will. In his bed. *All night long.* But at the same time, she was terrified that it would change everything for her—that it would make it even harder to stop wishing for *more.*

She'd vowed that night in his '57 Chevy that she wouldn't be scared anymore, that she'd just go with the flow and keep having fun. But the truth was that even though she was having the time of her life with Will, she didn't know how to shelve her worries. How could she, when she was falling so hard and so fast for him? Falling deeper and deeper with every kiss, every caress, with every sweet word he said to her, every smile he gave to her brother. Falling even harder and deeper after the barbecue. After watching him with Noah and seeing what a great father he would be. Someone she would have been proud to introduce to her own parents.

But when, outside of a fairytale, did the gorgeous billionaire actually fall for the normal girl?

"Does that sound good to you?"

She looked into his deep blue eyes, and despite all the worries and questions circling inside of her, she melted. Just like always. "It sounds amazing. I've been dying to see *Wicked.*" She was pleased by how calmly and steadily the words came out, as if she actually had any self-control at all where he was concerned.

* * *

Oh God, she thought on Friday night, *I am so not in control.*

How could she be when the evening was this fabulous? Will was utterly gorgeous in a black tux and white shirt. Dinner had been at an exclusive private club on Nob Hill that didn't even have a menu, where the waiter had recited delectable descriptions that left her mouth watering.

And so did Will. He was his usual can't-keep-his-hands-to-himself, first at the restaurant, and then at the theater in their private box. Almost as if he wanted to keep spinning her out on the delicious edge of pleasure every moment so that she couldn't spare one single brain cell to dwell on worries and questions. He'd made her feel special, desirable, irresistible, beautiful—as though she was the center of his world.

After she'd visited the ladies' room during the intermission, she found Will in the crush of elegantly dressed theater patrons, amid photographers snapping pictures of the beautiful, rich, and famous. He was waiting for her just down the hall, a champagne glass in each hand.

"You looked thirsty." He kissed the tip of her nose.

It was so sweet, something a man did to a woman who belonged to him. As though they were a real couple rather than just friends with benefits. As though he felt for her exactly what she was feeling for him. Despite all the reminders she kept giving herself, she couldn't help but be totally swept up in the romance of it all.

Until a male voice came between them. "Will, it's good to see you outside of the office."

The man was older, mid-forties maybe, and well-bred handsome. His short dark hair had very little silver in it, and his eyes were a steel gray that seemed to pierce through everything. Harper's hair wasn't exclusive-salon prepped, her nails weren't manicured, and her dress was off-the-rack among all the designer gowns floating around the mezzanine. She'd never cared about any of that before...but compared to the drop-dead-gorgeous woman hanging on the man's arm, Harper felt horribly out of her depth. Just the way she had several times before, when Will had swept her into his amazing world of fast cars and caviar.

"Cal, great to see you, too." Will's voice was warm as he held out his hand and the two men shook. "Monette." His voice became slightly less warm. "Please meet Harper." He slid his fingers around Harper's, then told her, "Cal is business manager for the Maverick Group."

The beautiful Monette was staring at Harper's hand clasped in Will's. She smiled, but despite her lush lips, perfect cheekbones, and expert makeup, the smile didn't move beyond that slight twitch of her mouth. Her manicured grip tightened on Cal's arm.

Will made polite conversation. "I'm so glad Harper agreed to come with me tonight."

"It's been such a treat," she said, hoping her smile looked genuine despite her discomfort beneath the other woman's laser-focused gaze.

When Cal smiled back, it filled his face and deepened the laugh lines at the corners of his eyes. "A *Wicked* treat."

"Oh Cal, you're so funny and smart." Monette spoke for the first time, her tone sultry, as if she'd whispered something naughty. Her gold dress sparkled with tiny jewels that Harper thought might actually be real.

She would *not* feel bad in her classic black cocktail dress, one she'd been so pleased to find on sale last year.

Will squeezed Harper's fingers as though he could hear her thoughts. Not wanting him to think she wasn't making an effort with his friends, she told them, "I haven't been to the theater since *The Phantom of the Opera*."

"That show was here ages ago, wasn't it?" Monette drawled, as though she'd scored a point in a game Harper hadn't realized they were playing. "I'm so glad Cal has been taking me to see *everything* lately." She stroked the arm she held and blinked bedroom eyes at him.

Cal looked at Monette, a line between his brows, then at Will as if a light bulb was going on.

Oh. Well then. The light bulb had just gone on for Harper, too. Clearly, Will had a history with this woman. A sexy history, if Harper had to guess.

"This is only our second show," Cal corrected politely, still smiling, still friendly.

But Monette's eyes narrowed like those of a Siamese cat. Harper couldn't say for sure, but she had the distinct impression this would be their *last* show. She was good at reading people, and the business manager looked like a man who, out of respect, wouldn't date a woman who'd already infiltrated the Maverick Group once before.

Will beamed at Harper as though he was oblivious to the byplay. "Monette's right. I've been remiss." He raised her hand to his lips and kissed her knuckles. "I should have been taking you out on the town instead of keeping you all to myself." His eyes darkened as if he'd forgotten there were other people in the conversation as he added, "But I haven't been able to help myself."

All right, Will definitely wasn't oblivious. But Harper stopped caring as her pulse raced and she couldn't look away from him, couldn't do anything but wish they were somewhere private so that he could strip her clothes off and make love to her. And she could make love to him, too.

"Cal, isn't that the mayor I see over there?" Monette's voice grated Harper right out of the spell Will had cast over her. "Didn't you say you wanted to speak with him?"

Over Monette's head, Cal raised a brow at Will, before saying, "Of course. It was lovely to meet you, Harper." He let himself be led away.

"Franconi, it's good to see you."

Another tall, well-dressed man, with an older woman wearing fuchsia taffeta, slid so quickly into the vacated spot that Harper didn't have a chance to ask Will about Monette. Which was a good thing. Because she *shouldn't* ask about Monette. It wasn't her business whom he'd been with before they started spending time together, and the very mention could come across as jealousy.

Except that when one conversation ended and another began as yet a different society couple poured into the empty space, she couldn't help but consider what Monette had been to him. Had he called the other woman *sweetheart?* Had he looked smitten as he'd introduced Monette to all of these people at similar events? Had he invited her to meet the other Mavericks?

Or was there any possibility that Harper was the only one he was always touching—her back, the nape of her neck, her cheek, her hair?

And was there any chance at all that Harper was the only one he'd taken for those fast and wild rides?

When the bell rang signaling the end of the intermission, Will finally led her back to their box, pulling her close as soon as the door sealed them in. "If I'd known it was going to be like that, I'd have brought the champagne in here and kept the door locked." He nuzzled her hair. "Sorry about Monette. She can be catty."

Harper couldn't think while he was touching her. Which meant she also couldn't remember to hold back the words, "You used to date her?"

"A couple of times." He shrugged. "She likes men with money."

Harper had enough experience with fortune hunters after Jeremy's trust to understand. But even though she still couldn't quite shake the jealous vision of Will sleeping with a woman like Monette, she needed him to know something. "She was a fool."

He turned to her with a surprised look that she was able to catch just as the lights went down. But when he kissed her—a kiss that was not only full of passion, but something more, something that seemed even bigger than desire—she didn't need to see his face to know how much he'd liked hearing those words.

CHAPTER TWENTY-SIX

Their limousine could have seated ten. Champagne chilled in a silver bucket on the center console, and a pot of Will's special caviar teased her senses as the limo maneuvered through the San Francisco streets, heading to Will's penthouse flat. The flutes were filled with raspberries, already half drenched in champagne.

This was the opulence she'd expected from him that first night—an exclusive restaurant, a private box at the show, a stretch limo. And yet, while it was still more than a little overwhelming, it didn't scare her away the way it would have back then. Because she *knew* Will. Knew the man behind the money and the power. Knew how kind he could be, how sweet. Sexy, too, but that had been obvious from the outset with nothing more than one look.

He filled the glass and handed it to her before doing the same with his, then tapped his glass to hers in a *ting!* of crystal. Flush against him on the seat, his exquisitely male scent went to her head like the champagne bubbles.

"Did you like the show?"

"It was wonderful. Thank you so much for taking me." The plot was a little fuzzy, though, since she'd been so taken over by him that she couldn't remember much of it. But what she did remember—all of his incredible kisses, the way he'd teased her with barely-there caresses—made her tingle all over.

"It was my pleasure. Being with you always is." He tipped the stem of her glass, and murmured, "Drink."

It was ambrosia, with a hint of almonds and the sweetness of the fruit at the bottom.

"Now try a caviar chaser." He unscrewed the lid of the caviar and dipped his finger into the pot.

No spoon, no cracker. Just him. His lids half-closed, he fixated on her lips as they parted, and she took his finger into her mouth.

He was a burst of flavor—the rich, buttery taste of the caviar and the saltiness of his skin. An ache blossoming deep in her core, she licked him clean, every last morsel. The sensory overload was already close to sending her over the edge, but when he trailed a kiss along the low neck of her dress, over the swell of her breast, she was sure she would die of wanting him.

Slowly, he pulled away, raining more kisses over her skin before saying, "Your turn."

Dazed with desire, Harper dipped a finger into the pot, retrieving a scoop of the luxury before Will set it back on the console. Then he captured her wrist, bringing her hand to his lips. His eyes on hers, he went down on her finger and sucked the caviar away.

The limo idled through the city traffic, but she no longer needed speed to get that wild, crazy feeling from racing fast in a car.

All it took was one touch from Will.

He licked her finger once more, his gaze smoldering. Then he tipped her champagne against her lips. She took a long drink, the bubbles bursting all the way down her throat. When she was done, he leaned in and tasted her mouth, licking away the drops of the champagne.

"I want you now," he whispered against her lips, "but I swore to myself I'd have you in my bed tonight. All night long. Over and over."

Moments later, the car stopped and the door opened, garage lights beaming beyond the driver's shoulder. Her knees seemed to wobble as Will helped her from the car. He carried the two champagne glasses in one hand as he walked her to the elevator, which he opened with a special key card. There were no floor buttons. Once inside, he simply inserted the key again. The doors closed as the limo rolled away.

His arm wrapped around her, he held the glass to her lips once more. "Eat the fruit. It's been sitting in champagne." He tipped the glass until the berries slid down into her mouth. They were rich with bubbles, sweet and sparkling.

Then Will's lips crushed hers. He held her tight against his body, pressing her up against the elevator wall as he tasted the fruit with her.

But though she'd truly had an amazing time at the show tonight and the fancy ride, complete with fruited champagne and delicious caviar had been seductive and decadent, she hadn't needed any of it to be happy.

All she'd needed was *him*.

* * *

Harper's taste on Will's lips lingered as the elevator doors opened and they stepped into his flat.

"Wow."

Harper's breathy exclamation of wonder called him to her. She glided to the wall of windows showcasing the vast blackness of a nighttime San Francisco Bay, with the blazing lights of the city, the Golden Gate Bridge, Sausalito, and the East Bay surrounding the water like a ring of fire. Abandoning the champagne glasses on the coffee table, Will shadowed her.

"It's so beautiful." She spoke to the inky night and to him.

With the room still dark behind them and moonlight falling across her, she was more beautiful than any landscape. He shifted to stand close at her back, seeing through her eyes. He'd bought the place because of the view, but he'd long since stopped noticing it. Harper made it fresh again as he shared her awe, revealing the beauty he'd forgotten.

She turned her head slightly to gaze at him over her shoulder. "Do you sit here at night just staring at all this?"

"I haven't." But he could sit here all night watching her. "But I see now that I've been missing something."

He'd been missing so damn much until she'd walked into his life. If only what he felt for her was enough to wipe out ten years of his past, from the ages of eight to eighteen...

She turned back to the vista, leaning against him. "Just looking out your windows would be like meditation after a long work day."

"Maybe I should rearrange the furniture and make this window the centerpiece."

"Yes, you should," she said, and her hair, still fragrant with some sweet shampoo, brushed his cheek, his chin.

He'd planned the evening meticulously, from dinner to the sold-out tickets for the two-week run, the limo, the caviar, the fruit in the champagne glasses. He'd wanted to wow her.

But he was the one wowed. From the very first moment he'd set eyes on her.

She needs to know how you feel. Trust her with your secrets.

Susan's words had been his constant companions since their talk. Wrapping his arm around Harper's waist, he pulled her back tightly against him, as he wondered for the hundredth time: Could she handle what was in his heart? Or would it send her running?

Rich men in fast cars, the teenager who'd run her brother down, the wealthy father who'd bailed him out—Will knew he embodied all Harper's fears and he instinctively stiffened at the thought of losing her.

"Will?" She turned slightly to look up at him again, her eyes meeting his. "Is everything okay?"

He brushed her hair aside to plant a kiss on the sensitive skin of her neck. "You're here." He sucked her skin, leaving his mark on her, then moved up to her ear, a sweet little hot spot, and nibbled. "Everything is amazing."

"You make me totally crazy when you do that." She twirled and wrapped her arms around his neck. "You're such a tease."

He wanted to tease her right up to heaven, wanted to give her so much pleasure that she'd never, ever think about leaving him. "The word *tease* implies no follow-through. And believe me, I intend to follow through." He kissed her lightly. "All—" *Kiss.* "—night—" *Kiss.* "—long." Then he parted her lips and took her mouth, hot need spiking through him. "You're absolutely perfect."

"So are you."

But he wasn't.

Not even close.

* * *

Harper was dying for him to tear off her clothes, throw her down on the carpet, and take her right in front of the window.

That was how he always made her feel— totally wild, crazy, and out of control. But this was going to be a night for firsts: the first time in his bed, the first time with him completely naked, the first time she'd have him all night long and wake up beside him in the morning.

They'd rushed everything else, but she couldn't bear to rush this.

Even if it killed her.

And yet, when she looked into his eyes, she saw shadows. The same shadows that had been there moments before when his whole body had tensed against her back.

"Will." She reached for his cheek. "If something's wrong—"

"No." The word sounded choked. "Nothing's wrong when you're here. Nothing's wrong when you're with me." But there was a storm in his eyes. "Let me love you, Harper. Please, just let me love you."

His words rippled over her, through her, tugging at her heart. So even though she knew this was just supposed to be for fun, how could she say anything but, "Love me, Will."

The next thing she knew, he tugged her dress off her shoulder and traced a finger down until it rested against her breast. Slowly pulling the material aside, he revealed the lace of her black bra. Slowly, so slowly that she nearly went crazy, he pulled the cup down until her aroused flesh finally popped free.

"Delicious," he whispered before he bent his head.

His thick, soft hair caressed her skin, and his tongue devastated her. She held him tight as he licked her, then closed his lips around the peak and sucked.

All her electrons were firing like crazy when he raised his head and said, "More."

He always wanted more from her. And she always gave it to him.

When she whispered *"More,"* he splayed a hand across her back and turned her insides to liquid with his lips and tongue.

Then his teeth scraped across her, like a live wire straight to her center. Her body shuddered, and she clung to him, gasping, writhing. It wasn't an orgasm, but a deep, needy quaking that made her moan, clutch him tight...and beg.

"Please."

"Whatever you want."

"I want you naked." Her need whispered out on a breath. "I want to see all of you."

He was always the one taking her clothes off. But she couldn't wait any longer to see every inch of that gloriously hard flesh.

She expected his usual grin, but just that quickly, the storm was back in his eyes as he suddenly lifted her in his arms to carry her through the dark living room. There was no hall, just a doorway off the central area. In his bedroom, city lights illuminated a four-foot rectangle in front of the window, hiding the rest in darkness. He walked unerringly to the bed and laid her down gently.

They'd been in the dark since they'd entered his apartment, but that wasn't enough for her anymore. "I need light," she said, "or I won't be able to see you." And she *had* to see.

He paused for a long moment, his face still grim in the shadows, before finally flicking a light switch. The lamp lit the bed, his scrumptious black tux, white shirt, and lightly mussed hair.

A dark wood bureau matched the nightstands and headboard. White tile glinted through the bathroom doorway, and a big jet tub two steps up lay just beyond in the shadows. His personal space was expensively furnished with a fabulous view and probably cost a fortune—he even had his own elevator, for goodness sake—but while it was rich, there was nothing that shouted Will's ownership.

Instead, it looked almost lonely.

He advanced on her. "You have on too many clothes."

He was still minus his usual grin, but the sensuality in his tone made her forget all about the room and its lack of a personal touch. There was only the huge bed and the gorgeous apartment.

And Will.

"So do you," she agreed. And this was her turn. All the other times, he'd managed to keep even his shirt on. "I want to see you, the way you've seen me," she insisted, her pulse throbbing.

He moved away from her then to snap the blinds closed, so that it was just them—no people on the street far below, no cars honking. And when he turned back to face her, she realized he'd never looked at her with such raw hunger...or such deep, tormented emotion.

"I'm all yours, Harper."

All hers.

At least for tonight.

CHAPTER TWENTY-SEVEN

Harper rose slowly, shrugging the shoulders of her dress up and letting it fall back into place. For once, she was going to keep her dress intact while Will was the one exposed.

"Shoes first," she directed.

He quickly toed them off and kicked them away.

She stepped close, talking as she undid his jacket. "I love your tux." She loved *him* in the tux.

Walking around him, she slipped her fingers inside the front lapels and pulled the jacket down his arms. She folded it, laying it across a chair in the corner. Even from this angle, he was strong, muscled. She trailed a hand across his back as she circled him once more. "I've never tied a bow tie."

"All you need to know is how to untie it."

She slipped the knot, smiling as she noted, "No cummerbund."

"I thought that would make it easier when you undressed me."

She *tsk*ed. "You didn't know I was going to undress you."

"Yes, I did." His eyes were hot.

Of course he did. Because she'd never been able to resist him, had she? But there was no time—and no need—to beat herself up about that now. Not when he was still waiting for her to undress him. And she was *dying* to see every last gorgeous, naked inch of him.

She cocked her head. "Hmm. Cufflinks first? Or shirt buttons?" She put a finger to her lips. He'd kissed her hard and deep, but the lipstick was long-lasting and wouldn't smudge. She liked the idea of her lipstick against his—

"Shirt buttons," he decided for her.

"Definitely." She wanted to feel his skin, the sooner the better.

She pulled the shirt from his waistband and slowly unbuttoned it, her fingers caressing his flesh. The dusting of hair on his chest was soft, silky. She trailed down, and when she looked up, he was anything but unaffected. A pulse beat at his throat, and his gaze seared her. She loved the power his eyes gave her, how potent he made her feel. She pushed his shirt aside and slicked her tongue over him, eliciting another telltale quiver.

"You like?"

"You make me crazy, I like it so much." Need turned his voice harsh.

She wanted to go straight for his belt, to see what she could only feel right now. To touch. And taste. But this was a strip tease, for *both* their pleasure.

Running one hand down his arm, she flicked the cufflink at his wrist and pulled it free. She did the same with the other, loving the soft plop as they hit the carpet. More touching, teasing, her hands on his skin as she walked her fingers up, to the top of the shirt, over his shoulders beneath the cotton, then down his strong arms. She let the shirt billow to his feet.

"You're beautiful." She stepped back to absorb him and couldn't resist touching. Muscled shoulders down to pectorals and tapering into washboard abs. "And you've got a tattoo."

His biceps hardened as she traced the ink's contours. A muscle car. And over it, the stylized phrase, *Road Warriors.*

"Very sexy. Like *Sons of Anarchy* or something."

He clenched his teeth and hissed in a breath. Then he said, "Or something."

"Was it a club you belonged to?"

Two long beats of silence. "Yeah."

"You're a bad boy." One who made her weak in the knees every single time he kissed her. "And you know how women feel about bad boys," she teased.

"Tell me how *you* feel, Harper."

Couldn't he tell already? Didn't he know? "It makes me hot. *You* make me hot."

The air soaked up his tension, raising the hair on her arms like static electricity. Until he blinked it away...and moved her fingers to his belt.

* * *

Harper unbuckled and unzipped while he watched. Her hands were trembling slightly, but she didn't stop, just tucked her lower lip between her teeth as she concentrated on taking off the rest of his clothes. And when her lips curved up in a little smile and she gracefully dropped to her knees...*oh hell*, he nearly lost it right then and there. Nearly tore her dress from her and took her the way he'd been wanting to take her all night long.

"You're gorgeous." There was no artifice in her voice, just reverent awe.

He kicked aside the pile of his clothing. "You've seen me before."

Still down on her knees, she tipped her head back, her hair falling in waves around her shoulders. Will's heart thumped hard knowing she was his for this night. He'd waited so damn long and now his hands shook, just as hers had when she was undressing him. He fisted them in her hair to hide it.

"Only parts of you." Her gaze was soft, her lips sweet. "The parts you've let me see. Tonight is the first time I'm seeing all of you."

Jesus, she had no idea what she was saying, did she? No idea that she'd just seen more of him than any other woman had. She hadn't balked at his tattoo. She'd thought it was sexy. But it would lose all its sexiness if she knew what it really meant.

She leaned in to swipe her tongue along his length and his thoughts scattered as everything inside him clenched, coiled, made ready to pounce. She smiled as though she knew exactly what she did to him.

"You still have all your clothes on," he somehow managed to say.

He wanted her naked. On the bed. Spread out. He'd never wanted anyone this intensely, with every cell primed, each sense attuned. Only Harper. Her scent was sweet, with the added spice of arousal. Her fingers were silk caressing his skin. Her kiss was a drug he couldn't get enough of.

"We're even, then," she replied, "since I'm always the one who's naked."

Susan had said he needed to let Harper know how he felt. There were so many things—need, desire, amazement, *love*. But right now all he could get his brain to manage was, "I need you, Harper." He pulled her to her feet and unzipped the cocktail dress. Pressing kisses to her spine as the material slid down and pooled at her feet, he licked the sensitive hollow at the base. The last to go was her bra. Standing behind her, he cupped her breasts in his hands.

"I need you so damned much." Her head back against his shoulder, she arched into his palms, silently begging.

Until tonight, he'd tried to play it cool with her, teased her, made her climax in ways he was sure she never had before. But he'd never completely let go. Not even the night in his '57 Chevy. Even then, he'd been aware of every action he took, calculating whether it gave her what she craved. Letting go was risky.

But if he didn't let go—and if he didn't let her in—then all he could ever be to her was some hot sex on the hood of his car or in the front seat of his Chevy. But he wanted so much more with Harper. Needed more with every cell in his body, with every heartbeat, every breath.

He reached around her and dragged the coverlet down the bed, tugging the blanket and sheet to the bottom. He picked her up and was so far out on the edge of reason that he all but tossed her onto the bed.

He went to her nipples first, licking, sucking, until she arched against him. "The way you taste." He swiped his tongue across a peak. "The sounds you make. The way your body begs for more. All of you makes me crazy, Harper."

She threaded her hands through his hair. "You make me crazy, too."

He crawled up her body, then rolled until she was on top. Spreading her legs over him, he pulled her hips down, riding her center without actually entering her. She was slick and hot. She curled her body around him, her hips moving up into his, quaking, gasping, her heart beating so hard he could feel it.

He'd never felt so wild with a woman as when he hauled her up, clamped his hands on her hips, and pulled her to his mouth. Jesus, she was sweet. Wet. He held her to him, drinking her in. He circled, spiraling down slowly until he touched the center of her pleasure.

Above him, she grabbed the headboard, her hips undulating, her body directing him, telling him how to move, where to kiss. He kneaded her hips in his hands, increasing the friction, the pleasure. Her sounds filled the room, gasps, sighs, little cries. He was voracious, consuming her as she shuddered, trembled.

And came completely apart for him.

But it wasn't enough. He couldn't let her go. Not yet. He had only enough thought left to grab a condom from the drawer before he came down between her legs. "Look at me."

She opened her eyes, fuzzy with sated pleasure. "I don't know who's crazier anymore."

"We're crazy together." Then he thrust home.

Closing his eyes, he held still, absorbed the feel of her around him. "So good," he whispered. "So perfect."

There was sex. And then there was *this*. One was merely physical. *This* was body and soul.

He pulled her leg to his waist and moved, slowly at first. She shuddered, circled his shoulders with her arms, and as she brought her other leg up, she looked into his eyes and whispered, "It's too good."

"It could never be too good."

He held her hips, falling into her, retreating, then moving in deep again. Every muscle bunched, his blood pounded. And he could feel her around him, taking him, holding him tight. He could stay here forever.

Then she moaned. Her breath hitched. And he knew she was climbing again. He had to go with her this time, needed to jump off right along with her. Pumping faster, harder, going deeper, he steeped himself in her, *"Harper. God. Yes. So good,"* falling from his lips.

Her heart thudded hard with his. He buried his face in the crook of her neck and smelled their salty-sweet scent, tasted her on his tongue. The heat of her skin became his heat. Her body was indistinguishable from his. And when she convulsed around him, she dragged him over the edge with her.

He heard her name on his lips. He heard her cry out his.

Then his voice saying, "I love you."

* * *

I love you.

Harper's body, her head—but especially her heart—were all spinning as she tried to make sense of what had just happened. And what he'd just said.

"Harper?" He eased to his side, taking some of his weight from her, even as his arm tightened around her. "I love you."

He'd put his hand on her cheek and turned her face to his as if he'd known she wouldn't quite be able to process those three little words the first time he said them. And it was so tempting to say them back, her own *I love you, too,* right there on the tip of her tongue.

But the words wouldn't come, almost as if they were locked up tight inside her, and she couldn't find the key.

She could tell him about her fears—that he'd tire of her and Jeremy, that surely he couldn't want to take both of them on when all the other men she'd come across had been horrified at the thought. But she already knew what he'd say—*I'm not like them.* And he wasn't, because she knew how kind and generous he was.

Unfortunately, that fact didn't change the others—his money, his lifestyle, or his ability to take whatever he wanted.

Harper knew her own self-worth, and yet, with the penthouse apartment, the limo, and the glittering jewels of all the people fawning over Will tonight... honestly, she couldn't help but feel out of her depth. It had been like being tossed straight into the deep end when she was only just learning to swim.

More than anything, she wanted to love with her full heart and soul. All the way, nothing held back. Wanted it more than she'd ever wanted anything in her life. And she knew he'd talk her out of every single doubt.

But how could she tell him she loved him unless *she* was able to talk herself out of those doubts?

When she looked back up at him, he was frowning. Her throat felt tight, her chest ached, and she wished she could tell him what he wanted to hear. Wished she was ready, that she was already there. "Will—"

Before she could try to figure out what else to say, he surprised her yet again by saying, "You're smart not to say it back to me, Harper."

Wait...he didn't *want* her to say she loved him? Why would she be smart to hold a part of herself back from him?

But before she could voice any of those questions, he said, "You should know I'm not a nice guy. That's why I haven't told you how I felt about you. Because I'm not good enough for you. And yet I can't make myself stay away even though I should."

Not good enough for her? Will Franconi thought *he* was the one who wasn't good enough?

All of this made her head whirl. It was happening so fast and was all so unexpected. Not just how sweet he'd been from the first day she and Jeremy had met him, but also how much he'd done for them since. And how much she wanted to let herself love him, all the way, with nothing held back. This was just supposed to be a thrill ride. But somehow, it had turned into so much more. And now that everything she'd been telling herself was true had spun on its ear, she didn't know what to think. Or how to feel.

She knew only one thing. "No one has ever been nicer to me," she told him. "Or to Jeremy."

"That's now. But back then—" He broke off and his chest rose with a deep breath as if he was trying to force himself to do something painful. "Remember when I said some kids were bullying Matt the day I met him?"

She could feel his heartbeat beneath her fingertips. "Yes. And you rescued him."

"Evan, Daniel, and Sebastian rescued him, Harper." He looked her straight in the eye. "*I* was one of those bullies."

CHAPTER TWENTY-EIGHT

Harper tipped her head back to look at him. The strong lines of his face were tense, the bedside lamp casting dark shadows across one half.

"*You* were bullying him?" She shook her head, unable to put the amazing man she'd fallen for in that picture, even as a boy. "I can't believe that."

His jaw flexed. "Believe it."

"But I've seen you with Matt's son, Noah. I've seen the way that little boy looks at you, and the way Matt trusts you. How could he trust you with his son if you did that?" No father would have let a son of his near the man who'd been his bully when he was a child.

He filled his lungs with another deep breath. "Because, in the end, I changed." He exhaled sharply. "I changed my mind."

"I don't understand." And she truly didn't—couldn't understand anything he was saying to her when it was the exact opposite of what she'd come to know about him.

"I belonged to a gang. In my neighborhood, you were either a bully or you got bullied," he said in rapid-fire bursts. "You had to act like them to be accepted. So I did."

His arm still bound her to him as if he was afraid she'd get away. Reaching up, she forced his palm against her cheek, holding him, too, as she tried to piece it all together.

"Road Warriors?" When he nodded, she said, "So if you felt you had to be a bully to fit in, then why did you change your mind about Matt?"

"Maybe I felt sorry for him because he was so scrawny. Or maybe there was just something in his eyes when he looked at me, like they were a kind of mirror that made me see myself in them. See what I was doing." His whole body was rigid along the length of hers. "I told them to leave him alone. So they turned on me." She felt his shrug, as if what the bullies had done to him was nothing and only what he'd been about to do to Matt had meaning. "That's when Daniel and Sebastian rescued *me*. They were always good fighters."

"I'm sorry." She understood bullying. She'd seen neighborhood kids pick on Jeremy. She'd put herself between them. But Will a bully? She remembered his defense of Jeremy at the grocery store, and, in a way, his story made sense of his reaction that day. He'd seen himself in that clerk. Cruel and demeaning. And he'd gone overboard to protect her brother. "But the gang took you back?"

"I *went* back. I thought they were my people. I thought they were my family, the only one that would ever want me. And that isn't all I did." He caressed her cheek with his thumb, his touch a contrast to what he was saying. "You need to know everything. Everything I've never told anyone but the Mavericks and my foster mom and dad. I was a burglar and a car thief, too." He moved slightly, indicating the tattoo on his arm. "I stole anything I thought I could sell. I was really good at picking out the good stuff." His laugh was more of a snort, angry and mocking. "I still am. I've made a fortune at peddling the good stuff."

Her lips parted. She couldn't seem to close them again.

"My dad sent me into houses. I was small and I fit through windows where he couldn't. He'd toss me in and I'd unlock the place for him. Since I was always able to spot the best stuff, dear old pops put that skill to excellent use. We lifted everything we could carry."

"Your father?" No one could do that to a child, especially not their own child, could they? Except that she wasn't naïve. She knew people did awful things to children all the time. But this was Will. Not some fifteen-second news bite about a stranger.

"He's in prison now. Three strikes and you're out."

It was hard to breathe, hard to hear, but she knew it was harder for him to tell. "How old were you when he made you steal for him?"

"It started when I was eight. A couple of years after my mom died. When my father figured I was old enough to follow orders without screwing up."

Her whole soul ached for him, as if she'd suddenly been shoved through a tiny window right along with him, shards of glass scarring her the way his father had scarred him. She'd wondered why he'd sidestepped all her questions, why he'd never told her his story. Now she knew: *This* was the truth he hadn't wanted her to pry up.

She'd told her story so many times that she'd ended up feeling as though it defined her, as though it had too much power over her. Whereas, even though Will had told almost no one else, she could see the enormous power his past had over him—and that he believed it defined him, too.

But couldn't he see? "None of that was your fault."

He pulled from her then, almost to the opposite side of the bed. So far, far away that even if her hand had been on his chest, his heart, she still wouldn't have touched him.

"Maybe I wasn't to blame at first. But all the stuff I did later was my fault. All the bad choices. Lots of bad choices."

She ached to run her fingers down his arm or to smooth the tightness from his forehead. Anything to ease his pain. But he needed to get it out, and she was afraid that he'd stop if she pushed him just then. Still, she needed to say again, "You were just a kid."

"I was a bully. I was a thief. I could hotwire a car like that." He snapped his fingers, a loud, sharp sound in the quiet. "Still can. I probably would have gone to juvie when they put my dad in jail if it hadn't been for Susan and Bob. Daniel's parents took us all in when we needed it. Except for Matt." He shrugged, pressed his lips together, the shadows taking over his beautiful face. "He never moved in officially, he was just underfoot all the time."

When he talked about Susan and Bob, his voice was reverent, rife with emotion and meaning. The Mavericks, Susan and Bob—these people were the most important in the world to him. No wonder they were bonded beyond blood relation. She didn't know his friends' stories or anything about their lives, but if they'd come to Daniel's parents, she now knew they must have seen things as bad as Will had.

She wanted so desperately to reach out. But Will remained untouchable. "They must be good people."

"The best. I should have accepted what they offered me long before I did." A wisp of wind could have carried the soft words away, but other than the rustle of sheets as Will moved, there was only the sound of his voice. "But I didn't stop doing the things my dad taught me." His fingers bunched in the sheet as he pulled it higher. "I loved speed. I loved drag racing. I loved cars. And I loved stealing them. I was one of the Road Warriors. And I thought they loved me, too. But I didn't have a clue." He turned his head, finally looking at her, one half of his face in light, the other in darkness. "*That's* what I did to Susan and Bob. To the people who tried to help me. Gave them heartache and worry."

"I'm sure they understood, Will." But she realized the useless platitude in that even as she spoke the words. Words that did nothing to ease his pain.

"I left the Road Warriors when I was sixteen." He paused, stared at the far bedroom wall as though he could actually see his life playing before him. "Or maybe it's better to say that they ceased to exist." Harper stretched out her hand, across the wide chasm of mattress between them as he told her, "That day with Matt, I at least learned I didn't want to be a bully. And I never did that shit again. But the Road Warriors were different. The lowest on the totem pole always got picked on. That was our way of life. It happened to me, it happened to all of them. Until you weren't the lowest anymore.

"We had this kid who wanted to be one of us more than anything. He was like a gnat, always buzzing around. And he couldn't do anything right. His name was Eddie, and they called him Eddie Munster after that old TV show." He shook his head at the wall, still watching the movie in his mind. "They didn't let up on Eddie. It was freaking endless. But he kept coming back for more. You just wanted to tell him to give up. It was never gonna happen. He'd never be one of us." Even his voice changed as he spoke, dropping letters off his words. "But ya gotta understand how badly you need a family out there. You'll take any kind of abuse just to belong."

She closed her eyes, held her breath as her heart broke in two for him. That was Will himself, the kid who'd taken any abuse just so he could be a part of them. She wanted to cry for him, scream for him, take care of him, never let him hurt ever again.

"Eddie couldn't drive for crap. And someone got the brilliant idea of giving him his absolute last chance to make it with us. They wanted to set him up in a car, let him race, and watch him crash. 'Cause they were all sure he'd crash. I saw Eddie talking to himself, a pep talk, psyching himself up. He was gonna do it. This time he'd get it right." He gritted his teeth. "Light—we called him that because he had the lightest fingers and could pick anything out of any pocket—he stood there telling the Munster he had shit for brains and he couldn't do it, he was nothing, would always be nothing, and this would prove it. On and on. And I watched. All I did was *watch*."

He stopped speaking, then stayed silent so long she thought the story had cost him his power of speech.

"He lost it," Will finally said in a soft voice, one she could barely hear. "The way they all thought he would. Sideswiped another car. That was it. His last chance. And he was out. I can still hear them laughing at him. Until he made them stop." He closed his eyes, shuddered. "I guess he snapped. He turned the car around, and he plowed right through them." His tanned skin had gone white, as if the memories were draining all the blood from him. "He killed Light and two other guys. Then he slammed into a wall head on. Killed himself, too."

She couldn't manage to hold in her gasp at Will's revelation, but less than a heartbeat later, she needed him to know, "You didn't bully him. You didn't do anything."

He looked at her then, and she swore she could see him shutting off the movie screen in his head. "That's exactly right. I did nothing. I let them drive him into the ground. I never stuck up for him the way I did for Matt. Matt was an outsider, an innocent. Eddie, he wanted to be one of us. So I let them haze him to death. Literally. And he took the guys I thought were my friends with him. If I'd done something long before then..."

"Could you really have stopped it? Or would they simply have beaten on you like they did when you stood up for Matt?"

He shook his head sharply. "It doesn't matter. I never tried. A crime of omission is still a crime."

She understood then why he drove so fast. It wasn't so much a love of speed as it was a way to run from his memories, his past. "And you're still racing after all these years," she said aloud.

His eyes were simultaneously full of emotion and totally bleak. "Yes. I still love speed. Still need speed. Still feel like I'll go off the rails if I don't have enough of it. Being with you is like that, Harper. A total rush. You fill up all those empty spaces. And even though I've known all along that I shouldn't let it happen, I haven't been able to stop. Haven't been able to make myself do the right thing and leave you alone."

She couldn't stand it anymore. She couldn't lie still in his bed. She either had to touch him—or run.

And she knew which one he thought she would pick. Almost as if every word he uttered was designed to make her leave. To force her out. To make her throw his words of love back in his face.

But how could she, when everything was now so clear? Will had been a small boy who was horribly used. And yet, he'd turned into a man who would champion her brother and teach a small child to swim. He'd been a broken little boy who, with help and love, had glued himself back together again.

And now, he was a man who *loved* her.

All along she'd been telling herself this was just hot sex with a super hot guy. Nothing more than a thrilling ride in a fast car. But the truth was that Will had managed to touch her in all the places she'd been afraid to let anyone near. Not since her parents died. Not even since she'd lost the old Jeremy. She'd never let anyone in. Not until Will had pushed past her barriers, her walls, each of her fears, one by one.

The honest truth? She was terrified. Terrified that if she truly gave her heart and then something happened to him, how could she possibly keep moving forward without him the way she had before?

"So you see, Harper, I'm really not a nice guy in any way."

As his voice thrummed like a chord inside her, she crawled across the expanse of his bed. She couldn't let him believe that horrible lie for one more second.

She straddled his lap and took his face in her palms. "I don't want a nice guy. I only want you. The *best* man I've ever known." Putting her hand on the tattoo of his youth, she bent to kiss the inked skin. "Susan and Bob forgave you no matter what you did. And so do I, Will. So do I."

But she knew she needed to say more, needed to explain why she wasn't echoing his beautiful words back to him. "My not saying those words...it's not because you aren't worthy. And it's definitely not because I'm too smart to fall for you. I'm falling, Will. You have to believe that. I just—"

She'd been planning to seal the confession with a kiss designed to ease his pain and loss, but he cut off her halting words, pulling her to him, his mouth a breath away.

"It's enough to know you're falling, Harper. And that one day, maybe, if I'm lucky, you'll let yourself fall all the way."

She kissed him then, with everything she had in her. Tasted him, savored him, and took his hard heat between her naked thighs, putting on protection at the same time. Then she took him deep inside. So deep that their coming together stole her breath, his breath, even stopped the beating of their hearts for one endless, perfect moment.

"Harper."

She drew everything from him then, with her body, her soul. Over and over, faster, harder, her hands, her mouth, taking him higher, deeper, until he cried her name, guttural words spilling out.

She recognized *love*, she recognized *you*. And for the first time, as she followed him over the edge of a greater bliss than she'd ever known, she let herself fully drink in his emotion...and the undeniable truth that he was quickly becoming everything to her.

* * *

Will had never known peace. Not until this moment. He'd always been fighting—to make more money, to best a business opponent, to drive the fastest car, to introduce his clients to the perfect caviar or the ultimate Swiss watch, to find the one thing in the world that everyone wanted and only he could provide.

He'd been fighting his whole life to erase the kid he'd left behind in Chicago.

Until Harper made love to him...and he realized he didn't need to fight anymore.

She hadn't said she loved him, had even told him she needed more time. He understood that Harper—and Jeremy—had been hurt enough by men like him that she needed to think, to process, and to make absolutely sure she trusted him. But he swore he could feel her love in the way she looked at him with such emotion, in her touch, in the way she'd taken him to heaven and wouldn't let him leave.

She rested her fingers on his tattoo. "If it bothers you so much, why haven't you gotten rid of it?"

"It reminds me of where I came from." He could have left it at that, but she'd just given him so much. More than he'd ever hoped for. So he forced himself to give her more in return. "And it reminds me of where I never want to go again."

He still couldn't believe she hadn't jumped from his bed and demanded that he take her home. That she didn't hate him.

"Is that why you never let me take your clothes off? Why you wore a T-shirt when you were swimming with Noah?"

"Almost no one has seen my tattoo. I'm careful to make sure they don't."

She pressed a kiss to the center of his chest, right where it felt as if his heart was beating only for her. "So that makes me special, doesn't it?"

Hauling her tight against him, he wanted her to feel the power she had over him. To know that she'd made his life good in a way it never had been before. In a way he'd never thought it could be. "So special you make me ache when I look at you."

Her gaze roamed his face. She followed the look with her fingers. "You changed your life, changed who you are. If you ask me, you should let everyone see it."

It stunned him that, like Susan, she saw his mark as a symbol of triumph rather than as the evidence of his worthlessness. She wanted him to recognize it, too. Just as Susan had said, Harper was good for him.

In that moment, as he held her tight in his arms and she held him right back, Will vowed to do everything in his power to prove he could be good for her as well. He wouldn't let her down.

No matter what.

CHAPTER TWENTY-NINE

"I still can't believe you rented the entire Laguna Seca Raceway," Harper said a week later. "How is that even possible?"

The man could do anything. He wasn't just amazing—he was completely overwhelming.

Will hadn't sprung this trip to the racetrack on her, but checked with her first whether it was okay before mentioning it to her brother. "I swear," he'd said, "we'll keep it to one hundred twenty, tops. Slower in the turns."

One hundred twenty. He'd said it as if she should be reassured by that number. She wasn't, of course, since one-twenty was *way* too fast. But he had promised to keep her brother safe, no matter what. And despite the blitz of fear at the thought of her brother going that fast in a car, she realized she trusted Will. Trusted him with Jeremy in a way she'd never trusted anyone else.

Will's mechanic, Leland, had trailered the Cobra down to the Monterey Peninsula. Its paint job gleamed in the summer sun as it sat on the track. They'd both taken Friday off work for this, but the raceway wasn't empty. There were people working, mechanics along pit row, golf carts whizzing by.

Jeremy and Will had helped Leland roll the Cobra out of the trailer. Harper had been expecting a gruff old guy with grease under his nails, but Leland was younger than Will, and reminded her of Elvis in some of his early racing movies.

In the pits, Will had introduced them around, never letting go of her hand, the same way he'd kept her close when he'd introduced her during intermission that night at the theater. She'd been half expecting pictures of her and Will in the society blogs after that night, but there'd been nothing. Most likely because she hadn't even been worth the question, *Who's the mystery woman with Will Franconi?*

Will, with his constant attention, erased any slight from the thought. Who cared about the society pages when he gazed at her with such heat, desire, and sweet emotion in his eyes?

Leland, Will, and Jeremy were leaning over the open hood of the car out on the track, a small crowd of onlookers two steps behind observing the precheck procedure as if they were preparing for a flight around the world.

"What do you think, Jeremy?" Will pointed at something Harper had no clue about. "Should we change the timing?"

"That sounds good, Will," her brother agreed, his concentration intense. It was serious stuff when Will asked his opinion—and it always made Harper smile. And fall just a little bit more for her deliciously sweet billionaire.

"Yep," Leland added. "Changing the timing will give you a little more torque and squeeze out a little more speed."

Harper had no idea what any of that meant. She wasn't entirely sure that Jeremy did either, but he nodded gravely. She felt another flutter of emotion in her stomach. Will was so good to Jeremy, making him feel a part of things, as if he were a man instead of a kid.

Leland was pointing into the engine. "But you'll have to watch out on the turns or you might lose the back end."

A bald man gave Will a wrench as though he were a nurse handing the surgeon a scalpel. Every visible inch of skin except his face was armored with tattoos. His name was Zeke or Duke or something with a hard sound to it. There'd been too many names for her to catch. Everyone watched in silence, as if they were all holding their breath, Harper included.

She didn't want the extra torque if it spelled danger. Before she'd worried only about Jeremy. Now her heart also went into a frenzy worrying about Will and his need for speed.

He laid his hand on Jeremy's shoulder. "Lesson one with fast cars: Sometimes you've got to decide between putting a few more digits on your speedometer or making sure you don't crash. Safety first, right?"

"Right, Will." Will was his hero, and Jeremy agreed with everything.

"We're not going to do it," Will said as he handed the wrench back to Zeke/Duke, who tossed it into the tool chest.

And Harper's tension eased. Will loved speed, but he wasn't crazy. He wouldn't take unnecessary risks, not with Jeremy. And now, she realized, not even with himself.

She didn't know if it was a change she'd brought about; she only knew it was a worry she didn't need to carry any more. Will wouldn't let anything happen.

"Okay, let's do it." Will slammed down the Cobra's hood. "Thanks, Dude." Okay, maybe the guy's name was Dude. "We're ready." He clapped Jeremy on the back.

"Are we gonna get on the track now, Will?" Her brother was vibrating with energy.

"We are. And we're going real fast today, too." But even as he said it, Will looked at her with silent communication, making sure she was still okay with it.

He was so careful with her and with Jeremy and it made everything inside her melt as she gave him the barest of nods. And a smile. The one he sent in return flipped her inside out with pure sweetness.

Their small audience lined the fence as Will handed a helmet to Jeremy. "There are rules for safety here, so you have to put this on."

"Cool." Jeremy beamed as Will helped him with the chin strap. "It's like *Grand Prix.*" Another of Jeremy's favorite old movies.

Her brother waved at her from the passenger seat, his smile filling the entire open face of the helmet. Will started the engine, and the spectators gave a cheer as the vibration of the motor rumbled in her chest. Harper couldn't even begin to imagine what it would be like on race day with a horde of high-powered cars on the start line.

And then they were gone, leaving only a rush of wind behind them and the phantom roar of a crowd.

The scream of the car carried across the infield of the racetrack. She counted seconds that seemed to go on forever, then a minute, two minutes. The air moved first, as if it were dragging the car, then they blew past in a blur, Jeremy shrieking with delight. Her heart was in her throat, but it didn't top out there, rising up until she thought her head might explode. Or maybe that was the rumble of the motor pounding against her skull.

They flashed by her four more times, raising her hair each time, until it fluttered back down in their wake. Will finally brought the Cobra to a stop right in front of her.

"Wowowowow." Jeremy was pulsing with so much energy he couldn't even get the harness undone. Will helped, then reminded him, "Don't forget the pipes are hot when you get out."

Jeremy climbed out with exaggerated movements. When he was free, he ran so fast he almost barreled right into her. Somehow Will was right there, too, a hand on their arms to steady both of them.

"Your turn, Harper, your turn." Jeremy was high on the thrill of the ride, his eyes shining brightly under the rim of the helmet.

Will didn't say anything, simply looked at her with those intense eyes that did amazing things to her body—a blush of heat, butterflies in her stomach.

I love you.

Even now, she could hear him saying the words in that beautiful, harsh, wild voice.

In those early weeks with him, Harper had tried to use common sense, tried to keep things under control. But since that night in his penthouse a week ago, she couldn't even remember the definition of *common sense*. With every touch, her resistance melted. Her head told her to go slow, but when she was with Will, she wanted to hit the gas, rushing headlong wherever he wanted her to go. And all she wanted, every moment of every day, was this wonderful, sweet, and incredibly sexy man. One who'd trumped an unimaginable past.

Which was why she couldn't say no, not to anything. Especially when she'd just let Jeremy ride beside Will. She shouldn't allow her brother to do something she wasn't willing to do herself.

As if he could read her mind, and knew that the answer was *yes,* Will said, "Jeremy's helmet should fit you." He tugged at the chin strap and helped Jeremy pull it off.

"Look at you." She fluffed the flatness out of Jeremy's helmet hair.

He wriggled away just like a kid whose mom rubbed dirt away with a lick of her fingers. Will smiled as he watched the exchange.

"Okay, Jeremy, back behind the fence so you can watch." Will pointed to the other side of the chain link. Then he pushed the helmet down over her head. She was glad for the open-face style, so she could see his eyes, memorize the lines of his mouth, catch his scent. He jiggled the helmet slightly, but the foam inside fit snugly against her ears.

"It's good." He tilted her head back and dealt with the chin strap, sneaking in a kiss before saying, "Hop in."

The car was low, the seats deep. "At least I'm wearing pants this time."

He glanced down at her legs. "I like you in tight jeans. But the skirt was fun last time, too." He gave her one of his wolfish smiles. "For me, at least."

Leaning over her, he drew the shoulder harness down on both sides. Where the touches had been light and fast that first day they'd met at the airport—a hint rather than a promise—now he caressed, lingered, made sure every single piece of nylon was in exactly the right place.

She forgot about the spectators. She forgot about Jeremy. Forgot about everything but the gorgeous man beside her as he reached down between her legs with slow, seductive movements. He hooked the strap into the harness, his fingers brushing her inner thigh. Heat, his hands, her body. Quicker breaths, as if she were anticipating the speed, anticipating his strong hands on the wheel. And on her.

"Ready?"

The question was loaded with alternate meanings, especially when accompanied by the look he gave her, the way his gaze dipped down to her mouth, held there, then slid back up to meet her eyes.

She was ready. So ready.

She gave him a standard thumbs-up. The engine roared through her chest when he pumped the gas, then settled into a steady rumble inside her. He started slow, increasing speed gradually. It wasn't an oval track with only four turns, but a road course with twists and curves. He'd shown her and Jeremy an aerial map.

They went into the first hairpin turn at fifty miles per hour. His speed climbed as they went up the hill by the lake where they'd entered the track. Then they were going faster, faster, *faster*. Though he braked and downshifted into the turns, he throttled up coming out of them. Despite the harness, her head was jostled and she had to hold onto the door so she wouldn't be thrown around in the seat. It was like a roller coaster, up, down, around. Adrenaline fueled her blood like gas fueled the car. The corkscrew turn barely slowed him down. Her eyes teared in the wind. Even with the helmet, the noise was deafening, the air whistling past them, the thunder of the engine as he powered up, its whine as he decelerated.

They blew through a short straightaway, then he braked into the next turn. She glanced at the speedometer as he came out of it. Sixty. Then he jammed his foot onto the accelerator on the long straightaway past pit row. She didn't see Jeremy. She couldn't make out faces or even bodies, there was just a blur. By the time the speedometer hit one-twenty, she was pressed fully into the seat, one hand on the door, the other wrapped around the harness so her neck wouldn't snap.

And they were *flying*.

Flying so free that she closed her eyes, and there was only the sense of speed, the rush of wind, and the shriek of the motor.

She was high. She was wild. She needed Will to touch her, but he couldn't take his hand off the stick shift. And yet he was so close she could feel his heat beside her as if it were burning right off the engine.

Speed was the drug. Will was her pusher. She'd wanted to control the habit, but she was starving for more as she shouted, "Do it again."

And he did, taking her around the track over and over, until she was nothing more than hot skin, hard bone, and exhilarating, utterly breathless sensation.

* * *

Later, Will had taken Jeremy around again while Harper watched. She'd stood on the sidelines, vibrating like voltage through an electrical wire. Will had felt the same, his body charged, his skin sizzling to the touch, his heart hammering in staccato beats.

As for Jeremy, he'd chattered like an excited squirrel. Speed affected them all. And when her brother said he wanted to drive back in Leland's truck to Will's house, where Mrs. Taylor was waiting for him, so that they could talk cars the whole way, Harper agreed readily.

Now, Will and Harper were headed up Highway 1 alone, the others out of sight. "Were you scared on the track?"

"Terrified." But even now, he could hear— could see—the thrill flowing through her.

He'd been euphoric. He never raced other cars on the track. He was always racing himself. But with Harper in the car, he hadn't felt like he needed to outrun his past anymore. She'd heard it all. And she was still here beside him.

For the first time ever, speed had been just for *fun,* rather than the need of a junkie desperately taking his hit just to make it through to the next day.

He touched her hand in the close confines of the car and he heard her breath hitch at his touch. Even her skin seemed to be humming with electricity as she suddenly said, "Take this exit."

With nothing more than three small words, she flipped his switch, turned him on, powered up his engine. Which was exactly what he knew he'd done to her every time he'd pushed his foot to the floor and blown past her speed limits.

He finally saw the same thing she had—a motel, one of the better chains, but nothing like his usual luxury.

"There," she said, pointing. And it required only that one husky word to throw him nearly to the edge.

He took the exit.

CHAPTER THIRTY

"I could have paid for the room."

"No." Harper had gotten a great deal of pleasure out of charging the bill on her credit card. It was fun, as if she were having an illicit affair with a slick race car driver.

All she'd thought about in the car was getting her hands on him. And his hands on her. The moment the door closed behind them, she fisted his shirt and pulled his head down to hers. Her blood was on the boil as she kissed him— deep, wet kisses that made them both desperate.

"Did you bring a condom?" She couldn't believe herself—Miss Timid making demands. Taking charge. Better than that, feeling totally comfortable doing both those things.

He patted his back pocket. "Always prepared, just like a Boy Scout."

"You—" She tapped his chest. "—were never a Boy Scout." Grabbing his shirt again, she turned and dragged him to the bed. "You're a road warrior." A fire flared in his eyes, one that she knew had to match the fire in hers. "*My* road warrior." With the flat of her hand on his chest, she pushed him down onto the mattress. "And I want you bad."

The curtains were closed, the room dim, and his eyes were as dark as blue midnight. And hot.

"Not as bad as I need you, sweetheart."

Harper slid out of her sandals and climbed onto his lap. With her thighs along his, she slid down hard against him. His hands on her butt, he hauled her even closer, until every ridge and bulge enticed her through their jeans.

God, she loved the feel of him. The hard muscles, slick skin, delicious mouth.

"I want to ride you the way I rode the Cobra today," she said, her lips almost touching his. "Only I want your hands, your arms, to be the straps keeping me safe."

"*Jesus.*" His breath caught in his throat as though even the idea of her being on top was too much for him.

She bit his lip. A love bite. Then leaned down and practically jerked the T-shirt off him. If she could have had him in the car at high speed on the freeway, she'd have done it. This was the next best thing.

They tore at the front of his jeans, Will undoing the button, Harper sliding the zipper. She stepped back onto the carpet to let him get rid of everything and swiped her T-shirt over her head. She'd never gotten naked so fast, and she didn't even let him climb fully up the bed before she was on him again.

Her hair fell forward, cocooning them. "You made me crazy in the Cobra on purpose, didn't you?"

He grinned a *Who me?* smile. But then his expression grew serious. And loving. "I want to give you everything," he said in a voice made raw with desire and emotion. "Everything you want. Everything you need."

The next thing she knew, he'd sheathed himself. In one desperate move, she took him fast. Hard. And oh so right. The rush shot to her brain as he gripped her hips, arched, and went so deep there wasn't any part of her that wasn't filled with him.

His skin was hot, his body hard. She was soft and liquid.

They were a perfect match.

"Harper." He looked up at her and let her see all the way into his soul. "What you do to me—"

She reveled in the sweet sound of his surrender. Bending to the tattoo on his arm, she licked it, her tongue rasping like a cat's on his flesh. "Mine," she whispered. *"Road Warrior."*

She lay flush against him and claimed his lips with another kiss. They were one, mouths locked, bodies fused. She took his tongue into her mouth the way she'd taken his hard flesh into her body, then angled her head for his kiss and circled her hips on him as Will groaned his pleasure again, a rumble against her breasts. She let him guide his hands on her—until she had to have more friction or she'd die without it.

She pulled back from his luscious mouth, his sweet taste, and planted her hands on his chest both to steady herself and because she couldn't stop touching him. His skin was hot, his muscles hard. He forced her to a beautifully punishing pace, knocking the breath from her with each slap of their bodies.

She clenched around him. "Oh God, Will, please. *Please.*"

He was so beautiful beneath her, his face taut, his hot eyes owning her. All her emotion welled up her throat, her cries spilling over. But she didn't care about the unladylike sounds she made. She didn't care that sweat turned her skin slippery. She didn't care about anything but the feel of him inside her...and the sound of his voice as he said, "I love you."

Again and again and again.

* * *

Having smoking hot sex in a motel wasn't why he'd taken Harper for a ride in the Cobra. He'd simply wanted to share the speed with her because he knew how much she loved it. But she was one surprise package on top of another, always revealing a new and different layer.

None was more surprising than the fact that she wanted the road warrior in him. For so long, he'd hidden that part of himself. He'd buried it with emotionless sex in the dark, always using his past to remain separate. But Harper had bared him. And *accepted* him. She'd taken him into that motel room—no luxuries, no gifts, no lies—and given over her whole self. He'd felt the gut-deep connection just the way he felt her thumb along the back of his hand right now as they headed home in his car.

He had one hand on the wheel, and one hand on her, as she said, "I want you to know I'm not like this with anyone else. Not ever."

He knew there was no way she'd ever done those things with someone else. She didn't have to tell him. She was in deep, just like he was...even if she still wasn't ready to say those three little words back to him.

"I love everything about you, Harper," he said first. And while she was still blushing, added, "I have to go to London for a couple of days. I'd like you to come with me."

"I can't take another day off so soon," she was quick to say.

As quick as he'd honestly expected her to. Other women would have leapt at the chance to fly to Europe with him. But Harper wasn't like those women. She was independent.

And still far too wary.

"Would the following week work better?" The plant tour he'd arranged could be postponed.

She found another excuse. "At this late date, a plane ticket would cost a fortune."

He had a fortune. And more. "I have a private jet."

Her expression shifted and he couldn't quite read her thoughts as she said, "You're forgetting about Jeremy. I can't just leave him like that."

"I haven't forgotten about him. You know I wouldn't do that. He can stay with Mrs. Taylor and my driver can take him to school, to work, and back home again."

"But..." She halted, and he knew her brain must be spinning as she looked at the situation from all angles, the way she always did. The way she'd always had to, ever since her parents had passed away and she'd become all Jeremy had. "I've never left him for that long."

"You've never even gone away for the weekend?" The shake of her head marked his peripheral vision, and he felt a tightening in his gut at the confirmation that Harper had never had a life of her own. "He'll be fine with Mrs. Taylor. He likes her."

"I know he does, but that's not the point."

He knew he was moving fast, that he was pushing hard. But he wanted this—and he knew she did, too. "He'll be fine. I promise. He can do this, Harper. It'll make him feel like an adult."

Jeremy was the biggest part of her life, he understood that. But Jeremy wasn't a seven-year-old child. Yes, he had limitations, but he would be fine for two days without Harper. It would be a vacation for them both.

"Jeremy and I are a package deal." Her voice was tight now, no longer loose, the way it had been at the motel. "You can't have one without the other."

"You know I want the package deal, Harper. But a little freedom won't hurt him. And it won't hurt you, either. You don't always have to be your brother's keeper. And I hope one day you know that you can always ask for help from me, too. *Always.*"

* * *

Harper wanted to tell Will she wasn't Jeremy's keeper. But before the words could make it out of her throat, she realized they would be a lie. Because she *had* set herself up as her brother's keeper, and that had directed every decision she'd made since. Even her career choice had been about Jeremy. She was happy to do it, of course, happy to take care of him. But it was scary to realize that her entire world really did revolve entirely around her brother.

At least it had—until Will had blasted into their lives.

"Let me relieve some of your burdens, Harper." His voice was gentle but firm.

Confident. As always. "And let me take you to London in my private jet." His tone changed, deepened, softened. Seduced. "I want to lay you down on the bed in my private cabin. I want to join the Mile High Club with you."

He took all the air out of her objections with a few words and an image that carried a big punch. Of course he would have a bed in his private jet.

"That's not fair," she whispered.

"It's completely fair," he argued. "Because we both want it equally."

God, yes, she wanted it, just as much as he did. Wanted it so badly that just thinking of it had her control ripping into even thinner shreds than it had out on the race track, and then at the motel.

"I'll make sure he's fine. School, work, home. He won't be alone. I've got it covered. I promise."

There was one big difference between Will and the men she'd dated, apart from his wealth: Jeremy loved Will. And from what she could see when they were together, he cared deeply for her brother as well. That alone should have been enough for her to say yes, but they weren't talking about one wild night together—this would be two full days and nights and an ocean away from her brother.

"Tell me what you're really afraid of, Harper. And I'll fix it."

She watched the parched brown hills of summer race by, felt the rumble of a semi as they whizzed past. "I'm not afraid of anything. I just worry."

What if someday Jeremy doesn't need me?

The thought surprised her. Surprised her enough that she was forced to ask herself whether it would really be such a terrible thing to take a couple of days for herself. If she let her brother fly freer.

"You need to tell Mrs. Taylor that he doesn't like the dark."

Will's grin was huge as her words made it clear that she would go with him, but he was smart enough not to gloat. "You can give her a list of instructions. And we'll be home in forty-eight hours. A *very* hot forty-eight hours."

He picked up her hand and kissed her fingers. Even the light touch of his mouth set her pulse on high speed. She hadn't a single defense against him.

A normal woman would question why she needed a defense against the perfect man. After all, Will had all the answers. He'd told her all his deep, dark secrets. And it wasn't that she didn't trust him.

She put her hand over his on her knee and stroked his knuckles with her thumb. Then she splayed her fingers and laced them through his. He'd told her he loved her—and she wanted to love him, too, wholly and without any lingering fears. But though she now knew where he'd come from and how he'd made himself into the wonderful man he was—and even though she'd never been happier with anyone else—she still couldn't shake her natural tendency to hold something back.

Just in case. Just for a little while longer, because everything had moved so fast between them.

From zero to a hundred in the beat of a heart.

Soon, she hoped, she'd be able to round the corner and feel sure about everything. Sure that Jeremy would be okay without her spending every waking minute watching over him. Sure that being a little wild, and unfurling her wings from time to time, wouldn't damage the life she'd built for herself and her brother.

And sure that when Will said he loved her, he meant that he'd love her *forever.*

CHAPTER THIRTY-ONE

It was far easier to clear time on her calendar than Harper had imagined. Jeremy thought it was a major adventure to stay at Will's for two days. He was going to watch all the *Fast and Furious* movies back to back, then all the *Transformers*. His tastes were simple. Other kids his age would have had a huge party and raided the liquor cabinet.

Just as Will had said, Jeremy would be fine. He probably wouldn't even miss her. But she was determined not to spoil the trip by thinking about that...or by worrying that she was wrong, and that something might happen to him while she was out sowing more wild oats with Will.

"This filet mignon is delicious." The luxurious lounge where they were served dinner aboard his private jet could pass for an elegant living room except for the seatbelts, the flotation devices, and the oxygen masks that would drop down if needed. "I should have known you'd serve gourmet meals."

Will poured more champagne. "If I'm going to do something—" He grinned. "—I want to do it better than anyone else."

Harper now knew that was no exaggeration. A limousine had driven them onto the airfield at San Francisco International Airport. Two flight attendants—a man and a woman, both in their mid-thirties, neatly dressed, attractive, and enough alike to be siblings—had greeted them, stowed their luggage, served cocktails, provided bowls of her favorite sweets, and disappeared. The captain, a seasoned gentleman in his fifties, had gone over the flight plan with Will, then returned to the cockpit.

Throughout, Will was polite and full of thanks, not only with the captain, but also with the flight attendants. With his driver. With a waiter. With everyone. He thanked big, tipped big, and showed respect.

"How is porcelain unique?" She went back to the conversation they'd been having. Tomorrow afternoon they were going to tour a porcelain factory he was interested in.

"Actually, I'm not sure right now how I'll make it unique. That's the purpose of the trip. To figure it out."

"But why?" She hadn't imagined Will would find china plates the slightest bit interesting.

"The truth?" He gave her a grin that was halfway between cheeky and embarrassed. "I was on Facebook and some guy had posted photos of his new set of French china. People went nuts over that post. And you'd be surprised how many comments were from interested guys, not just women." His smile still made her heart race every single time. "So I'm looking into it."

"You think there could be a lot of money there?"

"I see potential. You can show some people a five-hundred-dollar set of china and they shrug it off as merely department store. But charge them five thousand, and suddenly, they've got to have it."

"For the same exact thing?"

"With a tweak—something to make it unique." He nodded. "It's about perceived value, not actual cost."

It was a totally different way of thinking. She'd never bought the "most expensive." Although sometimes she had to agree that you got what you paid for when the thrifty alternative fell apart after two uses. So okay, sometimes expensive had its advantages.

She waved a hand over the crystal, china, and silver. Everything was first class on Air Franconi. "Speaking of all this fine china—"

"I didn't pay five thousand for it. So my testosterone is still intact."

"I never doubted that." Will had *way* more than his share of testosterone. "Actually, I was going to say I feel totally underdressed in jeans. I should be wearing an evening dress."

"You're perfect exactly the way you are. Besides," he said as he leaned close, "I intend to have you out of those jeans right after we finish the chocolate mousse."

A flush of sexual heat washed through her, but she couldn't help wondering what his flight crew would think when he took her into his private cabin. But since she'd decided to take this trip with him, she intended to relish every single moment until the trip ended.

Raising her champagne flute, she waited until he picked up his, too. "To the Mile High Club." She clinked the rim against his. "Let's save dessert for later."

His eyes darkened with the sexy glint that never failed to turn her insides to liquid. "You always have such perfect ideas."

He rose, came to her side, and leaned down, his mouth so close that his warm breath caressed the shell of her ear. She actually shivered. With anticipation. With lust.

And with an emotion she was terrified to put a name to.

"I'm going to tell my stewards to keep the mousse on ice and the coffee switch ready to brew." He nuzzled her cheek. "Then I want to walk in on a naked and willing woman in my bed."

Air speed wasn't getting to her now. She didn't need the power of a jet engine.

Will was all it took to make her crazy.

* * *

Harper was absolute perfection, her skin creamy and soft, her silky hair fanned across the pillow, her breasts taut and her body sweetly ready for him. "I should commission a portrait of you just like this." He would put it on the wall opposite his bed so that he'd see her the moment he opened his eyes. Until the day he convinced her to move in with him and he could just turn his head to look at her in all her flesh-and-blood glory.

She laughed, a slight touch of nerves mingled with pleasure at his compliment, sexy and a little shy all at the same time.

"Your champagne." He came down on the bed with one knee between her legs, tipping the glass until a dribble of sparkling wine filled her belly button. He sipped it away.

She held his head to her stomach and arched up, a little hum of pleasure in her throat. The sizzle of champagne on his tongue and the sweetness of her skin were the only sustenance he needed. But he needed to be skin-on-skin with her, so he backed away and stripped down. Fast. There wasn't any rush, but why waste a moment covered up by excess clothing when he had Harper in his bed?

The thought made him want to laugh. He felt as though not a single shadow was hanging over him anymore.

He felt *happy*.

It wasn't an emotion he'd truly known before. Not until Harper. And now, with everything in him, he wanted to make her happy, too. Happier than she'd ever been.

He stalked her onto the bed, climbing on all fours until he was over her. He hadn't turned off the overhead lights and the late afternoon rays swept in through the portholes as well. As they flew east, the sun would fall fast. Her eyes were a seductive shade of blue, her lips full and red, and for the next forty-eight hours she was all his.

"Beautiful." The single word was filled with awe. "You are just so damned beautiful."

He leaned down to steal a kiss from her lips, taking a sip of her. Then he went deep, kissing her hard, tasting her mouth like a man addicted to sweetness, giving her his entire heart in the kiss.

"You're beautiful, too." Her whispered words were almost shy. She traced his tattoo. "And so sexy. I've never known anyone with a tattoo."

"Maybe they kept it hidden." The way he had.

"I don't think so." She kept her gaze and her touch on the tattoo, the barest hint of a smile on her mouth. "I'd never been with a bad boy before. Not until you."

He flexed his arm, the tattooed car undulating as if its engine were revving, which made her smile. "I used to be a bad boy," he said, "but now—"

"You're still one," she said in a husky voice. "Every time you kiss me. Every time you touch me. Every time you look at me from across a room and I know that you're mentally stripping me bare. Or," she added with a sexy little smile, "when you've got me naked beneath you on your plane."

"Naked and so damned sweet that you blow my mind every single time." He licked her lips, then trailed his mouth along her jaw, down her throat. He tongued the sweet skin at the hollow of her collarbones. He worshipped her breasts, tasting them until she moaned and arched beneath him.

Thank God she'd said she liked being with a bad boy, because he couldn't stop himself from taking her with his fingers, hard and fast until her breath became sexy little pants that strummed his nerve endings. He bit her neck then, in the way she loved, and she tightened around him, her body rising, her breath falling, her pleasure sounds wrapping around his insides and pulling him in deep.

Until Harper, sex had never been more than a physical release. It hadn't been sweet. It hadn't had meaning. But now her pleasure meant absolutely everything to him as she writhed on the bed, brought her legs up around his back, fisted her hands in the sheet, and cried out. Her body bucked against his and tiny tremors rippled across her belly as she climaxed hard.

But she didn't cry out again, and he knew it had to be because she'd obviously remembered where they were. She'd thought about his cabin crew, and she'd shut herself down.

For so long, ever since she'd had to take charge of her brother, she'd shut down her innate passion, and along with it, so much joy.

But he didn't want her to ever have to do that again.

* * *

Harper had barely come down off her delirious high when Will said, "You were thinking."

She opened her mouth to reply, but he kissed her before she could. Framing her face with his hands, he delved deep. Her scent was on his fingers, his body was hard between her thighs. She was all skin and sensation.

When he lifted his head, he stared her down with hot, dark eyes. "No thinking. That's my only rule for you and me."

"I wasn't thinking." How could she when the pleasure he'd given her had turned her upside down and inside out, until there'd only been room in her mind for his touch?

"Then why didn't you let yourself cry out?"

Her answer came before she realized he'd been right. "Your crew."

"That means you were thinking."

He swept in for another long, hard, delicious kiss, making sure she couldn't possibly think anymore. He filled her up, every space, until there was no room for anything but his possessive mouth, his skin soft and rough against her, the electric hum through her body, and the warmth around her heart.

God, he did things to her. Made her *feel*. Hot and needy, soft and gooey. It was beyond getting physical, beyond his mouth on her, his hands stroking her. Beyond the climaxes.

He made her feel beautiful.

He turned her over, setting her on her hands and knees, and pushed up flush against her. Big and beautiful and dangerously sexy, he made her wild all over again. Wonderfully, perfectly wild, as he gripped her hips with his hands and was inside her before she could even take her next breath.

A moan escaped her as he plunged deep, clear to the very heart of her. Everything spiraled down to the connection between them, his heat, his hardness, his relentless movements. She braced herself on the bed and pushed back on him, meeting each of his thrusts.

He completely surrounded her then, leaning over her, a blanket, lusciously hot and heavy. They strained together, hard breaths, hammering hearts, rushing blood.

And this time, when she shattered, she couldn't think about anything but him, crying his name as he called out hers, too.

* * *

Will had never been more content as he hauled her closer, her arm splayed across his chest, her hand resting at his shoulder.

She fell asleep against him, and after they woke, he loved her again, head to toe, top to bottom, inside and out. He'd loved her with every inch of his body, touched, kissed, licked, and adored every inch of hers. He knew every scented hollow, each sensitive patch of skin.

But it still wasn't enough. He ached for more. And they had only thirty-eight hours left. He considered canceling the plant tour and holing up with her in his Knightsbridge flat. But he wanted to show her London. He wanted to give her something she'd never had before—that trip to Europe she'd been saving for but had never been able to take after her parents passed away.

"We'll be landing in a little over an hour. I ordered the coffee." They'd never gotten around to the mousse. "Do you want to shower before breakfast?"

She flexed and stretched before cracking one eyelid. "I'd kill for a shower." She opened both eyes and smiled at him. "Come with me."

"Can't resist me?"

The teasing curve of her smile faded. "No. How could I?" She put her hand over his heart and he swore it skipped a beat as she said, "How could anyone resist you, Will?"

He'd known she wouldn't say she loved him at the peak of her climax. Not when it was clear that she still needed to think, decide, determine whether letting him all the way into her and Jeremy's life was a good idea. But with that touch and those words, she gave him the promise of it.

Of *love*.

Hell, yes, she made him so damn happy his heart stood wide open and ready for her. And soon, hopefully, hers would be wide open for him, too.

CHAPTER THIRTY-TWO

Harper knew she should be exhausted, with the time change, the lack of sleep, and the way Will had loved her all the way across the Atlantic. Yet his touch was like a jolt of electricity lighting her up.

Even once they'd entered the factory doors, he didn't let up. A hand at the small of her back to guide her. A light caress on her arm to point out something interesting. He introduced her as his girlfriend, and everyone treated her with the utmost respect.

She found the porcelain factory fascinating. The owner and plant manager, Mr. Beacham, told them all about how porcelain was made, and the differences between it, bone china, and fine china.

"The cup is beautiful." It wasn't quite a teacup that you'd use on a saucer, but it wasn't a mug either. At least, not the thick, heavy ceramic kind she was used to. This was smaller, more fragile, and painted with flowers and swirls and curlicues highlighted in gold.

Real gold.

"Please, you must have it." Mr. Beacham was tall, with a bald patch, thick glasses, dense tufts of hair sprouting from his ears, and the hint of a middle-aged paunch beneath his three-piece suit.

"Oh, I couldn't."

"Please, ma'am, we insist," a young artist spoke up.

"You do amazing work." Will held aloft another cup, the light shining through the delicate pattern and glinting on the gold-trimmed rim. The workroom was large, exceptionally clean, with high windows set along the upper wall and curving into the ceiling to provide more natural light. Pieces in various stages of the process lined long workbenches. "It's amazing to think that each piece is hand painted."

"Thank you, sir." The woman was petite, her thick red hair pulled back in a bun and stuffed beneath a net. Her name was Rose, and she was obviously from another part of England, as she lacked the crisp city accent of Mr. Beacham. But she beamed beneath Will's praise.

"In the next room, we have our figurines." Mr. Beacham began to move them along.

But Will wasn't about to be herded anywhere. "We appreciate the opportunity to view your artistry," he said to the small assembly.

There were smiles all around from the five women and one man. Mr. Beacham had explained that generally men's hands were too big for the delicate work. The one gentleman was smaller than average, with thin pianist's fingers.

Will turned to Mr. Beacham. "Why are there no signatures on any of the pieces?"

The tall man hesitated for a moment before answering. "They're meant to be indistinguishable."

"Consider this." In his elegant suit, striped tie, and white shirt, with his dark hair and strong features, Will was a businessman to be reckoned with. "Each of your artists brands their work with a hidden symbol. Every set then becomes unique and sought after. People will be searching for the symbol. It will be the thing to talk about." He smiled at the pretty red-haired girl. "They'll say, 'I've got a Rose.'"

Mr. Beacham pursed his lips primly. "But what if everyone prefers the pieces made by one or two workers, and no one wants to buy the others?"

Will turned to Beacham's artists. "What do you think?"

Standing amid all the fine and delicate china, Will was amazing. He had so much money that he could stomp on these people. Yet he respected them enough to ask their opinion. He called them *artists* rather than workers. It was the way he treated everyone, from Mama Cannelli to his flight crew to the girl who'd served him coffee in the factory cafeteria.

It wasn't how she'd ever thought of men with money. But it was Will, through and through, heart to soul.

One after the other, the porcelain artists spoke up. "It could be a competition," Rose said first.

"There would certainly be no slackers." Cecily was an older woman with a tiny nose and extremely small hands, as well.

"I'm no slacker." That was the young man, one step behind the women. His name hadn't been mentioned. "My artistry would be valued as highly as anyone else's."

"I'm sure it would be." Will looked from one to the next. "I would like my wares to have a signature. Exclusively." Harper understood that this would be the detail that would set his commodity apart. This was why his clients would buy at a price ten times higher. "And I'm willing to pay for that exclusivity, of course."

With the mention of money, Mr. Beacham nodded as though his head were on springs. "Certainly. Of course. It's a brilliant idea."

Will's charm—and brilliance—were remarkable. He'd secured buy-in from the lowest level to the top without any fist-pounding. She was sure that when he negotiated the premium for the signature, he would drive a hard bargain, but the company would get its fair share.

Mr. Beacham, a very happy executive with a million-dollar bone between his teeth, spread his arm expansively. "Now that we've got that settled, let's move to our figurines. I think you'll find them most exquisite. We dip real lace into porcelain to create the period dresses." He expounded further, leading Will away.

"Ma'am?"

Harper turned. It was Rose, the petite redhead, with a box in her hands. "I wrapped two cups. One for each of you. They're my design."

"Thank you so much, Rose. You should be very proud of what you do."

"I am. But no one's ever appreciated our work the way Mr. Franconi does. Or you." She had a bright, sweet face that made Harper feel years older. "Please thank him for all of us."

"Of course."

With a wave and a smile, Rose went back to her painting table.

For a moment, Harper stared after Rose, her mind stuck on what the girl had just said. *No one's ever appreciated our work the way Mr. Franconi does.* Just as no one had ever appreciated Jeremy the way Will did.

And her. No one had every truly appreciated *her*.

Not until Will.

Every step of the way, he had shown her how special he was. He wasn't some ruthless billionaire CEO who raided pension plans. People—and their happiness—were important to him. They didn't have to be rich, they didn't need to have something he could use or exploit. She didn't doubt he could be a hardass when he needed to be, but Will never exploited the small cog.

He was a good man.

A man worth loving.

* * *

Soon, Harper found out that Will had done one better than even she'd imagined. He and Beacham had negotiated their contract over dinner, which Will had been very happy for her to sit in on. As if they had no secrets. As if they were partners. And he'd totally floored her—and Mr. Beacham—by adding in a stipulation about employee bonuses. The artists would earn a special commission on every piece of theirs that sold, above and beyond the generous amount he was already going to pay them to do the work.

And it made her love him even more.

She didn't know how she could have been so blind. Or so stubborn. She loved him, and she needed to tell him. But she wanted the perfect moment. The ride back to Knightsbridge wouldn't do. His driver would hear everything.

She'd planned to tell him the moment they entered his penthouse flat. But when Will lifted her into his arms while doing those incredible things with his mouth, she couldn't think, couldn't hold onto anything except how much she wanted him.

How much she *needed* him.

And when he took her again, holding onto her like he never wanted to let her go while stroking hard and fast inside her until they reached the peak together—the words were right there on the tip of her tongue. But she didn't want Will to think she was only saying them because her world was shattering in ecstasy.

The jet lag finally caught up with her as he gathered her into his arms, but all she could think, as sleep came to claim her, was that she needed him to know just how wonderful she thought he was.

"I love you."

And then, utterly contented, with his lips brushing her cheek—and his own words of love echoing back to her—she slept.

CHAPTER THIRTY-THREE

I love you.

Three simple words had just rocked Will's world in a way nothing else ever had.

He hadn't thought Harper was ready. He'd been telling himself he could wait. But when she said *I love you*, he'd realized he hadn't truly believed she'd ever come around to loving him—all of him, the good and bad, the past and the present.

Just hours ago, he'd been planning to show her his favorite parts of the city, like the old pub sitting next to some of the last remaining stones belonging to the original Roman wall of London. Special places he'd found and wanted to share with her.

But then she'd said she loved him, and suddenly everything changed. It meant he could bring her back to London again and again. He could take her to his house in Paris, his flat in Sicily, his cottage in the Swiss Alps. All the places he'd never shared with anyone special except his Maverick family.

Now he had Harper. And they had Jeremy.

And everything was suddenly so much better.

Better, at least, as long as she meant the words. As long as she felt them.

He tried to relax his muscles, tried to convince himself that it was okay to believe that Harper loved him...and that he was worthy of her love. But it was hard going when the truth was that he hadn't believed himself worthy since he was a kid.

"No one will ever love a little shit like you," his father used to say. *"Not unless you can figure out how to be faster and smarter and sneakier than everyone else. Then maybe you'll be worth something."*

So that was what Will had done—he'd figured out how to be fast and smart and sneaky. It wasn't until he'd finally come to trust Susan and Bob and the Mavericks that he'd figured out how to love. And of course he loved them with everything in him, even if he'd often wondered how they could possibly love a fast-handed, sneaky smartass like him.

Thankfully, the tension in his body didn't wake Harper. She stayed right there in his arms, her skin like silk against his, her leg thrown over him, her foot between his calves. And bells were ringing.

No, not bells. His phone.

Unwilling to let her go, he fumbled around on the nightstand, finally feeling it beneath his fingers. "Hello." Though his voice was low, it sounded sharp in the quiet room, with only Harper's soft breaths breaking the silence.

"Mr. Franconi, it's Benny."

His driver Benny was shuttling Jeremy to and from work. In an instant, Will's heart began to beat fast and out of rhythm. "What's wrong?"

"I can't find Jeremy."

No.

Please no.

Harper was still asleep. Still oblivious. While Will's lungs felt like they'd been flattened by a speeding, out of control car.

"He was supposed to be in front of the building," Benny said, his voice fast, nervous. "That's what we arranged. But he wasn't there. And I couldn't find him upstairs in the office. No one remembers seeing him after three o'clock."

Will glanced at the bedside clock. It was five-thirty in the evening back in San Francisco. Which meant that Jeremy had been missing for over two hours. It took everything Will had to figure out how to take that breath he needed so desperately.

"Will?" Harper finally shifted, his name sleepy on her tongue.

She'd just told him she loved him...and now he had to tell her that he'd lost the most precious person in her life.

"Have you called the police?" he asked Benny, each word sharp and hard.

"No, sir, we looked everywhere we could think of and then I called you."

"Call them. Now."

Harper sat up. "Will." Sleep was gone—terror had invaded. Utter *terror.*

"But sir," Benny said, "they won't look for missing persons until it's been twenty-four hours."

Will threw his legs over the edge of the bed, and planted them firmly on the floor. He clenched his teeth so hard, he thought they might crack. "Tell them he's disabled."

"Yes, sir."

"Will?"

Her strangled whisper damn near broke him in two. But he needed to finish. "And get Security to check every room, closet, bathroom, and stairwell in that building."

"Yes, sir."

"Will."

"Have your phone with you at all times. Call me back as soon as you have anything new."

"Yes, sir."

The need to roar, to blame Benny and everyone else back in San Francisco, clawed at his insides. But he managed to keep the phone in his hand instead of throwing it across the room. For Harper, he needed whatever cool he had left.

She'd stopped saying his name. He turned, just enough to see her. And, like a coward, he thanked God there wasn't enough light coming through the windows to show him her full devastation as he told her, "Benny can't find Jeremy. He wasn't waiting outside when Benny arrived, and no one in the office knows where he is."

She'd gone completely still, and he swore he could hear every single worry she was thinking. Every fear she was feeling. Because he was thinking and feeling all of them, too.

"You said he'd be safe."

His guts twisted. *What the hell have I done?*

He reached back to turn on the light. He couldn't keep hiding from her in the dark. "We're going back. Now. I'll call the flight crew. I'll call the cops myself. And I know a good private detective. I'm on it."

But that was a lie, because his nerves were on fire. Every inch of him, inside and out, burned with uselessness. Helplessness.

"How could he just disappear?"

Her question sounded so lost. She wasn't crying, was showing no emotion at all. There was just a slackness in her features, as if everything had drained out of her.

Will had never hated himself as much as he did in that moment, watching Harper break. *He'd* broken her. And Jeremy, too. They'd been doing just fine until he came along, until he punched his way into their carefully constructed lives and upended everything.

"We'll find him." He wanted to touch her, but he couldn't, didn't deserve a touch, didn't deserve to comfort her. He didn't deserve those three sweet, beautiful, damning words she'd given him such a short time ago. All he had left were the meaningless sounds falling out of his mouth. "I promise."

"You *promise*?"

If she'd yelled or screamed or thrown a lamp, maybe he could have pretended he hadn't heard. But the low hush of her voice said it so much more clearly than her rage could have.

His promises meant nothing.

How could they, when he'd broken the most important one he'd ever made to her? He'd wanted her to come to London with him, so he'd come up with the plan, laid it out for her, convinced her.

And now he'd failed her, because he hadn't kept Jeremy safe.

* * *

How could everything have gone so wrong in just twenty-four hours?

Harper was curled into a tight ball of stress in her seat as the jet flew out over the endless ocean. This time, there was no filet mignon, no mousse, no crystal, no china. No laughter. No talk.

And definitely no love.

She'd left Jeremy alone. She hadn't called him to check in since they'd landed in London. God help her, the truth was that she'd barely even thought about him in almost twenty-four hours. And now he was gone.

What was happening to him right now?

Where was he?

Harper thought she might be sick right there in Will's elegantly appointed lounge.

He was on his phone. He'd been on it almost constantly since they'd run out of his London flat. They'd slammed their bags shut, and whatever wasn't in them got left behind. It didn't matter. All that mattered was back in San Francisco. Somewhere.

God only knew where.

"Yes," Will said, "he has a cell phone. Unfortunately, my driver found his jacket in a locker at the office with the phone in it." Will listened to the person on the other end of the line and glanced at her. "Do you have any photos of Jeremy on your phone?"

"I didn't bring it with me because I don't have an international calling plan." Her voice was hollow, but she couldn't put any life into it. Not when she was so scared. "And I knew he had your number."

These past few years, her job had been to figure out every single thing that could possibly go wrong for Jeremy, and then do whatever she needed to do to make sure it didn't happen. But ever since she'd connected with Will, she'd taken her eye off the ball more and more. And now, for this trip, when she should have run through all the possibilities, all the things that could go wrong, she'd done the exact opposite. She'd let Will handle the details for her brother so that she could have fun in her sexy fantasyland.

"I've got a couple of pictures I can send," he said to his caller, "but we were working on a car, and he's not looking straight at the camera." He paused. "Yeah. Sure. As soon as I hang up."

They'd taken off half an hour ago, after Will had awakened the flight crew in the middle of the night and obtained clearance to fly within the hour. He had everyone back in San Francisco looking for Jeremy—his staff, the police, the detective.

But he couldn't change the fact that they had to sit on this plane for almost ten hours. While Jeremy was out there. *Alone.*

What if something terrible had happened to him?

What if she never saw her brother again?

"Anything to report?" Will had his phone to his ear again as he signaled the steward, pointing at the coffee service on the sideboard and miming that the man should pour a cup for Harper. Even now, Will was taking care of her, taking care of everything.

"Call the minute you hear anything, find anything."

She wanted to blame him. For making her come to London. For taking Jeremy out of the grocery store and into that job up in the city. She wanted to scream at him, shout that it was all his fault. If he'd never come into their lives, if he hadn't seduced Jeremy with his cars and his friendship, if he hadn't touched her, everything would have been fine. Had she been able to make the blame stick, she'd have done it in a heartbeat. She needed someone else to condemn so badly that she felt bile push up from her stomach.

But she couldn't blame Will. She'd understood who and what he was right from the beginning. A man who knew what he wanted and hacked through whatever obstacles stood in his way.

This was her fault.

Hers alone.

She'd forgotten the one thing she knew to be true in her life—Jeremy had to come first. Her mother had drilled that into her long ago, after Jeremy had come out of the coma and they'd known he'd never be the same.

"Jeremy's going to need all the help you can give, Harper. He needs you. And if anything ever happens to us, you're going to have to take care of him."

Harper had always done everything in her power to take care of her brother. Until now. Until she'd allowed herself to be wild and free.

To fall head over heels in love.

She was Jeremy's guardian. She was all he had. But she'd let the rush of speed, and Will's charm, blind her to her responsibilities.

Will didn't know how Jeremy sometimes reverted to a frightened little boy. Will didn't understand how utterly trusting her brother was. He would believe anything a stranger told him. Will had wanted to give him more freedom, more challenges. But *she* was the one who knew Jeremy's limits. And she'd let it all happen.

She'd seduced herself with the attention, with the nights in Will's arms, and she'd started wanting more than she should have. Started thinking she could actually *have* more.

The steward set their coffee down, with cream and sugar for her, black for Will. She looked at the milky coffee without picking it up, realizing that she'd forgotten the two china cups back in Will's London penthouse. And she was glad, because they would always remind her that while she'd been off having wild sex in foreign lands, something bad had happened to her brother.

Will laid his phone on the table between them and turned the handle of his cup to pick it up, thanking the steward. When they were alone again, he said, "We've got a long flight. Why don't you get some sleep in the cabin? I'll stay by the phone."

"I can't sleep." Her voice sounded dull and totally without emotion.

"There are some over-the-counter pills in the bathroom cabinet." His eyes were weary, his brow lined with worry, his features sharp. "You haven't slept much since we left San Francisco."

She hadn't. Because she'd been too busy making love with Will.

But she'd finally remembered her brother was her true duty. And she would never, ever let anything happen to Jeremy again. Because when they found him—*God, please let me find him, I'll do anything you want*—things were going back to the way they had been before they'd ever met Will Franconi.

CHAPTER THIRTY-FOUR

Harper's silence made Will's gut churn. He needed to know what she was thinking, what she was feeling. She meant everything to him—she and Jeremy both did—and he would give up literally every penny he had just to have her brother safe and sound again.

And to know that he hadn't lost her love.

Right now, he was praying for at least one out of two to come true, since he couldn't imagine Harper ever saying she loved him again. Not after he'd done the exact thing she'd been so frightened of...

"I'm so sorry, Harper. I shouldn't have let this happen."

The cords of her neck were taut, and mouth thinned to a hard line. She was biting on the inside of her lip, as if she was trying to keep everything in.

He didn't know what to do for her. He'd been so busy on the phone calling absolutely everyone he could think of to help that every other thought had been pushed out of his mind. But now there was nothing left to do but wait. Nothing left to say except that he'd screwed up royally.

Finally, she spoke. "This trip was ill-advised. I shouldn't have agreed." The coffee sat untouched in front of her, the steam fading, the cream rising to the top and coagulating.

He wanted to rewind back to the day he'd asked her to come with him. He shouldn't have pushed her to come. He should have accepted her excuses. "We'll find him, Harper. He'll be okay."

As if he hadn't spoken, she continued, "Letting him go up to the city to work every day, where I wasn't close by if he needed me—that was wrong, too."

Will had loved the routine and Jeremy's happy chatter when they'd picked up dinner on the way home to Harper. Those quiet evenings sitting with her on the sofa, her body tucked close to his, had been the best he'd ever known.

But she was regretting it all.

"He was better off at the grocery store," she said in a firm tone. "He was better off with his regular routines."

Will had been telling himself the same thing, that he should have had the clerk fired and left Jeremy where he was. Where everything was familiar to him. But no, he had to have what he wanted. He had to choose the method, the job, fix the problem. He had to stick his nose into her affairs.

And he'd screwed up every damn thing.

"I didn't even call him." Her voice was higher, harsher.

Every word out of her mouth killed another piece of him. "It's not your fault, Harper. I was wrong. I didn't think. We should have called him together."

"I'm not blaming you." Her cheeks were tinged an angry pink. "I'm talking about *my* choices. I should have listened to *my* instincts."

Instead, she'd listened to his. And now, they were here, waiting, fearing.

Just that quickly, the anger, the hardness, the grim set of her mouth drained away, replaced by a pool of tears welling at the rims of her eyes. "Oh God, Will, what if something terrible has happened to him?"

"He's going to be fine, Harper. We'll find him." But he knew they were useless words when they were stuck thirty thousand feet in the air.

And when her tears spilled over, he didn't think, just instinctively rose, stepping around the table, to reach for her.

Her hands shot out and she pushed against his chest before he could even get close enough to put his arms around her. She whirled in the swivel chair, away from him, getting out on the other side as she scraped the tears off her cheeks.

Will froze. Every muscle, every organ, the breath in his lungs, the beat of his heart. He wanted to calm her, comfort her, take her in his arms and stroke her hair. He wanted to promise her that everything would be all right. But he'd already broken every promise he'd made to her, because Jeremy was gone.

"You're right." Each word was raw. Broken. "I should take a nap. Or at least lie down for a while."

"That'll be good." He could barely keep himself from begging her to let him hold her. To let him try to do whatever he could to take her pain away. "Take the pill. Then you won't be lying there with a bunch of worries running through your mind." It was a pathetic offer, and he felt as helpless as he'd been as a kid, with no right words to say, no action to take, nothing to do to fix things. "I'll wake you with any news."

If anything happened to her brother...

No, he couldn't let himself think that way. He had to believe that Jeremy would be found, that he was fine, just as he'd told Harper. Because if Will allowed any other scenario into his head, he wouldn't make it through the flight.

Harper walked to his cabin with slumped shoulders. Defeated. He'd done that to her. He'd done it to Jeremy. He thought he knew best. He planned and arranged and argued until he got what he wanted. He'd dragged her into his life when she clearly hadn't wanted it, not in the beginning, at least. But he'd made her want it.

The bedroom door closed with a click he could hear over the jet engines, one that sounded so final. Like the lock closing back down on a heart that had only just been set free.

She'd lain in his arms last night and whispered that she loved him. But it hadn't taken Will more than a couple of hours to show her that he didn't deserve her love.

* * *

Harper didn't think she'd sleep. Yet she was aware of nothing until Will stroked her arm. He sat beside her on the bed, his phone in his hand, not touching her except for that one brief caress.

"They found him. Your brother is all right. He's just fine, Harper. Totally fine."

She put a hand to her mouth to stifle the cry. The sudden wave of relief was physical, a warm rush of sensation that seemed to flow up from her belly and wrap around her heart. *Oh God, thank you, thank you, thank you.* She'd been praying when she'd fallen asleep.

"He wants to talk to you."

She grabbed the phone. "Jeremy?"

"Hi, Harper." Jeremy's voice was loud, as though he wasn't still thousands of miles away.

"Are you okay?" Her pulse was like the roar of the jet engines in her ears.

"Yeah, Harper. I got lost. I was dumb."

"You are not dumb, Jeremy." She turned away from Will, rolling to her other side, hugging the phone close to her ear with two hands. "Where are you now?"

"I'm at the police station in San Francisco. Benny came to get me."

"Good."

"Are you mad at me?" came his plaintive question.

"No, sweetie, I'm not." Later, when she'd come down off the relief high, she'd probably do a bit of yelling about how badly he'd scared her. But for now, she only cared that he was safe.

"Is Will mad?"

She didn't turn, didn't look at Will. "No, he's not mad. But you'll need to tell him you're sorry."

"Yes. Promise." It reminded her of Will's promises, and her heart ached. "Hey, Harper, I have to go. They brought pizza. I'm really hungry. I didn't get to eat dinner."

He wanted pizza. She wanted to cry. But he was all right. Everything was all right. "Okay, honey. You better get home and get some sleep. I'll see you soon."

"Bye, Harper. Benny wants to talk to Will again, okay?"

"Sure, sweetie." She held the phone over her shoulder, not looking, until Will took it. "Benny for you." She lay there, her eyes closed, her back to him as she struggled to keep her breathing steady.

"We'll get in around six in the morning your time," Will said. "You can pick us up then." He paused, listening. "Yeah. That's fine. I'm sure Harper would like that."

When he disconnected, she rolled back to him. "He sounds okay. But I have to see him for myself, make sure he's fine."

"I know." Will's eyes seemed sunken, with dark circles under them and lines on his face that hadn't been there yesterday. "Jeremy wants to come when Benny picks us up. It's probably better if he takes the day off school as well as work and goes home with you."

"All right. That's good." She glanced at her watch, but she wasn't sure whether she was on London or San Francisco time and she was too tired to figure it out. "How long before we're there?"

"Six hours."

She groaned. They weren't even halfway there.

"Where was he? What happened?" She almost put a hand on Will's arm, before she stopped herself. "He said he got lost."

Will flexed his jaw. "He went to the Exploratorium."

"The Exploratorium?" That didn't even make sense. "But he was working."

Will blinked. He didn't move another muscle, not to touch her, not to lie down beside her. His lids were hooded, masking his expression, his voice a monotone when he spoke. "A guy in the supply room has been telling him the Exploratorium is awesome. So when he wasn't very busy in the afternoon, he asked his supervisor if he could leave early. That was about three o'clock."

"His supervisor just let him *walk out?*" The fury that wanted out trembled on the edge of her voice.

"Yes." No expression leaked into his tone, it was simply flat, no reaction.

"How could that happen, Will? His supervisor should have known better." And she should have called Jeremy during the day, before he asked to leave. He would have told her what he planned, and she would have told him to wait until she got home. God, she'd been so stupid. "And how did he get all the way over there from your office?"

"It's been moved into one of the pier buildings. It's not that far from Market Street, so he walked there."

"Without his jacket or phone." She'd always tried to impress on Jeremy how important it was to carry his phone everywhere.

"He made it there fine. But he got lost coming back, got himself turned around and didn't recognize anything. Eventually he found a cop who helped him. But Jeremy didn't remember our office address."

And the only phone number Jeremy had memorized was hers. She closed her eyes.

"You're tired. Sleep. That'll make the trip go faster."

Will's face had always been the most beautiful one she'd ever seen. From the start his eyes had given away everything to her—his appreciation, his attraction, his love. And now? Now she could see his frustration, his guilt, and his regret.

Regret so deep that it was tearing through both of them.

Unable to take any more of it in, she rolled away from him and closed her eyes. Jeremy was safe, thank God, but anything could have happened to him while he was wandering around San Francisco.

The last thought she had before pure exhaustion claimed her against her will, was that her mother must be rolling over in her grave.

* * *

Jeremy was safe. It was the only thing that kept Will from losing his mind.

He left Harper to sleep away the rest of the seemingly endless flight, and poured himself a glass of Scotch. It burned going down. But it couldn't burn away his thoughts.

His blood powered up with the need to fire every damn last one of them, from Benny to Jeremy's supervisor to the kid who'd told him about the Exploratorium. Every freaking one of them. Come out with his fists swinging, just like the Road Warrior inside him. Hit first, think later. Smash and hack his way through.

But he'd come far enough to know that the fighting had been a symptom of his powerlessness, his inability to truly control everything around him. It had never fixed anything. It never even made him feel better.

And the fact was, he should have prepared his employees better. Much better. He should have stressed that Jeremy was disabled. Only, Will didn't think of him that way, and the idea of putting any stigma on him by giving his issues a name hadn't sat well, especially after the grocery store incident.

Now, Will knew that the clerk should have called *him* an idiot instead of Jeremy. Because being clear regarding Jeremy's limitations wasn't about stigma. It was about ensuring his safety.

He took another slug, let it burn, then catalogued over and over the mistakes he'd made during the past two months. Mistakes that had just cost him the love of his life and a boy who had become very important to him, as well.

When they were forty-five minutes out of SFO, Will ordered breakfast, and his crew had it waiting so that Harper could eat before they landed. He knocked lightly on the door to let her know.

"Did you sleep?"

She nodded. She didn't talk much. She didn't eat much either. It would have been easier if she'd yelled it all out, reamed him a new one. He was used to Harper speaking her mind. But she was completely closed off from him now, the lounge of his jet seeming as big as a cavern between them.

He knew what he needed to do. He wasn't good for them. He didn't deserve them.

But how could he ever get the words out to let her go when she was everything he'd ever wanted? Everything he'd ever needed.

They landed. He thanked his crew. He didn't dare touch Harper, not even to help her down the stairs.

Benny had the car waiting on the tarmac. And Jeremy ran over the moment he saw Harper, throwing himself into her arms.

The lump in Will's throat grew larger, the tightness in his chest clenching harder. Harper and Jeremy were a family that he wasn't a part of. That he would *never* be a part of.

"I'm sorry, Harper. Don't be mad, okay? I won't do it again." Jeremy stepped back, his lips pressed together in a sad pout. "Mrs. Taylor said I scared everyone."

"You did." Will noticed how gentle Harper kept her voice, even though it was clear she was still right there on the verge of shattering. "You know you shouldn't go anywhere without your phone. We've talked a lot about that."

His head drooped on his neck, and he wagged it back and forth. "I know."

"And what do you say to Will?"

Turning, his shoulders slumped, he was like a puppy who'd been picked on by his littermates. "I'm sorry, Will. Do you still love me?"

His father had burned all the tears out of him years ago, but Jeremy's words brought him closer to crying than he'd come since his mother died. "Yeah, buddy, you know I do." His voice sounded odd, the words choked. "Let's get you home. Your sister's had a long night."

"Sure, Will." Jeremy skipped back to the car, where Benny was stowing their two bags in the trunk. "Have you ever been to the Exploratorium?"

"Once, years ago."

"It's so cool, isn't it?"

Will opened the car door for Harper, then let Jeremy climb into the back with her to give them time together, while Will took the front seat next to Benny. Jeremy chattered about his adventure for the entire drive down the Peninsula. He'd said he was sorry, and now he could be excited over everything he'd seen and done. It amazed Will that he could so easily forget how lost he'd been, how frightened.

It was what Will would always love about him—his boundless enthusiasm, and the way he never held onto anger or sadness. But just because he loved him, didn't mean he was any better for Jeremy than he was for Harper.

When they arrived at her house, Harper let herself out of the car. Reaching into her purse, she handed her keys to Jeremy. "Why don't you run and unlock the door for us?"

"Sure, Harper."

Benny retrieved her case from the trunk and pulled up the roller handle for her, before getting back into the car to give them privacy.

"Thanks, Benny." She took it with a slight smile that died when she turned to Will. "I think Jeremy should stay home from work for a few days while I reevaluate the situation."

He felt the nails of his coffin driving into him, even though he'd already known that he had to let her go. Let them both go. But Harper was doing it for him. Because they both knew what the result of her *reevaluation* would be.

"Right, I understand," he said, even though he didn't understand a damn thing—especially not how he could have lost something so precious. So amazing.

Jeremy waved at him from the front door. "'Bye, Will. 'Bye, Benny."

As Harper rolled her case away, Will climbed into the car and watched her through the window, her back straight, head high.

"Where to, sir?" Benny turned the mirror slightly to look at him.

But there was nowhere to go. Because everything Will had ever truly wanted, he'd just had to leave behind.

CHAPTER THIRTY-FIVE

"We have to talk, Jeremy."

Harper sat him down in the living room almost as soon as Will left them.

Left them.

She closed her eyes for one brief second, the impact of it hitting her as though her heart were being crushed inside her chest. There'd been something so final in their parting.

But she couldn't think about that now. Couldn't think about Will, couldn't want him, couldn't need him anymore. She had to think about Jeremy. He was her number one priority.

"You're going to yell now, aren't you?" Her brother slumped down into the sofa they hardly ever sat on in a room they rarely used.

It seemed like a metaphor for all the parts of her life she'd closed off when her parents died. And, like a metaphor, it was also the room Will had carried her to that morning he'd surprised her with a sexy visit. God, she really needed to stop thinking about him. Especially now that he was *gone*...and it felt like her heart had broken into a million, billion little pieces.

Turning back to Jeremy, she said, "Is that how you see me? Always yelling?"

"No." His brow knitted as he thought. "You don't yell." Then he shrugged. "You just tell me what to do all the time."

She did. She took him to school, to work, nudged him to do his homework, to clean his room, to go to bed because it was late and he'd be tired in the morning. But when he was with Will, they'd had fun. They'd raced around Laguna Seca a few days ago and ridden the Giant Dipper at the Santa Cruz Beach Boardwalk a couple of weeks ago on one of Will's fun Sunday excursions after the Saturday work on the car. Whereas she'd never even taken Jeremy to the Exploratorium.

She could suddenly see that Jeremy had been starving for some fun. Harper wondered how much more guilt—and how much more sorrow—she could handle before her heart collapsed beneath the weight of it.

"I'm not going to yell at you today, but we have to talk about your phone."

"I know. I was just so excited. And Ronnie— he works in the supply room—drew me a map of how to get there. And it was so cool and there was so much stuff to do that I forgot the time. Until they were closing, and they said I had to leave." He had done all that himself—found the museum, paid to get in, wandered the exhibits.

"I'm glad you had fun," she said, and she truly was. Still, she needed him to know how serious the situation had been. "Your phone is your lifeline. You could have called Will, and he would have told Benny where you were."

"I'll take it next time. I promise." He nodded expansively.

Next time? "You can't go wandering off by yourself like that. You got lost. You need to wait for me to come with you on your next adventure."

He frowned. "I should have had Ronnie draw me a map of how to get back, too." Then he brightened. "I showed Benny the map, and he said I would have been fine if I'd just turned right instead of left when I came out of the museum. That's what I did wrong. I can do it, Harper. Next time, I won't turn left."

He'd followed the original map. Jeremy had figured out the streets and he'd walked there. He'd made only one small mistake that had thrown him off. A simple mistake that plenty of people could have made in a part of the city that was new to them.

It was astonishing...and also horrible to realize that she, the sister who loved him and would do anything for him, was the one who didn't think him capable.

Will did. Ronnie did. Benny did. *She* was the only one who doubted him.

More tears welled up and spilled over before she had a chance to stop them.

"I'm sorry, Harper. Please don't cry." Jeremy's eyes grew wet, too, in empathy. That was the kind of boy he was. No, he was a young man, not a boy. But she'd never treated him that way.

Harper swiped at her tears. "I'm just glad you're home and you're okay. But we need to go over a couple of rules. What's the first rule?"

When she stopped crying, he did, too. "I have to take my phone everywhere." His voice echoed in the nearly empty living room.

They would have to start hanging out in this room again. Her mom would want that.

"And the second rule," Harper enumerated, "is that you don't leave work or school unless you talk to me first."

He was practically bouncing on the sofa. That was her brother, overexcited, racing toward the next fun and interesting activity, forgetting the fright as if it had never happened. "Or Will? Can I call Will?"

Will. She'd told him she needed to reevaluate whether Jeremy should work for him. Until this moment, she'd been positive she'd never let her brother go back there. Now, she wasn't sure what to tell Jeremy.

"For right now, let's just keep it that you call me, okay?"

"Okay, but Will always tries to help me. Always wants me to learn stuff. Always wants me to have fun."

She swore her heart swelled a thousand times bigger as she looked at him a long moment—really looked. Her brother had the exuberance of a child, but the look of a young man. He smiled wide, he loved big. He could forget the bad and move on to the good. She was supposedly his teacher, the person he learned from. But she'd never stopped to think that Jeremy had things to teach her, too.

Like how to stop living in the past. How to trust. And, most important, how to love without holding anything back out of fear.

"Were you scared last night?" She'd never even thought to ask. She'd just assumed. Because she'd been terrified, and because Jeremy didn't like the dark sometimes.

"I was scared." He nodded hard. "But then I found a cop. And he was really nice."

He'd been scared. But she didn't think he'd been *terrified*. He'd gotten through just fine. Yes, things could have gone horribly wrong. He could have met bad people. But he'd actually done quite well.

Will had always believed that Jeremy could do more than anyone expected. He'd never seen Jeremy as handicapped. Until that moment in his London flat, Will had never used the word *disabled*. And she'd seen then how it hurt him to say it.

Whereas she'd constantly set limitations, never let Jeremy expand, never made him test his capabilities. She'd confined her brother. And she hadn't trusted him to learn from both his mistakes and his triumphs. She'd been afraid that Jeremy wouldn't need her one day. So she'd *forced* him to need her.

It was Will's faith in Jeremy's abilities that had made him stronger.

And Will's love.

Will had showered her with that love, too. Every time she'd doubted his promises, he'd made them anyway. He kept on believing in her. He'd bared his soul to her, revealed all his dark secrets, trusted her to keep them and accept him. And when she'd shut him down from the moment Benny called to say Jeremy was missing, he'd still taken care of her. Taken care of it all.

Everything was suddenly so clear. Clearer than it had ever been before.

She'd been wrong, and she needed to make some changes.

Starting now.

She put her hand over Jeremy's. "Here's what we're going to do. First, we're going out to breakfast. Waffles—what do you think?"

"Yay, waffles." Jeremy punched the air. "Can I have whipped cream and stuff?"

"All the stuff you want." She smiled at him, feeling her heart fill. "And after that, I have an errand to run. It might take a few hours. Can you stay home and hold down the fort?"

His eyes went wide with wonder, a look he'd probably displayed with every new and exciting exhibit he found in the Exploratorium. "All by myself?"

"All by yourself."

She had to start trusting Jeremy.

She had to stop being afraid.

And she had to tell Will everything that was in her heart.

CHAPTER THIRTY-SIX

Completely hollowed out inside, Will stared at the frame in his barn. After nearly three thousand rivets, it was starting to resemble a car rather than a birdcage. Over the past weeks, they'd worked on Saturdays and saved Sundays for fun.

And his nights had been entirely Harper's.

But he didn't have the heart to finish the car without them. Not when it had lost its meaning.

Not when *everything* had lost its meaning.

Everywhere he looked, in everything he touched, he saw Harper and Jeremy. He couldn't be here without wanting Harper. Without loving both of them.

"Mrs. Taylor said you were working up here."

*Jesus...*even Harper's voice seemed trapped in the barn, sweet, seductive, taunting him. He dropped his head into his hands.

"Will."

Wait.

Wait.

That voice—the beautifully husky voice he knew would always haunt his dreams, especially the way she'd said *I love you* to him just one perfect time—wasn't in his head. Was it?

He lowered his hands and turned, half afraid he'd gone round the bend.

But she was there—*thank God*—backlit by sunlight. The sun shone through the fine fabric of her dress. He recognized it as the outfit she'd worn the first night he'd seduced her. Or she'd seduced him. He wasn't sure of anything anymore.

Only that he'd never stop loving her.

His heart was an unsteady thump in his chest. "How's Jeremy?"

"He's fine."

"You took him to school?"

She shook her head, moving closer, narrowing the distance between them so that he could clearly see her beautiful face, her blue eyes, her red lips.

"He's at home." There was a softness to her tone, laced with meaning.

"By himself?" She must be a figment of his imagination. He couldn't imagine Harper daring to leave her brother home alone after what had happened.

She shocked him again by nodding. "All by himself."

Her lips turned up a little bit at the corners as she said it, but it wasn't a full smile. So he didn't dare hope, didn't dare reach out for her.

But another step brought her closer still, until she had to tilt up her face to look into his eyes. "I have a story to tell you, one I've told you parts of. But I need to tell you everything this time."

The need to touch her was an ache inside him, but he'd never forget the way she'd recoiled from his touch on the plane. He tried to ease the desperate ache by digging his fingers into his palms. "Okay."

"I was seventeen when Jeremy was hit by the car. I was old enough to understand exactly who hit him, old enough to understand about the bills and why my parents accepted the money. I was also old enough to understand that I needed to help take care of my brother. And when my parents died when I was twenty-two, I wasn't just helping anymore. I was in charge."

His gut roiled for that seventeen-year-old girl who'd had to grow up the instant some joy-riding punk lost control of his car, and then for the twenty-two-year-old who'd been all alone, with no one to help.

"I watched out for him. I made sure no one hurt him. I told myself that if I didn't let anyone get too close, they couldn't hurt him. But the truth is that my brother is happy and loving and resilient." Emotion brimmed in her eyes. "The real reason I didn't want to let anyone close was to make sure no one got close enough to hurt *me*."

He moved then, three steps, close enough to touch, to hold. And it was the greatest moment of his life when she didn't shrink from his touch, didn't push his hands away as he gently cupped her shoulders.

But she didn't let him interrupt. "You were the first person, the only person, to show me that I was holding him back. And when he started to fly free, I was so scared that he might not always need me. Because then what was I supposed to do with my own life?"

"Harper, I never meant to make you doubt yourself. You've only ever been good to him."

She shook her head. "I have been good to him, but I've messed up, too. I know it's not going to be easy to start letting him go, but he's not a little boy anymore. And I want to show him that I trust him." She inhaled a shaky breath as her eyes held his. "And I want to show you that I trust you, too. Because I do, Will. I swear I do. He's blossomed in these last couple of months with you. Your love has made him stronger. So much stronger."

He wanted so badly to take everything she was giving him, to believe that it was real. Just as much as he'd wanted to believe it when she'd whispered *I love you* to him in the dark. But he couldn't deny the truth of who he was.

"I screwed up so badly. I should have known I would. I should never have gotten in your way, should never have forced myself into your life, and into Jeremy's."

"Listen to me." She held his face in her hands. "My brother has learned how to do more for himself in the last few weeks than in the six years since my parents died. I did the best I could, but Jeremy needed *you* to see him as limitless. He got all the way to the museum on his own by following a handwritten map. And he had a great time. He never could have done that without you. Without everything you taught him."

"Harper, it was all you. I was the one who didn't prepare my employees properly. And he got lost."

"Yes, he got lost. And I'm not going to lie and pretend I wasn't terrified when we both know I was. But that's also because I didn't have faith that he'd know what to do. He did, though, Will. He found a cop. He got help. He helped *himself.* You gave him the strength to do that by believing in him.

"I love you, Will Franconi. I love you for seeing my brother's worth when even I don't always. I love you for loving me, too. And I love you for all you've done for your friends, for Susan and Bob...and for yourself. You were once a little boy who didn't have anyone to take care of him, and now you're a man who always takes care of everyone around you. You make us all better people just by being in our lives."

She kissed him then. And he felt loved right down to his bones. This beautiful, intelligent, wonderful woman believed in him.

Could he dare—*finally*—to believe in himself?

"I never thought I could change my story," she said, her voice thick with emotion, "so when you came into our lives I thought all I would get to have with you were a few stolen moments of wildness. But now I see that you, Jeremy, and I have *already* rewritten our stories. And we've done it together. You're a good man, Will. The best I've ever known."

"Harper—"

She put two fingers to his lips. "Tell me one thing. On the plane, before we found Jeremy, you wanted to fire them all, didn't you? Benny, Ronnie, even your PI friend. You wanted to knock them all down."

How could she know? But he already knew how. Because she knew everything right through to the heart of him. She always had, even before he'd confessed his past sins.

When he nodded, she smiled, and everything inside him stilled a moment as he basked in the headiness of that smile on her lips. It warmed every part of him, heart to soul.

"But you didn't fire them," she said softly.

"No." He breathed deeply, drawing in the beauty of her essence, wondering how he could have lived so long without her. And praying that he'd never have to live without her again.

"You probably sent them a memo with a new plan on how to help Jeremy without limiting him."

"I haven't sent it yet." But he'd worked out the details. Despite the crushing certainty ripping him into bite-size pieces that he would never see Harper—or Jeremy—again. "But I will. I'll make sure he's safe, Harper."

She bumped his nose with hers. "I know you will. And don't you see?"

He saw only her, the sweet center of her, so full of heart and goodness.

"Your Road Warrior of old would have smashed them all so that he didn't have to feel guilty anymore. But you took responsibility. Then you figured out a way to fix it." She dropped her voice to a note that vibrated inside him. "That's what you've been doing for years without even giving yourself credit. You made the right choice. You *always* make the right choice."

She *truly* believed in him. And Will suddenly felt lighter than he had...ever.

That's what Harper did for him. This gorgeous, generous woman made him recognize that he had control over who he was. He didn't have to be a Road Warrior. He didn't even have to be his father's son.

Once upon a time, he'd done a hell of a lot to change his life for the better. But he'd never taken the final step toward real happiness.

Never believed he was worthy. Never thought he could write himself a happily ever after.

Not until Harper made him realize that he could believe in himself—and true love that would last forever—because *she* already did.

She was right. Together, the three of them already had all the makings of real love. And the family he'd been longing for his whole life. They just needed to have enough faith in themselves, and in each other, to grab hold of it...and never let it go.

"I love you." He hauled her against him as he kissed her passionately, lovingly.

His heart kicked into overdrive when she wrapped her legs around his waist and held on tight. Taking a couple of steps, he set her down on the workbench and she quickly unbuttoned his shirt, shoving it down his arms. Then she kissed the tattoo he'd always kept hidden.

From everyone but her.

"I love my sexy road warrior." She smiled up at him, sweet emotion shining in her eyes. *"Always."*

* * *

They were sated, at least for now. But Will knew he would never get enough of Harper.

Cell phone to her ear, she told Jeremy, "We'll be home in about forty-five minutes with Chinese. Yes," she added with a big smile after Jeremy said something to her, "Will is coming, too." Will heard the kid's *Yay!* all the way over on his side of the car. "And you should go to school and work tomorrow as well, don't you think?" She laughed at whatever Jeremy said. "Nope, vacation is over. Okay, we'll see you in a little bit."

She ended the call with her thumb on the button and smiled. A radiant smile. "He's doing just fine."

Four hours. The house hadn't burned down. The cops hadn't been summoned. And Harper had only called her brother twice.

The last knot of tension around Will's heart untied itself as he pulled her close to him on the bench seat of the '57 Chevy, which he'd chosen precisely so that he could put his arm around her as he steered down his long driveway. He'd have Benny drive her car over later. They'd already called in their takeout order, and he would make sure they got back to Jeremy before their forty-five minutes was up, but he needed to take one quick detour first.

Pulling into the spot outside the fountain's fence where they'd once parked, he turned off the ignition and drew her onto his lap. Her sudden burst of laughter had him laughing too, even as he said, "Will you marry me?"

Her eyes widened. "Will?" She searched his face, as if she couldn't believe what he'd just said.

"There's nothing I want more in the world than for you to be my wife and for Jeremy to be my little brother, too. Wherever we go, I want to do it together. As a family."

Tears filled her eyes, but even as they began to spill over, she was saying, *"YesYesYesYes,"* sounding just like her brother did whenever he was really happy and excited.

He didn't ever want to let her go, but there was food to pick up, homework Jeremy might need help with, and, he was all but certain, dishes waiting in Harper's sink.

With a grin on his face as they headed back down the road, with Harper's hand on his leg and the wind flying free and wild over them, Will decided nothing had ever sounded better.

EPILOGUE

The Fourth of July party at Susan and Bob's in Chicago was a family affair, and everyone always cleared their schedules for it. They were missing only Lyssa, who was taking a two-month trip across Europe before she started her new job in September. Susan loved holidays and family gatherings, and this year was extra special because Jeremy and Harper were there—and Will was clearly a changed man.

Jeremy was currently crawling around the lawn on all fours with Noah clinging to his back. Sebastian Montgomery wasn't sure whether Jeremy was supposed to be a horse or an elephant, but from the way he'd stuffed a snorkel tube in his mouth and bobbed his head, Sebastian was voting for an elephant.

"Now that's one happy kid." Bob was slow-drinking a beer and idly rubbing the top of his bald head.

It was damned hot out in the sun, so Sebastian and Bob were seated in two of the recently acquired patio chairs on the new deck, a fan blowing over them, as they surveyed the lawn and the adults braving the heat and humidity. Matt stayed alongside Jeremy making sure Noah didn't tumble off. Harper was snapping pictures, with Will standing close behind her murmuring in her ear the shots he thought she should take.

Then again, Sebastian figured Will could be saying something entirely different, if one considered the blush on Harper's cheeks.

"Yep," Sebastian agreed, "that's a whole lot of happy out there."

"Susan's got stars in her eyes, planning the wedding and grandchildren." Bob smiled fondly. He adored Susan, always had, always would. During the years he'd lived with them, Sebastian hadn't witnessed the usual skirmishes, battles, or wars of most married couples. That just wasn't Susan and Bob.

Sebastian was truly happy for Will and Harper. He believed in love...but he also knew it didn't necessarily matter. Not when love could sometimes be the worst thing for you.

Hell, look at Evan. The guy was miserable with his wife—thank God Whitney had opted out of this year's party—even if he never admitted it. On the other hand, Harper and Will looked pretty damn good together.

The screen door opened and Susan called, "Who's going to be my cook today?"

Evan and Daniel followed, carrying platters of hamburgers, hot dogs, buns, and fixings.

Bob rose from his chair. "I'll do it, dear."

At fifty-five, Susan's hair was a rich silver. "Did you put on your sun screen, Bob?"

"I did."

Sebastian chimed in. "I watched him."

"Good boy. Both of you."

Her eyes crinkled at the corners with her smile. She had laugh lines, not age lines. Her figure was still trim, and she was a fast walker. She used to help Bob shovel the snow off the driveway until Daniel insisted they accept a new snow blower.

Daniel laid the platter of meat next to the barbecue against the deck railing. "Mom, I seriously wouldn't let Dad barbecue. He burns the burgers."

"I do not," Bob said indignantly.

A chorus of "Yes, you do," sprang up from the lawn and the deck.

Susan smiled sweetly. "You can cook mine. I love them overdone. Jeremy, honey," she called. "Would you like a hamburger or a hot dog?"

Jeremy yanked the snorkel out of his mouth. "Both." Catching Harper's raised eyebrows, he added a quick, "Please." Then he went down on his elbows so Noah could dismount his trusty steed, be it a horse or an elephant.

The little kid raced to the first stair, where Matt scooped him up, climbing the steps with him. "Hot dog, hot dog," Noah chanted.

Susan chucked him under the chin and gave him a kiss on his nose. "A hot dog it is."

"Can we see fireworks tonight?" Jeremy clambered up the stairs behind Matt and Noah. "I've never seen real ones. We only watch them on TV."

Harper followed him onto the deck. "It's just all the traffic and everything trying to get back home after the show," she explained, her cheeks turning red, as if they'd all think she'd neglected something vital in Jeremy's life.

Susan put her arm around Jeremy's shoulder. "I feel honored to be able to show you your first fireworks display." She smiled at Harper. "We'll take deck chairs and hot chocolate. And it will be the best fireworks we've ever seen, all because you're both here with us."

"That sounds wonderful." Harper touched Susan's arm in gratitude, and Sebastian could see the emotion in her eyes. In Will's, too.

"Dad, it's settled. I'm cooking." Daniel had already fired up the grill, and the two were bantering back and forth about the state of Bob's barbecuing skills.

Still seated, Sebastian was the only who noticed Will pull Harper close. She sighed as he whispered in her ear. She was obviously still embarrassed about the fireworks, and as Will nuzzled her hair, she leaned in, kissed his throat, then tipped her head back to look at him.

Love simmered between them, in the softness of Will's gaze, the sweetness of Harper's lips. They could make it. They *would* make it.

But that didn't mean everyone should give love a try. With his luck, Sebastian knew he'd likely end up falling for someone like Whitney— a woman who would strip all his secrets bare, then kick him when he was down.

Love didn't always make you a better man. Or a better woman. He'd seen how bad two people could be for each other, how they could bring out the worst in each other instead of the best. So no, he wasn't going there. No matter how good Harper and Will looked together.

"Hamburger, please," he replied when Susan called to him. He was just about to get out of his chair and offer to carry stuff from the kitchen when his cell vibrated in his pocket. He pulled it out, glancing down at the screen.

Xander Smith. An art broker he used in San Francisco.

"What's up, Xander?" Sebastian wandered to the far end of the deck, away from the chatter.

"The dragon in Chinatown?" Xander spoke fast, his voice high with excitement. He obviously smelled a finder's fee. "I found the artist."

Will had discovered the metal dragon outside a Chinatown church. It had been formed from an odd assortment of parts that blended into a fierce sculpture of brute strength, with circular saw blades as scales, the tines of a pitchfork for its tail, a barbecue fork as its tongue, its coils spray-painted red, and yellow and orange flaming out of its mouth. The individual components had probably come straight out of a scrapyard, but when welded together, its lines achieved a flowing symmetry and sinuous beauty. It epitomized the metamorphosis of an ugly duckling into a magnificent creature.

"Is the artist local?"

"Yes," Xander said. "A local. I can set up a meeting." He wasn't about to hand over the contact information.

Not that Sebastian would go around him. Xander had an eye, and he appreciated a great deal.

"I'll be back on Tuesday. Set it up for three and send me the address. What's his name?"

"Her. Charlie Ballard."

Her? Sebastian was intrigued. Now, more than ever, he wanted to meet the woman who had created something so fierce. So brilliant. And yet, so beautiful. All at the same time.

"Just make sure the meeting is at her studio. I want to see what else she has."

"Will do."

If her other work was anything like the dragon, Sebastian intended to showcase her talent in the lobby fountain of his new San Francisco high-rise.

Charlie Ballard, you're about to become famous.

~ THE END ~

ABOUT THE AUTHORS

Having sold more than 4 million books, *New York Times* and *USA Today* bestselling author Bella Andre's novels have been #1 bestsellers around the world. Known for "sensual, empowered stories enveloped in heady romance" (*Publishers Weekly*), her books have been *Cosmopolitan* magazine "Red Hot Reads" twice and have been translated into ten languages. Winner of the Award of Excellence, *The Washington Post* has called her "One of the top digital writers in America" and she has been featured by *Entertainment Weekly*, NPR, *USA Today*, *Forbes*, *The Wall Street Journal* and, most recently, in *Time* magazine. She has given keynote speeches at publishing conferences from Copenhagen to Berlin to San Francisco, including a standing-room-only keynote at Book Expo America, on her publishing success.

Visit Bella's website at: www.BellaAndre.com
Follow Bella on twitter at:
http://www.twitter.com/bellaandre
Join Bella on Facebook at:
http://www.facebook.com/bellaandrefans
Sign up for Bella's newsletter at:
http://bellaandre.link/NewsletterSignup

New York Times and *USA Today* bestselling author Jennifer Skully is a lover of contemporary romance, bringing you poignant tales peopled with hilarious characters that will make you laugh and make you cry. Writing as Jasmine Haynes, she's authored over 35 classy, sensual romance tales about real issues like growing older, facing divorce, starting over. Her books have passion and heart and humor and happy endings, even if they aren't always traditional. She also writes gritty, paranormal mysteries in the Max Starr series. Having penned stories since the moment she learned to write, she now lives in the Redwoods of Northern California with her husband and their adorable nuisance of a cat who totally runs the household.

Newsletter signup: http://bit.ly/SkullyNews
Jennifer's Website: www.jenniferskully.com
Blog: www.jasminehaynes.blogspot.com
Facebook:
www.facebook.com/jasminehaynesauthor
Twitter: https://twitter.com/jasminehaynes1

Printed in Great Britain
by Amazon